The Dragon of Neston

#2 in
The Neston Novels
Series

Tess Adone

ALSO BY TESS ADONE

#1 in The Neston Novels Series:
Neston

The Neston Novels Series is written in chronological sequence. Each book builds on the previous one to form a long story. Reading the novels in order will provide the most enjoyment.

Respect and Respectability:
Susan Price at Mansfield Park

THE
DRAGON
OF
NESTON

The Dragon of Neston
Copyright © 2024 by Tess Adone
ALL RIGHTS RESERVED

Library of Congress Control Number: 2024922971
ISBN 978-1-7323955-7-2 Paperback
ISBN 978-1-7323955-8-9 E-book
ISBN 978-1-7323955-9-6 Hardcover

Published by Tess Adone
Essex, Vermont
www.tessadone.com

For Larry W. Richardson

And the great dragon was hurled down—that ancient serpent called the devil and Satan, the deceiver of the whole world. He was hurled to the earth, and his angels with him.

Revelation 12:9

CHAPTER 1

"KNOCK, KNOCK," SAID MARCIA as she barged into my room.

"You're supposed to wait until I say come in." I closed the three-ring binder I used as a prayer journal.

"The door was open."

Yeah, all of an inch, so I could hear Gabe in case he woke up from his nap and started crying. She watched me shelve the binder with all the other notebooks I kept.

"It's a waste of time studying your old notes," she said. "They won't help."

I shrugged. The notebook binder did exactly what I wanted it to do, which was throw off prying eyes, so I let her think what she wanted. I kept some of the notebooks just for fun, like to look at what I had done in third grade, although I did study the more recent vocabulary lists. She never missed an opportunity to poke fun at me for it.

"Let's get it over with," she said.

"Get what over with?"

"You forgot? Oh, that's right, geniuses are forgetful. No wonder you need to review."

"I'm not forgetful."

"I'll be back."

She snapped her finger, meaning I'd better snap to it.

I did. There was only one thing she would be doing with me: gussying up my wardrobe so I wouldn't look like the eleven year-old I really am when I enter junior high school in a couple of weeks, which I got special permission to do.

She'd been Keeper of the Wardrobe—her own—for years, and she planned on attending the Fashion Institute in New York, so she was the best person for the job, but I doubted she'd get away with her Mistress of the Manor attitude there.

I peeked in on Gabe, who was still napping soundly, and when I returned to my room, Marcia and Donna were already there.

"You can get undressed," said Marcia.

"All the way?" I moaned.

"Don't be a dumbbell."

"I'm not a dumbbell. Don't call me that."

She ignored me. "See what she's got for underwear," she ordered Donna.

Donna had the decency to glance at me.

I sighed. "Go ahead."

It's a good thing I didn't hide anything in my dresser drawers. They're the first place any sneak would look. Whatever I had to hide was in plain sight: the Bible on my nightstand, postcards from Dieter tucked in the seam of the bulletin board above my desk, and my prayer journal, covered with an A&P paper bag like all the rest of the notebook binders.

I took off my sneakers and socks and shorts while Donna sifted through my dresser and Marcia slid the hangers aside in my closet. She tossed a few blouses and skirts onto the bed.

I was pulling my shirt over my head when she snapped the panty elastic against my rump.

"Cut it out!"

"Somebody's got a Coppertone tan."

"I do not," I said. I hadn't bothered with lotion since I spent so much time in the lake that it would have washed off, but my undershirt did nothing to hide my bathing suit strap lines.

"You do so," said Donna.

Just because they worked all summer didn't mean I couldn't have fun, but I didn't want to rub it in, the way Marcia was egging Donna on. Donna knew I had been swimming with Dieter right up to when he went home for final practice drills ahead of the Olympic swimming trials. I figured she'd be sore about that for a long time, but since football and cheerleader practices had started ahead of the school year, she was suddenly a lot less touchy. Quarterback Peter Jarvis had asked her out twice. She claimed she said "maybe" the first time.

"What's the situation?" said Marcia.

"Undershirts, plain panties, one long half-slip," said Donna. "Nothing she can wear on Phys Ed days."

"What's wrong with undershirts?"

Marcia started a list. "Panties and training bras and full slips."

"I don't need a training bra."

"I can see that. Nobody does."

"That's not true," said Donna.

Marcia stuck to her guns. "It's the idea."

"What idea?" I asked.

Marcia huffed. "You're the gym rat," she said to Donna. "You tell her."

"All the girls wear bras," Donna said emphatically.

She knew what she was talking about, but I didn't want to hear it. "You mean they'd notice my underwear?"

"Not on purpose, but girls who wear undershirts after the first week of PE stick out like a sore thumb."

"You can get by with what's left in the closet," said Marcia, "but these have to go." She indicated the clothes she'd thrown on the bed.

"What's wrong with—"

"Stand still," she said, "so I can measure you."

"Do you have to?"

"No." She started rolling up the tape measure. "They can do it at Lehmann's."

"Never mind," I said. "You can do it."

Thankfully, she took the measurement from my back while I held the tape over my chest, but still being short for my age, of course she would have to mention that my hems needed to be taken up.

3

"Or you'll look like the women in The Old Timers band," she said, "and we can't have that. Our reputation is at stake."

I could see how that might affect "our" reputation, but I was more concerned that people might talk if I wore the wrong underwear. I couldn't have that. Like it or not, I was moving into training bra territory.

"You can get dressed now—changed. For shopping." She paused. "You too," she said to Donna.

"I know," said Donna defensively.

"What about Mom?" I asked.

"What about her," said Marcia.

"Never mind," I said.

CHAPTER 2

THE WOMEN SHOPPING IN Lehmann's lingerie department kept their distance and spoke in hushed tones. At the training bra section, Marcia set the clerk straight. "I'll let you know if we need anything."

I was just a pawn in their game, so I stood silently, waiting to be told my next move while Marcia and Donna picked bras for me. When they brought me to the fitting room to try on what they had selected, Donna balked at Marcia's choices.

"Not those," she said.

"Oh, if you're going to be the expert—"

"She's got to have the bras with the matching panties," insisted Donna.

"They cost twice as much."

"Since when do you care about how much anything costs," said Donna. "You stick to outerwear. I'll pick the underwear."

"Fine, but I have veto power," said Marcia smugly.

"Fine, then I have veto power over outerwear," Donna shot back.

"Fat chance."

They steered me into the booth farthest from the floor-to-ceiling mirror panels, so I figured that meant I wouldn't have to model front, sides, and back, at least not for underwear. They sat on the tufted divan, and through the curtain between us, I could hear them whispering.

"She's got to feel confident," said Donna.

"Who said she didn't? You don't have to be so hostile," said Marcia, dragging it out into three syllables with a long i.

"You've got some nerve calling me hostile," said Donna, two syllables, short i.

"I'm ready," I said.

They came into the booth and squeezed onto the bench. Marcia ran her index finger between the lacy straps and my shoulders, then again between the clasp and my back.

"Good fit," she said. "Just enough give."

"How's it feel?" asked Donna.

I thought for a second. "Okay, I guess. It's different." There weren't cups like a real bra, only stretchy material in their place, just in case I started growing.

"It doesn't matter how it feels," said Marcia.

"It does so," said Donna. "The last thing she'll need is her bra chafing."

"Let me rephrase that. You'll get used to how it feels."

Marcia wasn't conceding; she just wouldn't want Donna to blab that she said it doesn't matter if underwear is uncomfortable.

"I meant I like the lacy straps," I said. They feel good." They had nice side panels, too.

"Not like those other ones that scratch," said Donna, speaking of Marcia's picks. "Try the rest of these on. You'll need six sets," she said to me.

"Four," said Marcia.

"She's got to wear them in rotation," insisted Donna. "Six is the minimum. It's only enough for three weeks of PE."

"But less to spend on outerwear."

"She can still mix and match what she's got."

"Yeah, skirts she's worn since fourth grade. Underwear is so much more important."

"I didn't say that, but it is important. Anyway, it's not like we're shopping for the entire school year. She'll have enough clothes to switch around for at least a couple of months, and by then, it'll be time to bring out cold weather clothes."

By comparison, outerwear was a breeze. Donna really couldn't disagree with Marcia's point that dresses lengthened my figure, even if Marcia was implying that blouses and skirts made me look even shorter.

"All I need is a new lunch box," I said as we left. Mine was definitely elementary school. "I can get that at Woolworth's."

"You can have mine," said Marcia. "I'm getting hot lunch this year."

"So am I," said Donna.

"But then Mom will have to make lunch just for me."

"You could get hot lunch too," Marcia said in her let-me-explain-it-to-you tone.

"Well, I could try it."

The shopping trip took more out of me than bicycling and swimming on the same day, but I was happy that, for once, Donna had won a battle, although she'd never win the war. And I walked away with the spoils: soft and shiny underwear, nice jumpers with coordinating shirts and socks, and the confidence that I'd be well-dressed.

I just wished confidence could be bought so easily when it came to my biggest fear of entering junior high. It wasn't about school itself; I was looking forward to learning new and interesting things, although I was prepared for it to be more difficult than I'd been used to. It was my fear of facing Tina Henry and Janice Armstrong.

We used to be playground pals. We won our best marbles from each other and played until we won them back again. We played Double Dutch jump rope, even though I had the advantage, being short and light on my feet. Sure, we battled it out, but we played fair and square. We had fun.

Right up until they branded me Eddie, and then they changed their tune. They gave up marbles for the merry-go-round, which they knew made me dizzy. They gave up jump rope for tether ball. I didn't have a chance. I couldn't reach the ball when the tether got short.

I didn't figure out how serious they were until the day Tina asked me to go on the seesaw. I should have known better. Mostly the younger kids went on it, but occasionally, some girls would chitchat while they seesawed, so I thought she was making up. I was pretty happy, and it had been so long since I'd been on it, at first it felt exciting when she held me high up in the air. Janice, standing nearby, started laughing, and then I knew Tina wasn't playing fair. She pinned me there. Finally, she slid off, and I hit the ground. Hard.

CHAPTER 3

FOR THE FIRST TIME in my life, I stood waiting at the school bus stop with Marcia and Donna. Well, not far from them. Marcia cozied up to Alice Dubuque. Alice was sweet, and I never understood why she was Marcia's friend, except that with last names starting with Du, they'd been seated next to each other in school since kindergarten. Donna waited by herself, but she seemed natural doing it, so I tried to do the same.

You'd never know they had agreed completely on my outfit, a blue jumper over a short sleeved blouse, with matching socks and pony tail ribbon. They insisted I wear my broken-in saddle shoes, so I had polished them, and the white stripe coordinated with my blouse. The outfit was a lot better choice than I would have made for my first day of seventh grade. The clothing ordeal had been worth it.

But it was just the first. The next one was on the way. I sensed Tina and Janice walking to the bus stop before I saw them.

If the way they'd taken to treating me was only a stage they were going through, I'd know in a minute. I took a deep breath and turned toward them, looking as neutral as possible, waiting to see if they would say hi first. They had to. It was their move.

They were wearing the back-to-school window display from Lehmann's, even though it was too warm for thick corduroy, and they'd have heel blisters from their stiff new penny loafers before the day was over. They matched the mannequins to a T, although they were as different from each other as Mutt and Jeff. Tina was tall and thin, and Janice had a round baby face that made her look pudgier than she really was. She had grown over the summer, but not as much as Tina, who was on the very tall side for seventh grade, but then, I'd be surprised if anyone would be shorter than me.

They looked me up and down, icy-eyed.

My heart jumped out of my chest. *Oh no! Here it comes, God.*

"Well, if it isn't Eddie," said Tina, looming over me.

Marcia whipped around.

"My name is Etienne."

"Aren't you in the wrong place?" said Janice.

"Why would I be?"

"How should I know?"

Marcia stepped up so close that Tina stepped back.

"What did you call her?"

"What's it to you," said Tina.

"I'm her big sister, that's what."

"Well, if you have to know, I called her Ettie."

Donna jumped into the ring. "You called her Eddie, on purpose. That's why she told you her name."

"I did not. I called her Ettie."

"You liar, nobody calls her that, and if they did, it wouldn't be you," said Marcia. She slitted her eyes. "Wait until my parents find out that *our employees'* children are calling us names."

"I didn't call her anything," said Janice, suddenly looking scared.

"I heard what you said to her," said Marcia.

"So he can't do anything to me."

"That's for me to know and you to find out."

My heart kept pounding so hard they must have heard it. Somehow, I don't know how, I got cocooned between Marcia and Donna.

Thank goodness Alice was the only other person to witness this. It was the last thing I wanted at the start of my high school career.

The bus pulled up. Staring down Tina and Janice, Marcia swung her hair over her shoulder and laughed right at them. I went in after her and Alice, but before Donna, who kept Tina and Janice at bay.

"Morning, morning," Mr. Ted said optimistically, over and over.

"Hi," I breathed out.

"Well, hello there."

He was as surprised to see me as I was him. I never knew that the younger Mr. Tedeschi drove a bus during the school year, but it made me feel less shaky. And he didn't know I was going to junior high school early, since I'd always been a year behind his daughter Sophie. Now she and I were both in seventh grade. I was getting the drill: people weren't expecting to see me.

I looked down the aisle. Maple Street was on the route before our stop, and Sammy and Bobby Fortin had stationed themselves in the last row seats, one on each side, but their sister Peggy was right in front of me. She moved over.

"Hi, Ette! I saved the seat for you," she said with a great big smile.

Unlike her sister Debbie, who had gotten so crabby she didn't even want to be one of my best friends any more, Peggy was as cheerful as the sunny A-line shift she wore. The swirls of color in the calico fabric coordinated with her coppery hair, and the matching hairband kept her shoulder-length flip in place.

"Thanks." Another relief.

"We'll be near each other in home room."

She sounded very happy about that.

"Yeah, some classes, too," I said.

Things were starting out just as Debbie had angrily predicted they would. Instead of it being her, her sister Peggy would sit with me on the bus, and we'd be in the same classes, and the next thing you knew we'd be friends. I had thought she was jealous because I wanted Theresa George to join Paula and her and me in bicycling over the summer, but it was clearer than ever that she was jealous of Peggy. The year between the sisters really showed.

It was a good thing Peggy had saved me a seat because the cocoon had broken open. Marcia sat with Alice, and Donna only took the empty seat next to Martin Smith so she could swivel around to talk to her best cheerleader friend Kimmie Hart and Kimmie's sister Betsy. Of course, Tina and Janice sat together, but other people put a buffer between us.

We made another stop before the bus turned west onto Neston Avenue. As each kid got on, Mr. Ted chirped over and over, "Morning, morning."

"Make room," he added.

The last stop, on Lakeshore Drive, was just a little farther, and the group waiting at the turnaround was smaller, since very few families with high school age kids lived year-round on Lake Île de L'eau. Lisa Ward went away to boarding school, like her sister Eugénie had, so I didn't have to worry about her. Sophie Tedeschi, Mr. Ted's daughter, was waiting with Bucky and Roxanne Buckminster. They got on. Sophie, who I hadn't seen all summer, had also grown. Her face was rosy from the outdoors, but what we noticed was what wasn't there.

"Sophie?" said Peggy.

"Hi, Peggy," she said, making her way to an open seat.

Peggy and I turned around. Sure enough, her flopping brunette pigtail, which used to reach her waist, was gone. Her pixie cut was shorter than some boys wore their hair nowadays.

We were still in shock when, at the last minute, a black Lincoln pulled up, and Theresa George hurried out. Her brother Nikky saw her to the bus. "Have a great day, Princess," he called.

"Morning," said Mr. Ted. "Just in the nick of time."

"Hi, Theresa!" said Peggy.

"Hi," I said, too, when she stopped in front of us, but she was preoccupied.

"Make room," said Mr. Ted, looking in the rear-view mirror. "Full up now."

"What's the matter, Princess?" somebody said. "Wanna sit on my lap?"

Theresa blushed. We turned around. Only tripling was left.

"What are you looking at, pimple face?" said lap boy to Martin Smith.

I wasn't the only one starting off on the wrong foot.

Peggy slid closer to the window. "You can sit here, Theresa," she said.

"Yeah, come on." I was small enough that when I moved over there was enough room for Theresa to perch on the end of the seat.

"Thanks," she said. "Hi."

I hadn't seen Theresa since before she went away on vacation. Her olive skin was darker than ever from spending weeks on Cape Cod with her family. She also had on a navy dress, but it had white piping and a pleated skirt. She must have gotten it when they went through Boston. Like always, her shiny, heavy black hair hung in a perfect page boy, and I was pretty sure she had tweezed her eyebrows. She looked mature for her age.

"We'll be in the same home room," repeated Peggy, just as happy as when she said it to me. "I wish Sophie could be, but we get split up by last names."

No wonder Debbie was worried about her. Peggy and Theresa and Sophie had been pals for a long time, but it was obvious Peggy made friends faster than picking rocks. Unlike Debbie, Peggy knew how important it was to stick together. Seventh graders needed that a lot more than juniors and seniors. Things were pretty well settled for them no matter what they did, but everything we did would count.

There was a huge commotion when we got near the school entrance. Bulldozers with caterpillar tracks like army tanks were beginning to clear the empty lot next to the school, and a sign on the chain link fence said *Home of the Future Bowl & Grill*, with a drawing of alleys and a dining counter. The kids went wild.

"A bowling alley!"

"With a restaurant!"

The Sunday issue of the *Neston News* had run an article with photographs of the ground breaking and sign unveiling that took place late last week, but it seemed most of the kids had not seen it or driven by over the weekend.

"That is such a clever name," said Peggy. She sounded like she already knew about it, and she was glad. She saw it differently than Theresa and I did. We had nothing against bowling, but both our families were in the food business. Our restaurant, La Terrasse, was fine dining, but we had to keep our eye out for any competition. The Georges' business, the North Shore Restaurant, would definitely take a hit from the Grill. It was only a matter of how hard. Theresa and I just looked at each other.

The bus pulled in to the lot.

"Have a great first day of school," said Mr. Ted over and over. "See you later."

CHAPTER 4

WE GOT OFF AND Marcia and Donna were gone before I knew it. A bunch of kids, including Peggy, stopped to watch the work that had begun beyond the chain link fence. I stood by her side.

As soon as I'd heard about the proposed bowling alley, I'd bought a camera and taken photographs of the lot while it was still green pasture. Over the summer, I'd gone back a few times and tracked the changes. The chain link fence went up, a plain trailer was put in place as a temporary site office, and from then on mud-spattered pickup trucks came and went, and men walked around the lot pointing and talking. At the rate the lot was getting torn up, I'd have to bring my camera to school to keep up with the changes.

Theresa and Sophie went ahead, but Peggy and I were not about to be late, so we caught up to them, passing the stream of kids exiting the buses from the routes closest to the border.

They may as well have come from another world. Canfield is just a crossroads in rocky farm land on the back way to Billington Springs. Keenan, running along the border, has a crossing into Canada that's restricted to official use. Notch Gore is so small it doesn't count as a hamlet; the road over the notch is closed in the winter, so there is only one way in and out then. If it hadn't been for the need to keep up the roads for the farm tractors and heavy equipment, the buses never would have gotten through those routes.

Neston Elementary School is huge compared to where many of them had gone—tiny village schools, or combined grade classrooms inside town halls, even an old one room schoolhouse, but everyone from seventh grade up came here. And that's why the school is named Consolidated Union High School. It's a dull name, but it wasn't fair to call it Neston High, when the school was built for all the kids from the surrounding towns.

Some of the youngest kids looked really scared, and who could blame them? Seventh graders from Neston already knew each other, and plenty of us had been to the high school for games that older brothers and sisters played in, but the northerners didn't usually come to games. Not even many of the Billington Springs crowd—the middle ground between the northerners and the Nestoners, did. On the other hand, some kids were smiling, but none as brightly as Peggy. She looked like she'd just been handed cotton candy at the fair. Already I knew I could learn a thing or two from her.

Principal Gaudet greeted students entering both sides of the open double front doors. We were passing the ladies' room on the way to home room when I figured I'd better use it. All that riling at the bus stop made me want to pee. Mom said I had a sensitive bladder and not to ignore it.

I gagged when I passed a stall where somebody was throwing up. When I was washing my hands, Brenda Pratt came out of the stall and rinsed her mouth. Standing next to her in front of the mirror, as soon as she removed the paper towel from wiping her face, I saw what was left of a shiner, a faint purple and yellow line along the half-moon socket under her right eye. Had Sammy Fortin hit her? Debbie had spied him pushing her up against the gym wall to kiss her.

"Are you okay?"

"I hate school."

Her nerves were worse than mine, and she had already been here a year.

I hurried to home room. I thought I would have Mr. Fortin for home room, which I was counting on him to be a familiar figure among a sea of strangers, but instead a Mr. Shaw had it now. As we went in, he said, "You may take your assigned seat when I call your name."

We stood against the walls.

"Janice Armstrong."

"Present."

He touched his pencil's eraser to the desk opposite his. She'd be right under his eye.

"Alexander Buckminster."

"Here. I go by Bucky, Mr. Shaw."

Mr. Shaw winced. "Alex," he conceded reluctantly. "And you are here," he said, pressing the eraser to the desk behind Janice.

Mr. Shaw pronounced the next name Deh-nee Du-sharm.

"You got it right," said Denis Ducharme, loping toward his seat.

I'd never seen him before, so he must have come from one of the outlying towns.

Mr. Shaw raised one eyebrow. "I am aware of that, Mr. Ducharme."

The class giggled. Mr. Ducharme took his place behind Alex.

"Etienne Durand."

He got that right, too. "Present."

"Etienne, you make take your seat behind Denis."

I sat down, and Denis turned around and winked. "Tck," he said.

Mr. Shaw raised both eyebrows over his reading glasses. "Is everything alright, Mr. Ducharme?"

"Copacetic, sir."

The class giggled again.

"Margaret Fortin."

"I'm here!"

I waited to hear Peggy ask Mr. Shaw to change her name to Peggy. Nothing. He continued.

"Theresa George."

"Present."

She smiled as she passed us.

I was thrilled. No correction to my name. Two new friends at my back. Seat next to the windows, which was nothing to sneeze at, since they were squashed rectangles compared to the Neston Elementary School windows, which needed a long tool to hook into the ring pulls when the shades were rolled up. I was declared Etienne in front of everyone, and to my surprise, Peggy was declared Margaret.

I watched the others as they took their seats, trying to remember the names of kids I didn't already know, but mainly I was interested in my who my neighbors would be.

Adele Guerin, a really pretty girl everybody eyeballed, was behind Theresa. Another two kids I didn't know named Mary Halloran and Tom Hecker started the next row, and Tina ended up third from the front, only one seat forward of my right, but Patrick Humphreys, a big boy who also must have come from one of the outlying towns, was behind her on my immediate right. John Jakes, an even bigger boy, who I knew as JJ, was behind Patrick to my lower right. Since Mr. Shaw was a stickler with Bucky, he didn't even bother to ask to be called JJ. I don't know what they were eating, but the boys surrounding me seemed to be thirteen going on seventeen. There were too many others to keep track of, but I knew Alistair Kittredge, whose father was the big shot at Kittredge, Renaud, and White Law Firm, as well as Luc Lambert of Lambert Dairy. Unsurprisingly, the last kid was a Levesque, but I'd never seen him before.

Praying in the moment was new to me, but I knew this was one of those moments. *Thank you, God. I never would have guessed you operated this way.* My friends and the big boys weren't bulwarks that would never fail, but I felt comforted surrounded by them—and, least expected of all, that Marcia and Donna had been my defenders at the bus stop. Tina and Janice wouldn't be misbehaving toward me, here or there.

The first period bell rang. We were off to the races.

CHAPTER 5

IT'S A GOOD THING I got the ladies' room out of the way because English was on the second floor way over by the auditorium.

Expecting to be assigned our seats, everybody stood bunched around the doors looking at the teacher, who was in the back of the room sitting with one leg swung over the corner of the metal forced air cabinet. *Julian Picard* was written on the blackboard in big fancy letters, like he was a signer of *The Declaration of Independence.*

But we still weren't sure he was the regular teacher until he circled his arm all the way over his head and said, "Come in." Then he waved his arm like a dancer. "Take a seat wherever you like."

Naturally, I headed for the windows. Margaret and Theresa also took the window seats in front and back of me, and Luc sat to my right. Denis did a U-turn and took a seat in the back row next to the door, about where Luc was in home room. Tina and Janice teamed up across the room. The farther the better.

"Fancy seeing you here," said Luc. He smiled.

He was another one who wasn't expecting to see me. "Yup, fancy that."

"If you ever need any help, give me a whistle. You probably won't, but just in case."

"Okay, thanks. I might."

Mr. Picard strolled to the front of the class, nodding more to himself than at us. Maybe he was having poetic thoughts. His goatee gave him away as one of the beatniks I'd seen at the patisserie, where they nursed coffees while they huddled over worn books. They all wore black turtlenecks and berets, although berets are a common item in this neck of the woods. Here, he wore a tie because he had to, but it was loose, and he'd taken off his jacket and rolled up his sleeves sloppily. His shirt was as wrinkled as if it was the end of the day.

He started right in without taking attendance. "We are in for a treat this fall," he said, handing out slim paperbacks to the first person in each row to pass back. "The entire school, junior and senior high alike, is going to be on the same page in English class. We are reading the play *Inherit the Wind*, which will be produced by the Theater Department in November."

It's a rule of life that when a teacher hands something out, students look at it instead of paying attention to anything else, so naturally, we opened the book.

"This is exciting news!" he informed us.

Everybody looked up, but we just eyeballed him. After all, it was our first class of our first day of junior high school, and we were expecting to get down to housekeeping business; you know, something regular, like, "Good morning, I'm Mr. Picard, welcome to English class, I'll take attendance now, what's your name?"

Mr. Picard was surprised that we weren't excited.

"If you are of the thespian inclination," he said, "tryouts will be held soon."

I made my first note of a word to look up, although I had a pretty good guess from the context, which you always have to take into account with vocabulary.

When that still did not create any excitement, he added, "They are open to all students, and there are many jobs, both on stage and behind the scenes, such as building sets. I encourage you to get involved."

JJ, I mean John, raised his hand.

"No need to raise your hand," said Mr. Picard.

"Do you get extra credit?" asked John.

Mr. Picard laughed. "No, extracurricular activities do not carry credit, but in addition to the great enjoyment of being involved in a production, you will grasp theatrical literature much more richly. Of course, in the long run, it may help your grade."

I didn't much like that he laughed at the question, but his answer made sense.

Tom Hecker raised his hand.

"No need to raise your hand," said Mr. Picard.

"Is it like the movie with Spencer Tracy?"

From the reaction in the room, that rang a few bells.

"Indeed it is like it. The 1960 film is an adaptation of the 1955 play script, which you hold in your hand."

"I saw it," said Tom, although he and the others nodding their heads couldn't have been much older than eight or nine when it came out. Generally, people went to see whatever movies came to the Bijou, and the drive-in often ran movies again, so it's possible that plenty of kids had gone when they were older. I hadn't.

"Well then," Mr. Picard clapped his hands once, "that brings us to the perfect place to start. *Inherit the Wind* was inspired by a 1925 court trial so famous some people called it the trial of the century."

"The Scopes Monkey Trial, right?" Alistair Kittredge, the future lawyer, spoke up without raising his hand.

"Yes, it was called that because a man named John Scopes was tried for teaching evolution. Jerome Lawrence and Robert E. Lee used it as the basis for their play. The fictional character Bert Cates is modeled on John Scopes, and—oh, but I see we are running out of time. Let's introduce ourselves, shall we?"

Let's, and budget our time while we're at it.

"I'm Julian." Another sweep of the arm, this time placing his hand flat onto his tie.

Julian? Nobody said a word.

"Okay, let's start in the back, with our outpost near the door."

That would be Denis. Then the student in front of him said his name, and from there attendance continued, back to front, and when it was time for the next row, two students said their names at the same time, the one in the back, who must have thought we were supposed to keep going back to front, and the one in the front, who must have thought we were supposed to go the regular way.

"Oh, let's toss it up, shall we?" said Mr. Picard, so we kept going in reverse, which slowed things down because the next rows still weren't sure who should go first, and the last handful of us had to give our names standing up after the bell rang.

CHAPTER 6

MATH WAS IN THE opposite direction. Pretty much everything about Math class was the opposite of English class. Mr. Reilly got right down to his seating chart as we entered the room, the same kids as in home room and the same order of seating, although he was fine with nicknames. He also got right down to business.

I always liked arithmetic, mainly because numbers are important when your family owns a business, but I quickly discovered that elementary school arithmetic is not the same as high school math, which was kind of exciting. Mr. Reilly said the first week would be review, and I was glad, since it wasn't review to me, so I paid close attention and planned to start catching up right away in Study Hall. Even so, the class was a relief. You knew where you stood with numbers. And with the teacher.

Same with Mr. Swenson for Geography—but this time we really were in for a treat.

First of all, Sophie was in the class with some other kids with last names from the second half of the alphabet, and after Mr. Swenson took attendance, he said, "Do you think the weather is good enough for us to get out into the field?"

We sure did.

He had us form into groups of four. "Three is okay if you want," he said, "but I don't recommend five."

Margaret had Sophie and Theresa and me picked out in a jiff. We marched out in our little formations to "the field": the manicured grounds next to the parking lot on the side of the building away from the construction, although it was still destruction at this point, and you couldn't get away from the sound or the dust.

Mr. Swenson gave us an orientation to the land. He pointed us east. "What do you see?"

This time, nobody raised their hand. We spit out answers left and right: the river, hills, trees, roads.

Denis whistled. "That's a Ford Mustang. They just came off the line this year," he said, and we caught a glimpse of the red sports car.

He got laughs, but Mr. Swenson said if we saw it, it counted.

"A basic definition of geography is the study of physical features of the earth," he said. "Our focus will primarily be on natural features, but geography certainly includes features made by man rather than nature. To study the earth, we must begin by looking closely, or observing. Now, groups, each of you pick one physical feature you see and record your observations. You can break up and go as far as the ends of the parking lot. I'll give the signal to regroup in ten minutes."

This was fun. We picked Bald Hill, which is across the Connecticut River in New Hampshire. Its bare rock bald spot could be seen for miles. The road running along the Vermont side of the river had pull-offs called scenic areas so people could enjoy picnics with a view of it.

After listening to Reverend Bouchard's rock sermons all summer, it was only natural to remember that he said David called God his rock and his salvation. At first, I hadn't understood the connection very well, but there's nothing like observing to clear up the picture. Rock mountain tops are safe places from your enemies, which make them solid choices.

We flipped opened our composition books and took notes. Now that I looked more carefully, I saw that there was a spot with a fold, just as if it had been icing piped onto a cake, and the baker changed direction to keep squeezing it on.

I had always noticed how the rock face looked tilted on its side. That was partly due to sharp cracks slicing through it, but observing it carefully, like Mr. Swenson said to do, I could see other things gave it that slant. Differences in color shaded the rock like the grain in a piece of wood. The tilted look also came from some white rock running through the gray like the icing between the layers of the cake.

From this distance, the individual features were clear even though the surface was ragged from boulders splintering off onto the road below. A yellow *Falling Rocks* sign warned of the danger, but you can't see a rock falling onto your car until it's too late, so it was about as helpful as warnings for moose crossing the road, which could dart out and crash into you before you knew it. When too many rocks started to fall, usually in the spring, a crew would come along and chisel away any clumps in danger of splintering off in order to help smooth out the surface a little. It was always ragged, though.

I decided to draw a picture. I turned my pencil on its side to shade the directions of the layers.

"That's clever," said Margaret. "Do you mind if I do a drawing?"

Of course not, but just then Mr. Swenson signaled for us to go back to class. Each group had to choose one person to write their main observations on the blackboard. The four of us had noticed similar things, but I was chosen to write them on the board because they wanted me to draw my picture also.

I got the notes down first. Right when I broke the piece of chalk to get the same drawing effect I had with my pencil, the class laughed. I took it personally, but I shouldn't have.

Denis's group had taken cars.

I kept going with my picture. When the blackboard writers sat down and the class could read what each had written, ours was the only group with a drawing. That got quite a reaction.

"No, it's good," said Luc, convincing his group, which had also picked Bald Hill. No surprise. The sun rose over it onto Lambert Dairy farm just up the road. He nodded his head and smiled at me. "Our observations are the same," he said, "but the picture really helps."

Check. A picture is worth a thousand words, not that I was an artist.

"Drawing is another way to record field observations," said Mr. Swenson. "Often it clarifies written notes. As you'll see in your textbook, drawings and pictures usually accompany descriptions, so they are important supplements to writing notes. They go hand in hand."

The kids liked that. Who doesn't like a book with pictures?

Well, most of them liked it. Janice and Tina had teamed up with Mary Halloran and a girl named Martha Zeno, and let's just say only half of their team was happy.

"But just as important is Luc's point that both groups made the same observations. We can see how having more than one group of observers can confirm certain features," said Mr. Swenson. "However, differences between groups reporting on the same feature often lead to further research as to why some groups see things a certain way and other groups see things in different ways. Sometimes we have to agree to disagree, in which case observation and research continue. In any event, our work as observers is always ongoing. Geography changes over time. A physical feature we observe today may be different tomorrow."

Mr. Swenson pointed out our homework assignment written in the upper right corner of the blackboard.

"You can sit in your groups when you arrive tomorrow," he said, "but choose a different person to write your observations on the board as soon as class starts. We'll be rotating so that everyone will get a chance."

Mr. Swenson actually accomplished what Mr. Picard tried to do—involving the kids, getting them thinking and cooperating. I wouldn't have guessed geography was such an interesting subject, but Mr. Swenson's class just whizzed by. The bell rang and the stampede to the next classroom began.

Except it was lunch.

CHAPTER 7

SEVENTH AND EIGHTH GRADERS were required to take the earliest lunch period. While I looked through the glass partition at the cafeteria serving line, kids grabbed their trays and slid them along. I realized there weren't any choices, so I got in line.

I arrived at the table last. Peggy, I mean Margaret, had saved seats for all of us. Thanks to her, we were already four peas in a pod. I just hoped she wouldn't mention it to Debbie. It was one thing for Debbie to toss out her friendship with me, but Margaret shared a bedroom with her.

Sophie and Theresa had brought their lunches, and of course the cucumbers with fresh oregano in Theresa's pint Thermos smelled great. Mom and I had figured school lunch would have the balanced food groups. Technically, they were all there on my plate, but the scales were tipped to the heavy carbohydrate side. A small serving of overcooked green beans sat next to a pile of macaroni and cheese and an oval meat patty topped with gravy that held its shape like a dollop of whipped cream.

I bowed my head and prayed silently, trying to be grateful. *Bless us, oh Lord, and these thy gifts, which we are about to receive from thy bounty, through Christ, our Lord. And thank you for Margaret and Theresa and Sophie. And Dieter. Amen.*

When I looked up, they were looking at me.

"Don't stop," I said. "Lunch is short enough as it is."

Everything was almost as soft as Gabe's food, only blander. It practically went down without chewing, but I chewed it well anyway. Mom always said it was important for digestion.

I wasn't sure if I should bring up Sophie's haircut, since some girls went bug-eyed and covered their mouths when they saw her, so I caught up on news with Theresa.

"You got a great tan," I said. I hadn't seen her since Paula and I had finished our bike ride around Lake Île de L'eau, which wouldn't have happened if Theresa hadn't gone with us after Debbie had bailed. "Did you like Cape Cod?" I asked her.

"I loved it," she said. "I can't wait to go back. We chartered a boat and went out to watch whales."

"Did you see any?" asked Margaret.

"Plenty. They travel in groups called pods." She forked a piece of cucumber, and the vinegar zinged across my taste buds. "Different kinds, too. Humpback and Minke and some Pilot whales. They're so beautiful. Some of them swam right next to the boat. I could almost touch their flukes."

"Their what?" asked Margaret.

"A fluke is the two sides of the tail fin. Flukes are all so different, they're like fingerprints. It's how whales are identified."

"Wow," said Margaret.

"Yeah, they were terrific."

She took the words right out of my mouth.

"And we saw dozens of dolphins and porpoises and seals— and guess what else?"

"A shark," I guessed.

"Not just one," she said. "A whole school."

"Wow."

"Were the passengers scared?" asked Margaret.

"There weren't any passengers. The first time, it was just my oldest brother's family and me. Tony pulled in the fishing lines and we went to another spot, but I went out again twice more with my other brothers when they took their weeks at the beach house."

Naturally. The Georges also ran the North Shore Marina, and all the brothers were licensed marine pilots. Theresa would have had to pull her weight on board as well, not just help looking after their kids. She was getting to know her way around a boat almost as well as her brothers did.

"You mean you spent three weeks there?" asked Margaret.

Theresa nodded. "I saw so many whales, by the time Nikky got there, I could point out a few I recognized."

"By their flukes?" said Margaret.

Theresa nodded. We were amazed.

"Sharks are beautiful, too," she added. "I'm definitely going into marine biology."

I'd heard her say so before, and all of us were as awed by the thought now as I'd been then. She probably would have enjoyed explaining the difference between a dolphin and a porpoise to me, but I wanted to ask her about Stu, so I gave her a hint.

"Did you see the Sturgeon Moon last night?"

"Did I ever! It seemed to fill up the whole sky. I've never seen such a bright orange moon."

Sophie jumped in. "We went out to look at it. The reflection on the water was beautiful."

"I saw it, too," said Margaret, "but I didn't know it had a name."

"All the full moons have names," said Theresa. "The Sturgeon Moon is named for a fish that was usually caught in the Great Lakes during the August moon."

"Stu was just a little early," I said.

Theresa got my drift.

"Speaking of which," she said, "Stu is Sue."

"He is? I mean, she is?"

"You lost me," said Margaret.

Sophie, being a Tedeschi, of Tedeschi's Bait & Tackle, knew all about the Georges' big catch, but Theresa was eager to tell Margaret, and of course, fill in what none of us knew yet.

"This summer, my brothers caught the largest sturgeon ever found between here and the Great Lakes. We thought it was a male, so we called it Stu, short for sturgeon, but we found out it's a female. The females live much longer. Sue's at least a hundred years old!"

More wows all around, even from me, and I'd been with them when they hauled Sue to the Marina for official weighing and measuring. There really was no end to how amazing that fish was.

"How did you find that out?" asked Margaret.

"We let the state biology lab take samples for research. The first report just got sent to us."

"Have you got Sue back yet?" I asked.

"No. She was frozen to be preserved, and when they were done taking samples, she went to the taxidermist, a special one who only works on fish. That will take some time. She's too big to go on the wall, so a table with a glass case is being built, but it won't be finished until she can be held perfectly in place. The taxidermist said she'll have to be set just like a diamond in a ring. After that, we'll have photographs taken. We're in no hurry, though. The report is really technical, and Mr. Vieth, the state biologist, said he'd come over to help us understand it. We have to get ready for a lot of interviews. Everybody is interested."

"Where will you put her?" asked Margaret.

"At the Marina. Mr. Vieth suggested we exhibit her, and he has some ideas for other things we could put in an exhibit, so we're going to apply to build an addition. Gregory says he expects the selectmen will approve it, but if they don't, the worst that could happen is we'll move some furniture to bring her home."

Now an exhibit would also be very good for the North Shore Restaurant business. I could picture framed newspaper articles next to the cash register, photos slipped between the glass and the counter. No Bowl & Grill could compete with Sue the Sturgeon.

"When will it open?" asked Margaret.

"If everything goes smoothly, we're hoping for next June, after school lets out. Would you like to be my guests at the grand opening?"

Would we! Not even Sophie minded. The Marina competed with Tedeschi's Bait & Tackle for boat rentals, but only for the choice between an outboard or a rowboat. In fact, she'd just been given the inside scoop, not that it would be a secret. Unlike the villages of Wortham County, permit approval is needed for everything within the Neston town limits now. The selectmen review meetings, which are listed in boxes with fine print in the *Neston News*, are open to the public, and I'd heard they were well attended.

As far as other news went, Margaret's trip to Plimoth Plantation and Sophie's summer away at camp couldn't possibly top Theresa's three weeks of whales and sharks, much less Sue, but their stories would have to wait. So would mine.

I was still figuring out how to tell it. I had spent a good chunk of the summer swimming and talking with Dieter. Given our age difference, the amount of time we spent together took some explaining to Debbie and Paula. I never told them how much we talked about God. From the moment I met Dieter, I knew that he was different. He was a Christian, and he made me see God in a whole new way. Before Dieter returned to Connecticut, I prayed to receive Jesus as my savior. Being born again is just like it sounds, starting new, and I was growing in my faith. I felt all fresh with the Holy Spirit living inside in me. God was not only real to me but had actually become interesting. We had a relationship. It wasn't the usual How I Spent My Summer, and I wasn't sure how anyone would take it.

Lunch was the shortest period and included recess, if you had the time or interest, after trundling through the line and gulping as fast as you could, to walk around the courtyard, which didn't even have swings. A few boys did. They also didn't seem to care that the construction ruckus echoed in that area or that the dust fell like snow. We were seated near the glass doors and got a dose every time someone went in or out.

"Next time, let's sit farther away from the doors," I said, trying to finish my lunch. It was too close to breakfast, too filling, and there was too little time to eat it in.

I looked over my schedule again before the bell rang. They say the first day is the hardest, and I still had plenty of jitters.

CHAPTER 8

MORNING STAYED THE SAME all week—English, Math, Geography, lunch—and so did final period, Social Studies. But the two periods after lunch changed subjects on different days of the week. Study Hall alternated with Physical Education, but I had to give up my midweek Study Hall to meet with my guidance counselor, Mrs. Richardson, to make sure I was adjusting to high school normally. Then the next period rotated between Home Economics, Health, and Art. I felt more confident about the rotating classes. How hard could they be?

Study Hall was just the breather I needed. I digested lunch physically and the new material mentally and was ready for the bell to ring to trek to Home Economics.

If there was any class I was excited about, it was Home Ec. Besides loving the subject, I already liked the teacher. Helen Trombley and Mom had been roommates at college. Helen was from Neston, and after college she returned to marry Gordon Spaulding, her high school sweetheart. They knew Dad and Carl from way back. There was only one cloud over Mrs. Spaulding's class.

If there had been a trophy for sewing, Marcia would have won it. Considering that she was headed for the Fashion Institute, Mrs. Spaulding obviously had been a big influence on her. If it crossed Marcia's mind, she would have been happy to think I had to follow in her footsteps. Of course, I would never measure up—

in the sewing department. But sewing wasn't my main interest in Home Ec. Cooking was, and I might make my mark in that area of study. So it was just a passing cloud.

We started right in on learning to sew the simplest skirt pattern possible. No doubt Marcia would point out that the elasticized waist made me look short, but that wouldn't stop me from enjoying sewing. In addition to learning something completely brand new and interesting to me, I'd have something to show for it. Plus, picking out the fabric for the skirt would be fun, and maybe I could find something with a vertical stripe that gave the impression of making me taller.

Home Ec put me in my best mood all day. I could face Social Studies. Not only had Mr. Fortin switched home room with Mr. Shaw, he had taken over Mr. Shaw's junior and senior History classes, and Mr. Shaw took his seventh and eighth grade Social Studies classes.

Sammy Fortin was a senior, and I wondered if the changes had anything to do with the trouble he had gotten into over the summer. Although I had been looking forward to having Mr. Fortin, the more I thought about it, the more I liked the changes, since I was the one who had turned Sammy in to the police. Nobody besides Mom and Dad and Dieter knew—and Detective Pecor and the police.

I didn't think it would make the slightest difference to Margaret if she knew, but I wasn't about to spill the beans. If it ever slipped out, Sammy might want revenge.

He would be right under his father's nose for his final year, and if things stayed this way, Bobby, who was a sophomore now, would be under it for the following two years. From my point of view, keeping a close eye on them was a good idea, although Sammy and Bobby probably didn't share it.

Anyway, the changes were more likely because of what they call policy. They always have their reasons, which I'd probably never find out. In any event, I got the advantage of returning to home room. Back at my own desk, after Social Studies ended, I wouldn't have to rush to grab what I needed and get to the bus on time.

Mr. Shaw already had our names memorized from home room. Talk about getting down to business. We hardly had our notebooks open before he started.

"Given the situation," he said seriously, "we will begin with a special focus on current events in—"

He pulled the large set of maps down in front of the blackboard and flipped to one near the back.

"—southeast Asia."

Southeast Asia! At the Fourth of July parade, a group of kids had been chanting "No war!" Dad had explained it was in southeast Asia, and he'd said it was still called a conflict, not a war, not officially anyway. But then why had the protesters called it that? I still didn't know.

"This—" Mr. Shaw placed the wooden pointer tip on the map, "is the Gulf of Tonkin, a place many Americans had never heard of before August fifth. That was the day President Johnson informed the public that two United States destroyers had been attacked while supporting South Vietnam in its war against Communist North Vietnam."

You could have heard a pin drop.

"Subsequently, the Gulf of Tonkin Resolution was signed into law, which allows, and I quote,"—he looked up from his half-glasses at each emphasis—"'Commander in Chief Johnson to take *all* necessary measures to repel *any* armed attack against the forces of the United States and to prevent further aggression. The United States is, therefore, prepared, *as the President determines*, to take all necessary steps, *including the use of armed force*, to assist any member or protocol state,' etcetera, etcetera, 'in defense of its freedom.'"

He removed his reading glasses slowly, crossed his arms, and jiggled his glasses under his left arm pit.

I raised my hand for the first time all day.

"Etienne."

"Does this mean we're at war?"

"War must be declared by Congress, not the President."

"But this sounds like he can."

"Indeed, there would appear to be a fine distinction between congressionally sanctioned 'war'"—he gestured quotation marks with his fingers—"and presidentially sanctioned 'repelling and preventing by armed force.' As Shakespeare's Juliet says, and I quote, "'What's in a name? That which we call a rose by any other name would smell as sweet."' End quote. Although never sweet, one might be forgiven for thinking armed force in this instance smells the same as war."

I finally had my answer.

CHAPTER 9

DONNA AND KIMMIE WEREN'T on the bus. I remembered Donna said the cheerleaders were going to work on pep rally signs after school, so they were taking the late bus. That left enough room for everybody, and the ride home was a lot calmer than the morning had been, but the bully was still all jacked up.

"I've got room on my lap, Princess," he said as he passed by and slid in a seat adjacent to us.

I was thinking we could get away from him if we took the late bus, too. It wouldn't solve the morning problem, but it would end the day better, but Margaret took the matter into her own hands. She turned to him and said, "Shut up."

"Who's going to make me?"

She turned back around.

"Mr. Ted," she hollered.

Mr. Ted looked up in the big rear-view mirror.

"That boy's bothering us." She pointed.

Mr. Ted waited until everyone was on and stood up. "I'll report anybody who makes trouble on this bus. Three strikes, and you'll be walking for the rest of the school year."

It worked like avoiding the bully never would have. He shut up, but he was steaming like a tempest in a tea kettle. Margaret would have to watch her back.

The bus rumbled off, and the kids returned to chatting about their first day of the school year.

"Thanks, Peg—Margaret," Theresa corrected herself.

"I never knew your name was Margaret," I said.

"I like it better than Peggy, but Mom and Dad have always called me Peggy. I hope they pick a good nickname for the baby."

"You mean Larry?" I asked. I thought Larry already was the nickname for her younger brother's real name, probably Lawrence.

"No, the next baby."

"Your mother is having a baby?"

"January. Mom says there's a chance it might be the first of the new year."

"Congratulations," we chorused.

"Do your parents want a boy or girl?" asked Theresa.

"They don't care, they've got three of each," said Margaret, "but Debbie hopes it's a boy."

"How come?" I asked.

"Sammy says he's moving out after he graduates, so there will be room for a boy as soon as he's big enough to sleep on his own. It's either that, or us girls' room will be more crowded."

"If she does have the first baby of the year, it will be in the news," I said.

"You'll get lots of free things. That's what everybody told my brother Nikky and his wife Lina. They would have had Neston's first this year if he hadn't arrived a few minutes too late," said Theresa. "Jason's really adorable," she added.

"That would be great," said Margaret.

Sophie returned to the name change. "I like Margaret better than Peggy, too," she said.

"Do you want to use Peggy with your friends?" I asked.

"No. I'm sick of it. Bobby and Sammy call me Piggy."

And I thought I had problems. She was actually on the skinny side.

"Will you call me Margaret?"

Of course we would.

"Just like the Princess," said Theresa, "Queen Elizabeth's sister."

Check. One princess thinking of another.

It was good to hear that Theresa wasn't resentful about her youngest nephew, since it probably meant she had to babysit at Nikky and Lina's house now, too, like she chipped in at her other brothers' houses, not her favorite thing to do. But if her grandparents' anniversary was any indication, the Georges wouldn't have nearly as much fun if all four generations weren't living next to each other.

The Georges and the Fortins—in a flash, I got the picture. Debbie turned on Paula and me this past summer exactly at the moment when I suggested Theresa join us bicycling around the lake. Paula was all in, but Debbie didn't want to be number four with her friends. She was already number four with her family. She just wanted to keep it the three of us.

On the surface, Debbie made Theresa out to be the problem, but at the time, she must have just found out her mother was pregnant. That would make her number four of seven instead of number four of six. It wouldn't change her number place, but it would make her the middle child, more left out than she already felt, more crowded no matter where the baby slept.

What's more, she had told Paula and me that her mother had asked for a fire pit, and the kids were roasting hot dogs and marshmallows over it until they were sick and tired of them. And they'd gotten a kiddie pool. I saw now that both saved her pregnant mother from cooking a few meals and giving a few baths. With another baby, Debbie, as well as Margaret—whose name change Debbie wasn't likely to be happy about—would have to keep an eye on their younger sister and brother, Cathy and Larry, more than ever. Sammy and Bobby sure wouldn't.

And the fire pit and kiddie pool had been put in right before we'd crashed Theresa's party. At the Georges' there was food galore and an in-ground pool, with enough adults to go around to look after the kids, even if Theresa did have to pull her weight. No wonder Debbie jerked her leg impatiently the whole time. She couldn't wait to get away.

I didn't blame Debbie for wanting to feel special in her family or for wanting some privacy. Sammy leaving would do more than provide a little breathing room, it would remove one of Debbie's problems. He was not nice to her. I suspected I only knew the tip of the iceberg.

Now that I understood the reasons behind Debbie's jealousy and anger better, I wouldn't have to wrack my brain, wondering what I'd done wrong to make her throw our friendship in the trash. But it was a real shame that she was so resentful that she couldn't let another friend into her circle.

Paula had insisted that Debbie was being selfish, and in a way, she was. She wanted something just to herself at home, and the next best thing to getting it was having her closest friends just to herself. She got a little confused along the way, is all.

Another baby brother or sister was the last thing Debbie wanted. I, on the other hand, felt sick merely imagining Gabe not being in my life. I wouldn't mind if more baby brothers and sisters came along for him to have close to his age, and I'd said so to Mom, but she said he was her last.

Chapter 10

I PASSED BY JANICE and Tina in front of the bus before we went our separate ways, sure that they wouldn't say anything bad to me, now that they'd been put in their place. I thanked God again. *You really are my rock.* I went on my way alone with my head held high.

I heard Gabe crying as I turned the corner to the house. He was with Mom and Dad on the kitchen porch. I dropped my book bag and held out my arms for him even before I kissed them.

"Baby Gaby! What's the matter, Gabe?"

"He wouldn't go down for his nap this afternoon," said Mom. "I think he missed you, Ette."

"Did you miss me, Gabe? It's okay. I'm home now."

He swatted at me, but he said "ahh," so I knew he was mad and glad at the same time, like when your parents scold you for making them worry but they hug you because you're safe and sound.

After a minute he stopped crying. "Atta boy," I said, and I sat down between Mom and Dad on the glider bench with him on my lap.

Mom pecked me on the cheek.

Dad rubbed my arm. "How was school?"

Because I'd skipped second and fifth grades and was the youngest seventh grader by far, this wasn't a run of the mill question. They'd be asking it a lot.

All in all, it wasn't the grand opening I had hoped it would be. I shrugged. "*Comme ci, comme ça.*"

"It is only the first day," said Mom consolingly, tucking my hair behind an ear. "The first week is often the hardest. Things will iron out."

"Ahh," said Gabe.

"Gabe." I gave him an Eskimo kiss.

I may be just learning to turn to God as the perfect antidote for the everyday poisons of life, but since Gabe was born, there has never been a time when he didn't fill me with happiness. He clung to me, already getting sleepy. He missed me! He and I both had some adjusting to do.

"How about if we talk about it after dinner?" said Dad.

I figured I had to, since I had made a promise to him and Mom that I would, but I wanted to anyway. Besides, I didn't think Marcia was faking it when she said she'd tell on Tina and Janice.

While I did my homework, that's exactly what she did, and Donna backed her up, so I wouldn't have to repeat the bus stop episode. They holed up in their room after dinner, and Mom and Dad and I settled in the den.

"Has this name calling happened before?" asked Dad.

"Yes."

"For how long?"

"Almost all last school year."

"A year!" said Mom. "Why didn't you tell us?"

"I guess I thought they'd stop. They got mean all of a sudden." My chin wobbled. "I don't know why they ever started."

"I think I do," said Dad.

"You do?"

He looked at Mom and they both nodded.

"From time to time, certain employees need some constructive discipline. It's a way to keep them as employees while they correct their problems, but it's their choice to go on probation for a time and come up to snuff or leave without a reference. That's what happened with Janice and Tina's fathers last fall. They stayed on and completed their probation. I won't go into it any more than that, Ette, because it's a confidential

41

matter, but I suspect that Tina and Janice did hear the details from their fathers."

"They were probably embarrassed and assumed you knew," said Mom. "They took it out on you."

"You mean...it wasn't me?" The tears I'd held back for so long spurted out.

Dad gave me his handkerchief and put his arm around my shoulder. "No, Ette, it had nothing to do with you."

Mom stroked my back while I whimpered, and when I calmed down, Dad said, "I know Marcia used their employment at the Arms as a threat, but I can't fire anyone without just cause. On the other hand, I won't tolerate having you suffer because Janice and Tina took up an offense against you—whether it was because of this or some other misguided ideas they may have. Ette, if they mistreat you in any way again, we'll have to inform Mrs. Richardson we think a problem at work is what started it, but you can't say anything about that to them."

"I won't," I promised, "but I don't think they'll bother me again. What Marcia said scared them."

"It should. You can rest assured, I will not allow my children to be picked on and called names. I'll address the matter with each of their fathers, first and foremost as one parent to another, but they'll know we'll be keeping an eye on them to see if it affects their attitude or performance at work."

I heaved a shaky sigh of relief. "Okay."

"Patience is a virtue, Ette, but not an excuse," said Mom. "Stand up for yourself."

"I will," I promised. It was easier said than done, but now I had seen it first-hand. I told them how Marcia and Donna stood up for me, and Margaret stood up for Theresa.

"Deputy Fife was right," I said. "You have to nip it in the bud."

"That's my girl," said Dad.

"Does nipping it in the bud include hot lunch? If it's going to be like today's lunch, I don't think I can take more than a week of it." We had paid in advance, and I wouldn't let a week's worth of food go to waste.

Mom laughed. "Of course it does."

"I'll make it myself so you don't have to make it just for me."

"No, that should be the least of your worries. I still prepare for us at home, Ette. We eat lunch too, you know."

She made me smile.

"Gabe had beans and vegetables mashed in the minestrone broth today."

He'd had a good nap. He perked up at his name.

"Gabe, you had minestrone!" I missed his first minestrone. He was at that stage when a lot of things happened for the first time, and sadly, I'd be missing most of them. I took him from Mom and bobbed him up and down on my knees.

"That was way better than I had," I informed him, "but I learned lots of new things today," and I launched into the interesting parts so Mom and Dad wouldn't think the whole day had been a washout.

They were relieved. After all, at this point none of us wanted to ship me back to sixth grade. That would be a lot worse than me learning to cut the mustard.

I went to my room when I heard Dad dialing the phone and saying, "Hello, this is Raymond Durand. May I speak to your father?"

I didn't want to hear any more. I closed the door and picked out my clothes for tomorrow. It was enough to know that Dad was my bulwark.

Then I locked the door and took out my prayer journal. Dieter had showed me that writing out requests and answers helps you be more specific in your prayer life. I honestly had not expected to have some answers so soon, and in each instance of progress that I jotted down, I wrote *Thank you, God.*

What I figured out from Margaret's news about her mother's pregnancy led to part of an answer to a prayer Dieter had made for me this past summer. He had asked God to heal my hurting heart. My friendship with Debbie wasn't restored, but understanding its loss truly began to heal the hurt and lift the heaviness off my heart. So did knowing that the situation with her wasn't all about me.

It was a lot like the situation with Tina and Janice and their fathers. I wasn't the problem, I was just the scapegoat. I'd suffered over them a lot longer, but I suffered over Debbie more deeply. She was—had been—one of my two best friends. Being shunned by Tina and Janice and Debbie still hurt, but the sting wasn't so sharp. And it was really them who were hurting.

Sometimes you think you know people's reasons, but it turns out, sometimes you just never know. Maybe the way they react against you has more to do with them, what's going on inside them, than it has to do with you, at least not directly.

Like Mom said, this was only the first day. There's a pile of ironing out to do, I wrote in my journal. As I was adding new prayer requests, something Jesus said that Rev. Bouchard mentioned in one of his sermons came to my mind. *Love your enemies, and pray for those who persecute you.*

The way Dieter had showed me how he prayed, it really wasn't too hard. I could pray for Janice and Tina like we had for Debbie and Sammy and the whole Fortin family.

Loving them was another story. We couldn't go back to the good old days. Playground games really weren't on the menu any more for kids our age. We had outgrown them, but I didn't have any ideas of what to replace them with, not that they would have made a difference.

How can I love them when they want nothing to do with me? You'll have to show me how.

CHAPTER 11

THE NEXT MORNING, JANICE and Tina steered clear of me at the bus stop, which was no surprise, but the challenge of loving them was complicated by it, and the fact that I also promised to stand my ground in the event they aggravated me. Like Mom said, being patient didn't mean being a pushover. I was definitely between a rock and a hard place. God really had his work cut out on answering this prayer.

Yesterday's changes to the bowling alley construction site had been so great from the time we'd arrived at school to the time we went home that I had decided, if I was going to keep up with them, I'd have to take photographs every school day, both morning and afternoon.

"I'm going to take some pictures of the bowling alley work," I said, before we got off the bus. "Will you wait for me? It'll only take a minute."

"What for?" asked Margaret.

When I explained my new hobby of photographing Gabe and Neston to see how they grew and changed, Theresa and Sophie were also interested enough to wait while I snapped a couple of shots.

We entered the school building, where the hallways were plastered with posters for the pep rally on Friday. *CU there!!!* they blazed in black and yellow, the team colors of the Hornets. The cheerleaders sure made the best of the school name.

I ducked into the ladies' room again. My first day jitters were over, but I decided it was a good policy since there was so little time between classes, and you had to get a hall pass if you went during class, and who knows what you might miss.

Brenda Pratt was puking again. I scrammed before she came out of the stall.

In home room, Denis slid into his seat and swiveled around. Since Mr. Shaw silently checked off our names as we came in, Denis wasn't interrupting him taking attendance.

"Tck," he winked. "Hi, Amber."

I laughed instantly but said "Etienne."

"It's my nickname for you."

"No, call me Etienne," I said, nipping it in the bud, although it was a good nickname because of my amber eyes, not a make-fun name.

"Whatever you say, Etienne." He gazed at the flowers embroidered on my Peter Pan collar. "Your wish is my command."

I think he meant it. He was funny, nice for a boy his age, already had enough fuzz that he could have started shaving, and if you excluded Dieter, who was completely outside the norm, was cute. I figured a lot of girls would like his attention, but I wasn't one of them, even if I appreciated having him sit in front of me.

In English, I stayed by the window with my friends. So did Luc.

"Did you finish the play?" he asked.

We hadn't.

"Did you?" I asked.

"Almost. I will today."

"Already? We have until next week to finish it."

"No big deal, it's short. If I can't get my homework done during Study Hall, it's easier to finish it right after school and take the late bus. I can read on the bus, too. Once I get home, I start milking."

And then it was early to bed and early to rise again at Lambert Dairy. If I wasn't in a tearing hurry to get home to Gabe, I'd stay after school and take the late bus, too.

It took forever for Mr. Picard to take attendance, since most of the kids had shifted seats, but then he did get down to teaching, and like math, it was new material to me. New material was a big reason why I wanted to enter junior high early, and I hoped it would be interesting, too. He wrote *Types of Conflict* on the board, and I started taking notes.

"Alright, people." He clapped his hands one time.

People? Okay, well, we were.

"Who can name a character in conflict with another character?"

Theresa raised her hand.

"No need to raise your hand," he said.

She put it down. "Cinderella."

It was the match that lit a bonfire. Suddenly, kids were calling out all sorts of examples from the story. Mr. Picard listed other types of conflicts, and in no time flat, we picked out examples of them, too.

"Excellent! Great! Good example." He wrote furiously on the board, trying to get all the answers down.

It worked, we were participating, but it wasn't like Mr. Swenson's class, where he was in control. While Mr. Picard's back was to us, a paper airplane flew across the room, and then there was so much nonsense cross talk and laughing, the room turned into a circus.

The back door to the classroom closed mysteriously.

A couple seconds later, Mrs. Steinmetz, the German teacher from across the hall, closed the front door. There was a sound, the sound of a whole classroom of kids sucking in their breath. Before Mr. Picard could explain—or apologize, she was gone.

Nipped in the bud. Or so I thought.

Math kept me on my toes again, but you could count on things staying steady in that class. I just had to catch up completely.

The best part of the morning was Geography. We sat in our groups and picked a different person to write on the board. Margaret drew a better picture of Bald Hill than I had, but the class paid more attention to what Patrick Humphreys did.

He was in the group with Denis and Bucky, who was Bucky to everybody except Mr. Shaw, just like John was JJ. He gave them a name, The Traffic Group, and he changed the observations that Denis had written yesterday in the form of a numbered list, which we all had done, into a table. It trumped our drawing again.

Margaret didn't take it personally. "That's clever," she said.

The whole class thought so.

"As we can see, observations can be recorded more than one way," said Mr. Swenson. "So far, we have lists, a drawing, and a table made up of rows and columns. The heading of the horizontal row is called the X axis, and the vertical column is the Y axis."

The Traffic Group's X axis had two parts: North and South. The Y axis had Cars, Trucks, and Other.

"North is traffic turning from Connecticut River Road onto Neston Avenue from the north, and south is traffic turning onto it from the south," explained Denis.

"What's Other?" someone asked.

"A motorcycle and two tractors," said Denis.

"These are just the totals," said Bucky. "We kept track of the makes and models and colors."

How did they know all those cars and trucks?

"My folks own a gas station," said Bucky.

In fact, they owned Buckminster Fuels, which delivered all over Wortham County, had a filling station and garage on Neston Avenue, and had just opened their second station and named it after him, Bucky's Garage. He had plenty of reasons for being in the group.

"Patrick and I have been tinkering since we were old enough to pick out the tools to hand his father. He owns an engine repair shop in Hinton," said Denis. "Makes are easy, but Patrick's the one who knows all the models."

Patrick, the big boy who sat right next to me in home room, blushed at the attention.

No wonder they chose traffic. If they weren't already friends, most likely they had met over the summer. We had gassed up at Bucky's Garage, which is on the Connecticut River Road, usually just called the River Road. Denis and Patrick's families probably had, too. Hinton is south of Neston, and they'd pass it before the turnoff onto Neston Avenue, where everybody for miles around went to shop. Bucky would have washed their windshield, like he did at the family's Neston Avenue filling station, while the hired man pumped the gas and checked the oil.

"Traffic is physical feature all over now," said Bucky.

I knew from Neston history that it hadn't always been that way, and some people would just as soon have liked horses and buggies instead, although, technically, they were traffic, too, since they weren't that unusual to see on back roads, and most farms used horses and wagons in addition to tractors.

"It isn't like a hill or a tree," said Denis, "but you said other things counted," he added, looking at Mr. Swenson.

"That's right. Natural physical features can change on their own, but manmade objects like roadways also change physical features."

Like bowling alleys where pastures used to be.

"I get how building the road changed things, but how is the traffic changing anything now?" asked JJ.

"Well, see the total number of vehicles at the bottom of the two columns?" said Bucky. "It seems like there's less traffic turning on to Neston Avenue from the south, but that's because of the left turn. The line was backed up, so it took longer for that traffic to get through, especially when there were trucks."

JJ cocked his head as he listened. "I still don't get it."

Patrick finally spoke. "A lane with its own left turn traffic signal might ought to be put in," he said. He looked down and scratched his neck with one finger.

"You've arrived at a conclusion based on observation and the information you collected," said Mr. Swenson, "which is a logical progression."

Like how much more crowded Neston Avenue would get after the Bowl & Grill opened.

"It's also another case for repeated observations and further conclusions."

The Traffic Group certainly had done a lot of observing in a short amount of time, and I thought what Patrick said hit the nail on the head.

"Another lane would change the physical feature again," I said.

"And the traffic," said Adele. "It would help the drivers turning left." She had a soft voice, but since it had taken all of a day to decide she was the prettiest girl in seventh grade, she had the floor. "It would fix the problem."

She looked at Patrick. He turned beet red.

"Yeah, widening the road would fix the traffic problem all right," said JJ defensively. "There's just one other problem. The road would come right up to the door of the Sawmill Apartments. My door. No thanks."

Somebody piped up, "Yeah, you wouldn't like it," but Martha Zeno said, "I think it's a great idea. I'm on the Hinton bus, and two days in a row, the wait to make the turn was something awful, and anyway, there's plenty of room to widen the road."

Mr. Swenson left it to us to duke out making a physical change that that was nowhere near happening, but Adele poured oil on the water.

"Then maybe a police officer could direct traffic when it's busy," she said.

"It would help," Denis agreed, "but," he added ruefully, "somebody would have to direct traffic most of the day. There's always a line to turn left."

JJ must have noticed the traffic problem, but he didn't say anything. Bucky nodded. Bucky's Garage wasn't that far from the intersection, so he would notice, not that it would be bad for their business. If Denis and Patrick came into Neston very often, they would have waited in the line every time they wanted to turn onto Neston Avenue. Considering that heavy traffic of the motorized variety was pretty much unheard of in Hinton, it would get their attention.

"The police at least ought to direct traffic before school," said Martha. "I don't want to be late because the bus can't get here on time."

Now that was another personal problem nobody would want, so it got some sympathy. Despite what he'd said, Denis had to see a traffic cop would help.

Whoever would have thought Geography would be a controversial class?

CHAPTER 12

AT LUNCH, I GOT in line with Margaret right away, and although I had said not to wait, she and Sophie and Theresa did anyway while I bowed my head to thank God for the Sloppy Joe sandwich overflowing its squishy bun onto limp French fries.

Margaret got the question I'd been wondering about out of the way. "Why did you cut your hair?" she asked Sophie.

Sophie shrugged, as if it wasn't the big deal to her that it was to everyone else. "I was in the water almost every day at camp this summer, and when I got out my hair was so damp all the time, I couldn't stand it any more, so I asked a girl who plans to go to beauty school to lop off a few inches. It dried so much faster, I had her trim a few more inches."

Theresa and I nodded. She spent the summer in her pool, and I spent it swimming in Île de L'eau. We understood that constantly wet waist-length hair had to be annoying, but we also shared in the fascination of such a drastic change. It would be like Linus giving up his blanket, except hair really is part of you. I wondered if Sophie had some other reason.

"She did a great job," said Margaret.

"She only cut it to a bob. I got the pixie done at a fancy hairdressing salon in Portland."

"*Très chic,*" I said.

"Thanks. I'd never been to a salon before. I'm looking forward to going to Annette's Beauty Shop here in town to keep it up." She stabbed a fry. "I feel free."

So that was it. People had always been possessive about Sophie's long hair. They tugged on her pigtail, for fun and for mean, and when she wore her hair out, even strangers petted it all the way down her back, none of which is very polite.

"What did you say the name of that camp is?" Margaret asked.

"Pine Tree Camp. It's named after the state tree of Maine, and because the camp has its own lake, and pine trees circle the entire lake."

"You were gone a long time," I said, wondering if she liked that.

"Most of the summer. Next year, too. I'll be a junior counselor."

That answered my question.

"Is it like Neston Campgrounds?" asked Margaret.

"Sort of. Pine Tree is a lot bigger, so there are a lot more choices."

"Like what?"

"Tennis, volleyball, archery, separate buildings for arts and crafts and putting on plays. All kinds of boating and water sports. The biggest difference is there's an equestrian center."

"That's for horses, right?" asked Margaret.

Sophie nodded. "Stables and riding arenas, and there are miles of trails for horseback riding. Or just walking."

Pine Tree Camp was huge compared Neston Campgrounds, but even without all those extras, I had gotten the basics and done the usual camp things, including learning to swim, building a fire and cooking over it, and canoeing over to the island of Île de L'eau, where we hiked.

"What did you like best?" I asked.

"Hands down, the backcountry trip."

Her eyes lit up. With the short bangs and wisps surrounding her face, her eyes looked bigger and bluer, her cheekbones more curved, her lips fuller.

"Four days, hiking from one spot to another, cooking in the open, sleeping under the stars."

"It sounds like you had a lot of fun," said Theresa.

"You'd love camp," said Sophie. "I wish you would come next year. You have to go at least once in your life," she said pleadingly.

Now that was a surprise. Like us Durands, all the older Fortins and the Bouchards had gone some time or other. What reasons could the Georges have for Theresa not going to camp? Could they really not spare her for one week? Sophie was right. It was high time the Georges budged.

"I'd be so old compared to the other girls there for the first time," said Theresa.

"No you wouldn't, and especially not if you go next year," said Sophie.

"Do you really think so?" Theresa asked doubtfully.

"I'm sure of it."

"I'd stand out," Theresa persisted.

"Only if you're really good at something. Nobody pays attention to how old you are the first time you go to camp. Except the counselors. They have to. It's on the application. I could have a brochure sent to you."

Theresa's mouth twitched. "Alright."

"I'll send you a postcard first. I have lots left over. That way, when your family gets the mail, they can see how beautiful the camp is."

"They'll notice it was sent from here."

"Then just say I forgot to send it when I was there. I mean, really, I did."

"Okay," said Theresa.

On the other hand, from the way she talked, Theresa sounded like she needed her own convincing. If she really wanted to go, she would have insisted. Had she held herself back? She must have her reasons.

Going to overnight camp the first time was frightening enough, and it must be a lot worse when camp is far away from home. Theresa seemed independent because she held her own with her brothers, but the Princess did everything with her family. Now she faced the fear of not fitting in as a first-time camper. Did she need to budge, too?

"Can you get a brochure sent to me?" asked Margaret. "I'd love to go."

"Sure. Word of mouth is how most campers go to Pine Tree."

That was another surprise, since I suspected Pine Tree Camp cost a pretty penny compared to Neston Campgrounds, and it would be hard for Mr. Fortin to afford it with his teacher's salary and a growing family.

"Do you want me to have a brochure sent to you, Ette?" asked Sophie.

I thought for a second. I wasn't sold on going.

Just like that, four fingers pointed back at me. *Who's the one who needs to budge?* But I had my reasons, too. I had gone to camp three times before Gabe was born. Admittedly, I could see The Neston Arms from one of the lookouts on Île de L'eau Island, but it still counted as away.

They were waiting for me to answer.

"Okay."

It was only for a brochure in the mail, not that I'd go.

"Maybe we'll all go together," said Margaret excitedly.

Sophie jotted down our addresses.

"Look at the time!" said Margaret. "I've got Phys Ed next. What have you got?"

CHAPTER 13

IT WAS OBVIOUS FROM the group going into the gym that the same girls from Geography class who had surnames from the end of the alphabet were also in PE class. There was no question Sophie would stick together with Margaret and Theresa and me again.

"Donna says to get into the locker room as soon as they take attendance," I said as we put our books into cubbies, "so you can get first dibs on your locker."

So we stood closest to the locker room entry while Miss Williams, the assistant teacher, called our names and issued shapeless one-piece gym uniforms. They were as fashionable as coveralls, only short-sleeved and lopped off at the knees, and meant to fit everybody, which meant they might actually fit nobody, least of all me.

"Ladies, listen up," she hollered above the griping. "We're starting the year with softball instead of field hockey due to the construction next door. We'll warm up with one lap around the track and meet behind home base."

The varsity football team wasn't about to cancel competing with other schools, but making the girls play field hockey right next to that construction mess was another story. Sophie was disappointed. Not me. Running the track around the field was close enough.

Miss Williams blew her whistle. "No lollygagging!"

We charged the locker room. There were small sections of locker areas, and based on another of Donna's tips, I led the four of us to the last section. It was farthest from the teachers' office, which opened to both the gym and the locker room, which made that end Grand Central. We'd also be away from the shower entrance and exit in the middle. There wouldn't be any girls bunching up or passing by. In other words, no people traffic.

I was trying not to notice anything while we got changed, but it was true, you just couldn't help it. They all had on regular bras. It wasn't my imagination that Theresa looked more grown up. She was more developed in the bust than Margaret and Sophie, but they were all developed. Naturally. They were thirteen. I was still only eleven. Of course, they noticed my training bra, too. I sure was glad I had listened to Donna and worn the best bra and panty set.

I spun my combination lock, and for a second, I thought of Dieter. It was the lock we had used at the beach during the summer. I prayed a quick prayer for him.

We dashed outdoors. The bowling alley lot thundered so loud you could feel it. The bulldozers heaved dirt, and choking clouds of dust blew over. I jumped at the sharp bleep of a siren and the roar of trucks gearing up. We all got distracted by the police cruiser with its lights flashing, blocking traffic as two haulers carrying bucket loaders screeched into the lot. They were so big, they needed the entire width of Neston Avenue to make the turn through the opening in the chain link fence.

"Let's go, girls," said Miss Williams.

What with all the ruckus and the distraction and the Sloppy Joe repeating on me, I did not get off on my best foot. I had been active all summer, but bicycling isn't the same as running. After the first few yards, my legs were as heavy as wet cement. Margaret came alongside, and we kept pace together. Nothing fazed Sophie. She sprinted way ahead of us. Theresa fell behind but hung on. Several girls lagged. Most of us huffed and puffed when we came to a standstill.

Miss Gendron, the regular gym teacher, lined us up and eyeballed us like troops under inspection. She didn't bother using the class roster.

"Alright, Shrimp, you're the captain of the Small Fry team."

I looked around to see who she chose.

"Heads up," she bellowed, pointing her finger at me.

"Me?"

"Do you see another shrimp?"

I looked at Miss Williams. She was consulting her clip board.

"My name is Etienne Durand," I said to Miss Gendron. *And God is my rock, so you better watch out.*

"Over here, Etienne," said Miss Williams.

I stood next to her.

"And you, Green Giant," Miss Gendron barked at Tina. "You're captain of the Giants."

Great. Just great. I needn't have worried about being picked last. The gym teacher picked *on* me! Shrimp! Small Fry was insulting, too.

It was a setup. The captains should have picked the teams, but Miss Gendron picked the team members and their positions, pointing and barking, "You, you, you!" until she had stacked Goliath against David.

Mom and Dad would hear about this.

Except for Sophie and a couple of timid but large girls, you could see the Giants gloating. The girls next to me, even Theresa, looked dejected. Janice, who had been swept into Small Fry, stood with her arms wrapped around herself like she was cold. I had one chance to do something as team captain before we took the field.

"Our team has a new name," I announced, shaking in my boots. "We're the Sharks."

Miss Gendron was just registering my saucy lip when she got upstaged by the assistant teacher, who waved and yelled, "Sharks on the field!" Miss Gendron's veiny sausage legs couldn't handle running at all—she had walked out, so she donned the umpire gear while Miss Williams trotted out to run the field. We followed.

It may have been the only power I could grab as captain, but it worked. Theresa perked up at the name, and the Sharks scrambled like mad, which meant Janice had to pull her weight, too, or the whole team would go against her. No matter what happened, I couldn't get blamed because she and Tina had been pitted against each other. It was out of my hands, for a few weeks anyway, until indoor volleyball started. Who knew what would happen then?

The Sharks' pitcher was Melissa Pelkey, a Missy if there ever was one, and I don't mean that unkindly. Missy's very feminine and particular about her delicate appearance, which is exactly why Miss Gendron picked her. She must have figured Missy wouldn't be a very good pitcher, and she wasn't, but the first two Giants up to bat swung at everything she threw, so they struck out quickly. Missy's first pitch to their third batter looked really good to me, but Miss Gendron called it a ball. There was nothing I could do. In any event, the batter hit the next pitch. It so happened that Mary Halloran was a crack left fielder, and we got the last out because of her catch. The Giants never got a player on base. Tina looked unhappy as they took the field.

"Batter up! Hustle, hustle!" yelled Miss Gendron.

Wouldn't you know it, she put Janice first up to bat for the Sharks.

Janice took one look at Cindy Young, the Giants big-boned pitcher, and stepped out of the box for a practice swing.

"Keep your eye on the ball!" I called out, just like any team captain would.

She gave me a dirty look as she stepped to the plate.

She let a pitch go by.

"Good eye!" I yelled. The ball was obviously too high for Miss Gendron to call it a strike, but I could be encouraging, just like any team captain would. Janice stepped back and took another practice swing, but this time she was more confident.

Another pitch came. She let it go by.

"Good eye! Good eye!" The whole Sharks team was yelling.

"Ball two," Miss Gendron growled in a low voice.

She was mad. She'd made a mistake with Cindy. Cindy looked sturdy, but her pitches weren't any better than Missy's, and Janice caught on to it quickly.

But the next pitch looked to be Cindy's best. We held our breath. It was headed for the strike zone, but the ball petered out and sunk just before going over home plate. The Sharks shrieked "good eye" over and over. I couldn't believe she held on for that pitch. Janice really did have a good eye.

"Ball *three*," said Miss Gendron furiously.

Cindy must have gotten rattled because her next pitch went over Miss Gendron's head. A walk-on! We went wild.

"Way to go," I said, like any captain would.

Janice dropped the bat nonchalantly and trotted to first base.

Adele was up to bat next, and she had learned from what just happened. She held still on Cindy's first pitch, another ball, but she knew a good pitch when she saw it. She made clean contact on the second pitch. "Go Sharks! Go Sharks!" we screamed as she ran to first, but Sophie, who must've played softball at camp, was just as good a left fielder as Mary. She backed way up and caught the ball. For a second, I hoped it would fumble out of Sophie's glove. These things happened, but Sophie caught the ball and held it up so it would be clear Adele was out.

"Good run," I said when Adele returned, and the others chimed in.

"Yeah, you're fast."

And Adele didn't linger on disappointment, either. She cheered Margaret on just as much as the rest of us. We had a regular chorus by now.

"Come on, Margaret! Keep your eye on the ball! You can do it! Go Sharks!"

She did. She hit the ball, which flew between first and second bases and landed, and the time it took for the center fielder and right fielder to decide who should scramble after it and throw it back was enough for her to reach second safely and Janice to score a run.

We jumped up and down and hollered. The team held up their hands for Janice to slap. She was as pumped up as a Macy's day balloon—but I was last in line and she turned away from me before she had to slap my hand.

Miss Gendron blew the whistle. "Game's over."

From the way Miss Williams was staying out on the field, we could have played to the end of the inning. After all, we had a Shark on base. The inning probably would have been over in three minutes, but Miss Gendron blew her whistle again.

"Great job," I said as Margaret came off the field smiling.

"We scored!" She grinned.

"You're a good sport." She truly showed what it meant to be happy for the team even though she got taken off the field.

"You're a good captain," she said.

I couldn't really take credit for how the team played, but that made me feel like a million bucks anyway. "Thanks."

"The Sharks won!" hollered Margaret. As the batter who got the credit for driving in the winning run—the only run batted in—she deserved to crow.

And better her than me. I started out on Miss Gendron's bad side. I had no doubt she wanted the Giants to win in the first place. Why, I don't know, but renaming the team the Sharks and then cheering Janice on so she wouldn't swing and miss bad pitches didn't help my cause.

And since Tina was the Giants team caption, I'd stay on *her* bad side as well.

We raced back to the gym and stripped down. Like cattle herded through the chute, we went single file through the communal shower corridor, holding our towels above our heads while water sprayed from the sides so we wouldn't go to the next class with BO.

I was right behind Theresa. She cried out like she had stubbed her toe badly.

Lo and behold, Miss Gendron was standing at the shower exit, grinning like the Cheshire Cat.

As soon as Theresa saw her eyeballing us, she covered herself and her towel got soaking wet.

Miss Gendron laughed. "Put your used towels in here," she said, indicating a rolling canvas bin.

I kept my towel up, but I felt just as embarrassed as if I were as developed as Theresa. My whole body burned as Miss Gendron looked me over.

In our section, Theresa was squeezing the wet towel over her chest with one hand and fumbling with her lock with the other. She was crying. Theresa George was the last girl on earth I ever thought I'd see cry.

The clean towels were gone, so I grabbed a used towel from the bin and handed it to her. It was better than the sopping wet one. She tied it over her bosom and let the wet one drop. I threw it in the bin.

Sophie came in shaking her head, and Margaret had fire in her eyes. We got dressed in silence.

Miss Gendron marched back and forth past the locker sections. We were in that last section, but she made a point of strolling by, stopping, smiling, watching us struggle to tug dry clothes over our damp bodies.

Mrs. Richardson would hear about this.

CHAPTER 14

EVEN IF THE MISS Gendron episode hadn't happened, I would have had enough to report to Mrs. Richardson about how I was doing so far. Today was supposed to be the first of our individual weekly meetings, but wild horses couldn't have kept Mom and Dad from being here.

They were standing in the waiting room of the Guidance Offices when the secretary let me in. She closed the door lickety-split. There was an outburst behind Mrs. Richardson's door, and seconds later, Tony George blew out of her office.

"I'll take this to the superintendent," he threatened. "The whole school board."

He halted at the sight of us. Principal Gaudet was on his heels.

"Here's the one who was with Theresa! You tell them," he ordered me.

"Now, if you'll calm down, that's what she intends to do," said Dad.

Tony huffed and backtracked.

"We're a bit crowded, but if you don't mind, it will be best if we continue meeting in here," said Mr. Gaudet.

Mom and Dad shook hands with him. "Of course."

Papa George and Gregory were also in the office, and when we came in, they vacated the chairs in front of Mrs. Richardson's desk and sat on a bench with Tony. I sat next to Theresa, who sort of sniffled a hello. She had a wad of crumpled tissues in her lap. Mom and Dad sat next to us, and Mr. Gaudet closed the door and stood guard.

Theresa pulled fresh tissues from one of the boxes on the desk. It had felt like a funeral since the moment we came out of the gym shower, but I was still too angry to cry.

"Good morning, Etienne," said Mrs. Richardson calmly.

"Good morning, Mrs. Richardson."

"Theresa has told us what she experienced in your Physical Education class yesterday. Can you tell us about your experience?"

"Yes."

They might have been expecting me to start with Miss Gendron eyeballing us naked, but I started at the beginning.

"Shrimp?" said Mrs. Richardson. "Did I hear you correctly?"

Theresa and I both nodded. She made a note, and as soon as she looked up, I went on with Green Giant and Small Fry and how the name-calling was just one of the ways that Miss Gendron stacked the teams unevenly and played favorites.

"I don't know why. It's not like it was a playoff game. It was only our first PE class."

Papa George looked down and shook his head, Gregory rubbed his forehead like he had a headache, and Tony looked about to burst an artery.

"This isn't a school, it's the Coliseum!" he said.

"Put a lid on it," said Dad.

Tony looked none too pleased, but he did as told.

"And then what happened?" Mrs. Richardson prompted me back on track.

I looked at the clock.

"Take your time," she said, "as long as you need. We're not on any schedule, and you needn't return to class until you feel ready."

I wish I'd thought of that yesterday. Why hadn't I run to the front office right after gym class? Why hadn't any of us? The upset we felt hadn't gone away just because the PE bell rang. I'd stayed so burned up during Health class that all I got out of it was that Mr. Gilbert said his wife was the head school nurse, but I'd cooled down during Social Studies. "The situation" took all my attention. But this wasn't the moment to take my mind off of the upset. Now was the time to let it all out, like cutting the poison out of a snake bite.

My face turned red just repeating how Miss Gendron looked us up and down when we came out of the shower. That stare. That smile. Theresa covered her face with tissues.

I had to stop for breath before I could tell how Miss Gendron made a point of watching us get dressed, too. Mom squeezed my hand. My voice wobbled, but I got through it.

"You can ask Sophie and Margaret," I said. "They were in the same locker section with us. And all the girls who went through the shower. They'll tell you it's true."

Theresa and I knew for a fact that Margaret and Mr. Fortin had met with Mr. Gaudet after school, and Sophie's father, Mr. Ted, had called him.

"We believe you," said Mrs. Richardson, looking up at Mr. Gaudet, "and their word as well."

It sounded like he had told her, and she trusted what he said. He left his post by the door and stood next to her. "Yes, we do."

Then he said, "Do you recall seeing Miss Williams during this time? When you showered and changed?"

Theresa uncovered her face and looked at me. We both thought for a minute.

"No. I don't remember seeing her at all." I said. "Do you?"

Theresa probably knew as well as I did what the question meant: was Miss Williams an accomplice?

Theresa blew her nose and cleared her throat. "Only in the gym. After we came back from playing softball, she unlocked the door to let us in, and she was there when I left. Miss Gendron...was the only one who stayed in the locker room. When the bell rang and we were leaving, some girls were coming in for the next class, and Miss Williams was showing them where to put their books."

She'd obviously replayed the scenes in her head more than I had. I'd been next to her and hadn't noticed all that. Shock hadn't wiped out her powers of observation like it had mine.

"Do either of you have anything else to add? Anything at all?" Mrs. Richardson asked.

Theresa shook her head.

"No," I said.

"If you think of anything else, let us know," said Mr. Gaudet.

Mrs. Richardson put her hand over her heart as if she was about to say the Pledge of Allegiance. "Thank you, both of you, for being so courageous to tell us what you experienced." She nodded at us.

I took a tissue then.

Gregory leaned toward the desk. For attention. He got it.

"Let me be clear," he practically whispered.

"No one shames my sister without answering for it."

All of Tony's grandstanding couldn't add up to the impression Gregory left. He meant business.

"The Georges, we are people of honor," said Papa George quietly.

"As are the Durands," said Dad. "Isabelle and I are here for Etienne, as well as for Theresa, but also for all the girls who've had to suffer mistreatment in many ways."

"That's right," said Gregory. "This woman—" he tapped the desk with his index finger, "this woman isn't just a voyeur. She's a sadistic pedophile."

A what? What?

"I agree," said Dad. "Mr. Gaudet?"

"Our goal is to ensure the honor of every student."

It was the kind of thing a principal had to say.

Tony shook his head and Gregory crossed his arms and Mr. Gaudet added, "I will personally remind each and every teacher of that goal."

"That's not enough, and you know it," said Gregory.

"I do believe everything the girls have told me," Mr. Gaudet repeated. "However, teachers are not dismissed automatically on the basis of charges." He held up his hands so Tony wouldn't explode again. "But given the seriousness of these allegations, Miss Gendron has been placed on leave while we investigate."

"While you investigate," said Tony scornfully.

"For your information, I apprised the superintendent and the entire school board of the situation as soon as I learned of it. We are acting in accordance with the law, and according to that law, she has a right to be heard," said Mr. Gaudet.

They fumed, but Mrs. Richardson said, "It *won't* happen again."

CHAPTER 15

THE NEXT MORNING IN home room, the announcements had been made and we were waiting for the bell to ring for first period when Mr. Gaudet came on over the intercom with an extra announcement.

"Miss Gendron is out due to an injury and we all wish her the best during her recuperation. Miss Williams has taken over as the Girls' Physical Education teacher, and classes and games will continue as usual."

Injury, my foot.

The bell rang, and late to class or not, I went to the landing beside the stairwell.

"She won't be coming back," I said.

"Not ever," said Margaret. She had the look of sweet revenge.

Theresa didn't need to say a word. Not if the Georges had anything to do with it. She closed her eyes and heaved a breath, gathering relief. Atta girl.

Adele, who must have gotten the lion's share of ogling, joined us. "She can't afford to risk it," she said.

If Miss Gendron ever set foot in the school again, her dirty laundry would be hung out for the whole world to see.

It won't happen again.

That should have calmed my nerves, but my stomach didn't catch up to the news in my head. Having Miss Gendron gone would not cut any ice as far as Janice and Tina were concerned.

They kept their distance at the bus stop, but Janice had refused to give me the high five, and Tina gave me the evil eye when she handed papers back to Patrick. I thought ignoring them would keep the peace—for the time being, until we'd inevitably have to work together—but PE pitted them against me every time. Sports are competitive, and they'd take advantage of it whether we were on the same or opposite teams. I expected the situation would drag on in every sport we played.

All morning, the closer PE got, the more my stomach knotted up, and that was even before the salty ham at lunch. I got a hall pass to the ladies' room. I understood how Brenda felt. She vomited. I urinated.

Theresa and Margaret were already eating when I got to our lunch table.

"Where's Sophie?" I asked.

"Over there," said Theresa.

I looked and found her sitting with girls from the Giants. They were all in the same home room, the same sections of certain classes.

We weren't peas in a pod after all.

If she stuck with them, we'd need to find another person to make a foursome at our table. Who would fit in as easily as Sophie had?

I was surprised that she'd give up our fab four so quickly. I was just getting the feel of belonging, and I liked it. I didn't like the idea of having to work at it a while longer.

The empty seat was like losing a front tooth. Your tongue keeps going to the hole in your gum, and of course everybody has to say something about the new space.

Didn't Theresa and Margaret care? I thought Theresa did. After all, she had noticed. But I didn't think Margaret would. Like everything else, it was water off the back of a duck, something I couldn't quite learn from her. Maybe you were born that way. But then she also looked around to see who else could sit with us. Janice came by.

"Janice, you want to sit with us?"

Janice looked like she'd been asked to sit on the bus bully's lap. "I'm sitting over there."

"Okay. Maybe next time."

Margaret didn't know about Eddie. Janice and Tina had been very careful to make sure nobody else did, so they wouldn't get caught.

I looked around the cafeteria again, wondering who else noticed the hole at our table. They had their own feelers out, not only watching who fit in where, but also checking to see if they truly fit in where they already were.

First, like Gabe's peg and hammer set, you had to get a basic fit, round peg in round hole, square in square. But after that, you have to fine tune, like a piece in a puzzle. Sometimes a piece almost fits, but not quite, and you can't force it. Not just any vacancy would do. You have to fit in with the others just right.

All the same, it looked like I wasn't any different from most of the kids in seventh grade who wanted to pigeonhole themselves as fast as possible—as if it would keep any of us safe once we fit into our slot. Sophie proved it could be easy come, easy go, as long as there were other good enough slots available.

The cafeteria, which also included eighth graders in the earliest lunch period, was pretty well divided between the kids who'd gone to Neston Elementary School together and those who hadn't, but there were exceptions. Adele was from Keenan, but the girls at her table came from three other towns, which I only knew because Mrs. Spaulding had us say where we were from when we introduced ourselves. The Traffic Group, which was from Hinton and Neston, sat together. Brenda was sitting with two girls who must've been out of towners because I'd never seen them before; there was a hole at her table, too.

I recognized a few kids. I didn't know them by name but by their family farm names, even the far-flung ones. Mom and Dad, as well as Frieda and Carl, often shopped at farm stands in summer. It was a good excuse to get out for scenic drives during nice weather, when the roads were in their best condition, and I was always eager to go. We bought what we didn't grow in our own garden, but we also gave those places our patronage because they supplied the Arms. Business and pleasure could mix once in a while, and as the adults jawed, I watched the kids. It wasn't unusual to see them running produce stands.

Like the rest of the world, we made a point of getting out and about in Wortham County in the autumn. Farmers took advantage of the foliage traffic to hold open houses, which were as entertaining for us locals as for tourists since they included plenty of tasting samples. Sure, the farmers wanted to promote their products so people would become loyal customers, but the samples did more than that. People got to know the farmers and their farms. Just as they worked stands, the youngsters took part in their family's farm tour. I learned a lot.

But even sleet and mud up to the axles couldn't keep people away from sugaring-off events. We only trekked as far as Wheeler Farm at the other end of Stony Brook Road. The Percherons hauled in vats of maple sap, which were boiled down in evaporators. It was a big to-do to get the first of the season Sugar on Snow—boiling maple syrup that freezes as it's drizzled onto a scoop of clean snow. There's no competing with nature's Sno Cone; you can taste the wood fire in the sweet sap.

I'd also tagged along to visit our meat suppliers. Many grazing lands were so far off the beaten path, the residents waved to people driving by, just because, well, because they were people, and people were few and far between, and if the people driving by had out-of-state plates, that was enough to flag them down for chitchat. The kids on these farms did way more than run stands. I'd watched them feeding and handling animals, and they watched me watching them.

Truth be told, the handful of the kids I now recognized in the cafeteria had helped grow the crops and raise the cows and sheep and pigs and chickens that ended up on the plates at La Terrasse.

I hadn't realized it was them getting off their buses the first day of school because, besides all the distractions, they'd grown since I'd last seen any of them, but on closer inspection, I recognized them now. I wondered if they remembered me. I looked pretty much the same for the past two years.

I was thinking how the puzzle pieces already fit into place for those kids when one of them saw me staring. He must have said something to the other boys at his table because Luc Lambert looked right back at me. He stood, and they ribbed him loudly, but he picked up his tray and came to our table.

"Ladies, is this seat taken?"

Margaret looked at Theresa and me. "Is this seat taken?"

"No," I said. "Hi, Luc."

"Hi." He sat down. "How's school treating you?"

We froze. Well, we weren't about to discuss the wringer we'd been through. A couple of seconds went by.

"Yeah, it's not Neston Elementary," said Luc, "but I'm getting the hang of it." To me, he added, "You sure you don't wish you were still there?"

"Too late now," I said. I picked up my Lambert Dairy milk carton. "To high school," I said.

"Cheers," he said, pleased that I gave him the nod.

We clinked cartons and drank.

We ate in silence like perfect ladies and gentleman until our cafeteria neighbors stopped watching, but their heads leaned in close to each other and their conversation dropped as low as the ladies in the lingerie department. Luc was the only boy in the entire cafeteria sitting at a girls' table. That took courage.

I wasn't going to let Sophie's departure keep me from continuing to catch up on summer news. "What did you like best about your family's trip to Plimoth Plantation this summer?"

It didn't take much to get Margaret rolling.

"The plantation is like a whole town, so there are all kinds of activities. We played some games, but mostly it was a lot of work, like feeding animals and cooking and milling wheat and grinding corn. They make it fun, though, so I liked it all." She glanced at Luc. "But it's probably not that interesting to you, having a farm and all."

"No," Luc objected, "it sounds interesting."

"Well anyway, if I had to pick one favorite out of everything, it would have to be the *Mayflower II*—it's a replica—mostly because the other activities are pretty much everyday things, but the long voyage on a ship to the New World was completely different, you know?"

We knew.

"The tour guides said two babies were born on the ship, one during the voyage and one after they anchored, and since Mom is expecting, we asked some questions about them. You'll never believe what they named the one born at sea."

We all took the bait. "Mayflower?"

"Oceanus."

"Really?" said Theresa. It was good to see her perk up again.

"The plantation is on the way to Cape Cod, if you go back there again."

"I hope so," said Theresa. "This place sounds like fun."

"Yeah, there's so much to do, kids don't have time to fidget. Larry and Cathy loved it. Anyway, when Daddy said he was a history teacher, the guides talked with us for a long time about how hard the Pilgrims had it coming over, but when Mom and I went in where they had to stay, it was so cramped, that's when I really felt like what it must have been like. And—"

She paused for a bite of pineapple with her ham, which I also did and must admit, made a nice sweet and salty combination. We nodded and chewed, all ears.

"—Daddy bought a bunch of things to put in the school library display case for Thanksgiving, and he's going to include a spoon I bought, just like the one Governor Bradford's ancestors used. It's only a reproduction, but I found some other spoons at an antique store, and I'm starting a collection. I know, collecting spoons doesn't sound that exciting, but it is to me."

"It sounds interesting," Luc reassured her.

Margaret must not have been back to the Neston Historical Society Museum since the Lamberts had donated personal items for the Civil War tableau display. She'd have known just how interesting it all was to him.

"If you see a spoon rack anywhere, let me know," she said to the table. "I already saved up for it."

CHAPTER 16

SOPHIE WALKED WITH HER friends to the gym, but she stayed in the locker room section with Theresa and Margaret and me. Maybe it was better not to put all your peas into one pod, at least not the whole day long. I was already pegging myself with only three girls, and look how jangled I got as soon as one dropped out. It was like touching the zebra on Gabe's crib mobile; the elephant and giraffe and lion moved, too.

We changed in the privacy I had wanted in the first place. When we went into the gym, the girls had gathered into two familiar groups.

A woman I hadn't seen before was standing next to Miss Williams, who had gotten an overnight promotion to regular gym teacher. She was all smiles. She blew her whistle to quiet us down. Standard procedure.

"Girls, this is Miss Brennan. She'll be taking over as the assistant gym teacher," she looked at Miss Brennan, "hopefully permanently."

Miss Williams was no slacker in the physical fitness department, but Miss Brennan, who was about four inches taller and very slender, had her beat in calf muscle development.

"Good morning, girls! Now, who have we got for teams here?" she said in a chipper way, and everybody snapped to attention. She had an English accent.

Tina didn't skip a beat. "Giants!"

"Sharks!" We interrupted their cheer with our own.

"I see. Well then, shall we keep our teams?"

"Yeah!"

We shall.

So, she and Miss Williams were not going to fix the situation. I didn't doubt that Miss Gendron had meant to stack the teams, but the way the game played out, it hadn't mattered, had it?

Miss Brennan took attendance. You never saw so much interest in attendance being taken. She had a smile for everyone. Closing her metal roster case, she said, "Captains, Miss Williams and I will set the pace. Lead your teams out."

We started out slow, Miss Williams alongside me and Miss Brennan next to Tina, but they called out to pick up the pace as we passed the construction. With the grassy topsoil razed from the site, the dust blew worse than ever onto the track. We slowed again, and at the softball field home base, our teams lined up opposite each other, hardly even winded.

Miss Williams took over, like she probably would have if she'd been allowed to in the first place.

"Softball, like any sport, is a game of skill. If we're to play well, we've got to have good skills."

Unlike our first game.

"That takes practice. And team work."

"Shall we start with throwing and catching the ball?" said Miss Brennan. "Miss Williams and I shall demonstrate. Each of us shall take five practice throws from the distance of home to first." She trotted to first base like she was floating on air.

"Before you throw, take a good stance with your legs," instructed Miss Williams. "You want stable footing, but with your body flexible enough to be ready to move."

She pivoted to show us how. "Now, take a good look at your target before you throw. You've got to gauge how hard to throw for the distance. You want to aim for the ball to land in her glove."

She showed us the arm movement. Then she showed us how to hold the glove and get good solid catches. All simple enough, but breaking it down was going to make this a whole other ball game.

"Not all throws are the same." Miss Brennan demonstrated the longer stretch for throwing between first and third or from the outfield.

"All right, count off now, one two, one two. Captains, start the count."

"One," I said.

"Two," said Adele, who was standing next to me.

It was simple. We spread out and took turns throwing. After two reps, as Miss Williams called them, we moved into positions for longer throws. Both teachers came around offering suggestions and compliments like, "Try this," "That's it," and "You've got it."

Adele and I were pretty accurate by the time we got called back to home base, plus we'd had a chance for a bit of chitchat. She had milk chocolate eyes and golden honey hair, but she wasn't stuck-up pretty at all. She said she'd been to Sunday Brunch at the Arms and enjoyed it. I said I was glad and asked her if she had any brothers and sisters and she told me she was an only child. Her mother drew portraits. Her father was a border patrol agent, smuggling operations.

"Is it dangerous?"

"Sometimes."

Smuggling has just about always been a way of life in Wortham County, especially since the War of 1812. Some people probably never went back to regular business. I figured it was best not to mention that I was on the side of Chauncey Smith, who ran a smuggling operation during that war, but he was just trying to stay alive after the blockade prevented him from doing business as usual. He skipped town before getting caught, so in the end he lost everything anyway.

"Next week, we'll round out skills on hitting and sprinting," said Miss Brennan, but if we use all our time on drills, we won't have time for an inning, now will we?"

"Captains, coin toss," said Miss Williams.

We stepped up, I called "heads" before Tina had a chance, and won the toss. The Sharks went to bat and the Giants took the field.

Just a little practice throwing and catching improved the pitching, but that meant better swings and hits. The inning was scoreless, which, as far as I was concerned, was a tie. We all had played much better. And at home plate or on the field, Miss Brennan and Miss Williams made fair calls, coached us through swings, and urged us when to run to the next base.

I hadn't expected things would turn around so quickly or so well. Miss Williams just beamed, and Miss Brennan turned out to be as nice as you could want. With teachers who encouraged us instead of bringing out the worst in team rivalry, I began to feel I could rub shoulders with Janice and Tina the same as with anybody else. Almost.

I trusted God to be my rock, but I was just getting used to the idea that God used all sorts of people, including sisters and teachers, to be there in that way. Really, every teacher should be a rock for their students.

All the same, my tummy reminded me that I had some unfinished business with Miss Gendron. It wasn't just what happened with her that kept me riled. Why had Marcia and Donna never warned me, especially Donna, who was a cheerleader and had played intramural sports since day one?

I'd never had a fight with Donna, and I didn't want one now, but the issue didn't go away just because Miss Gendron was gone. I got myself all lathered up about it by the time Donna and Marcia came home from school.

"How come you didn't tell me about her?" I lit into her.

"She's been called a pervert as long as I can remember. I thought everybody knew."

"How was I supposed to find out? All this time, everybody let her—"

"Ignored her, not let her."

"I did not," retorted Marcia.

"What did you do?" I said.

"The first time she gave me that once-over, I asked her if she liked what she saw. I said there was a strip bar just over the border if she couldn't get enough from the students. She steered clear of me after that."

Marcia really knew how to nip it in the bud. No wonder nobody ever gave her any guff. Sometimes she nipped sooner than she ought to, but her quickness worked in my favor when she stood up for me against Tina and Janice.

She hadn't solved the Miss Gendron problem for everybody else, though, only herself, and maybe the girls in her locker room section.

It was solved now, the hard way: after a lot of girls had been shamed for years. Why had no one ever spoken up?

Well, I hadn't spoken up, not for the past year. I never forced Tina or Janice to tell me why they decided to snub me and call me a name. I gave up, and I never complained, never told anybody, just let myself get hurt. I'd been patient alright. A patient coward, too scared to say or do anything.

I couldn't believe all those girls who had been humiliated in PE were cowards. They must have been afraid. Just telling others what happened was embarrassing.

But plenty of girls, especially those on the sports teams, the ones who got the worst of it, really had ignored it.

Including Donna. And she didn't sound like she'd been afraid or embarrassed—but if Marcia dared to snot off to Miss Gendron, Donna must have felt something the first time it happened to her—and once the shock was over, she got used to it—and in the end, they did let Miss Gendron get away with it.

Yet I couldn't stay mad at her. It was easier to forgive Donna than a lot of other people. She should have said something, but Donna was never mean on purpose. And I got another reason to be proud of her.

CHAPTER 17

AS THEY SAY, THANK God it's Friday, and I really meant it when I had my morning prayer time. The first four days of school had hit some rough sailing. Not just regular rough—I'd been expecting that—but storm rough.

I was better off pouring my heart out to God than keeping it bottled up, but I still wished I had Dieter to talk to. He said I could call. I looked at the slip of paper he had given me with his dorm number at school on it. If today hit another awful rough patch...

But he'd just be settling in, and catching up at the same time, since he had a pass from his classes to compete in the Olympic swimming trials in New York City. He was behind the eight ball from the get-go. It wouldn't be right to dump my problems on him just before he competed.

I felt battered, but he had a lot more on the line. I returned the piece of paper to the front flap of my prayer journal.

Please, God, at least let the week end on a happy note.

But it started out off-key.

"Denis? Ah, there you are," fumbled Mr. Picard, taking attendance.

Without a seating chart, Mr. Picard was having a hard time remembering our names, and every day, Denis had sat in a different seat in English class. Today he had moved to where Luc had been sitting near me all week, although you couldn't call it bumping when you were allowed to sit wherever you wanted. Luc moved a seat forward next to Margaret.

"Just mixing it up, Julian," said Denis. "Variety is the spice of life."

The class giggled.

Denis was not taking liberties. That's what Mr. Picard kept insisting we call him.

Now, I understood what it was like to be called the wrong name, but calling teachers by their first name wasn't the model of respect I'd been taught, or any of us had, for that matter, so all week, we kept calling him Mr. Picard. But he didn't want his first week of school ending that way, and I was the one he chose to make that point.

I was going to ask him when the play would be put on, and I still wasn't used to not raising my hand, so to get his attention, I said, "Mr. Picard?"

"We're supposed to be on the same page, Etienne," he said. "If I call you by your first name, you call me by mine. Julian, remember?"

The way he talked to me, I felt ashamed, but I said, "Okay, Julian."

He wasn't like Frieda and Carl, the only adults not related to me that I called by their first names. Well, except for Leo, of Leo's Pizza, but all the kids called him Leo. And Frieda and Carl and I really were on the same page. All the same, I saw his point. If he wanted Julian instead of Mr. Picard, like I wanted Etienne instead of Ettie, he'd get it.

I wasn't the only one who felt uncomfortable calling him Julian, but given an inch, the students took a mile. They had stopped raising their hands, as he wanted, and called out answers, but they also asked questions whenever they wanted even if the questions weren't on topic, and already more hall passes were issued for the bathroom from that one class than all the others combined.

I also wasn't feeling comfortable with *Inherit the Wind*. We had been assigned to complete Act I so we could begin discussion, and our weekend homework was to read the rest of the play. I love to read, so it wasn't like me not to get ahead and finish a book, especially a short one, but I put it off. All week, I broke my own policy of doing what I liked the least, or what I found the hardest, first. Not even math was such a challenge. I thought, maybe things will look up in Act II or III.

They must. After all, when I'd told Mom and Dad the whole school was reading the play and the Theater Department would be putting it on, they suggested I find out when, so we could plan well in advance for kitchen coverage for Dad and have a fun night out. They hadn't seen the movie with Spencer Tracy in it.

After he put me in my place for calling him Mr. Picard, Julian never bothered to get to my question.

The prospect of the week ending on a happy note was not looking up, but it was already obvious that Math was going to be the antidote to English. As usual, I concentrated enough that it worked. I was motivated to buckle down and get completely caught up.

Geography was good, too. Although we got weekend homework, nobody minded, since it was "out in the field," the first assignment of a long-term project. All we had to do was pick any spot we wanted to observe for several weeks, at least once a week, and present our findings to the class.

I knew instantly that the Bowl & Grill would be my project. Not only had I taken photographs before work started on it, since Tuesday, I had taken at least one morning and one afternoon photograph—the physical changes were happening that fast. Mr. Shaw let me keep my camera in his locked desk drawer during the day. When I'd asked him if I could and explained what it was for, he was only too happy. It was history in the making, he'd said.

But Sophie stuck with the other girls at lunch, and Luc went back to his crowded lunch table, so the hole was back. Fine. It could be like a spare tire. You don't need it all the time, but when you need it, you really need it. Maybe someone would need a seat some time. Our spare could take the place of their flat. If Luc could pop over just for a short ride with us, anything could happen. It wasn't so bad keeping the option open.

81

I hiked over to Art class, a cluttered and colorful room. Mrs. Casey had the most crooked nose I'd ever seen, a smile tilted in the opposite direction, and a heart of gold. Behind her desk was a framed poster of a pencil drawing in a weird style: her nose was fragmented into triangles and her teeth were a wide rectangle of piano keys. We had to be a ways from learning that technique, but I quickly understood how the student who made that drawing got away with it.

"Our first lesson is learning proportion of the body. You may use any subject you like as a model," said Mrs. Casey, "a photo you bring in, a picture from a magazine, another drawing or painting, so long as it is full body and lifelike in proportion and the subject's limbs are visible. I'm also available as a live model."

I decided I'd use Gabe. The photographs I took of him propped up next to the measuring tape every Sunday would be perfect. In the meantime, to get started on practice drawings, I went to a pile of magazines and cleanly tore out a page, which you were supposed to do if you wanted to use it. The nice thing was, it was an advertisement of a model wearing a Butterick dress pattern, with the cover of the pattern package in the corner of the ad.

I was surprised that all we had to do was copy a model, but as Mrs. Casey walked us through the steps, it only proved how much we had to learn. After fifteen minutes, we were laughing at our own drawings. Adele's was the only one completely in proportion.

How'd she learn to draw so well?

"My mother paints portraits, and she also draws composites for law enforcement agencies."

Composites?

"When a person describes a criminal suspect, she puts together the suspect's type of forehead and nose and eyes and mouth and chin—all the parts of their face, and their whole body, if possible, until the drawing looks like what the person remembers."

Like the *Wanted* pictures in the post office?

"That's right. It's called forensic art."

"A lot of crimes are solved from it," said Alistair.

Adele nodded. "Sometimes because of the composite alone. If a match is made and a photo is as good as the composite, the photo will replace it, but if a criminal is older than the photo, a composite can show what they might look like now."

Wow didn't quite express how impressed we were.

Things were looking up for Friday to end on a happy note but, given the situation, as Mr. Shaw put it, I couldn't really expect it in Social Studies. Once he had introduced Vietnam, he backed up to get us to look at the big picture from a distance. It was another lesson in proportion.

"Wars do not happen in a vacuum," he said. "Conflicts arise in cycles of causes and effects. Context is everything."

Already, we'd had daily homework reading assignments, with questions to answer about the history and geography of the area, and the weekend reading assignment was long. I regretted not finishing the play. It might be a long time before I didn't have to take any work home. Maybe never.

"Background reading is essential," explained Mr. Shaw. "It will form the foundation to connect the dots"—he jabbed air dots with his reading glasses—"between *politics* and *colonialization* and *militarization*."

He spent half the period reviewing and summarizing what we knew of the big picture so far. It helped, and that was a happy half note. The last half of the class was cut short for the school-wide pep rally, and I hoped it would round out to a whole note.

The first Friday night football game was against Bestbury High, and thanks to the rally, I got some pep for myself.

The main gymnasium was full, the band was playing, and a roar went up as the team mascot, Robbie "The Hornet" Underwood, swooshed around like he was flying, with a sign that said Bestbury stuck in his oversized stinger. The football team was right behind. Each player got some sort of hoot or holler as he trotted out, but none so much as Peter Jarvis.

The second the cheerleaders came out on the floor waving *CUHS is the BEST* flags, the screams raised the rafters. I covered my ears and screamed right along.

They looked sharp. And Donna, I wouldn't be surprised if she was homecoming queen next year.

Just when she turned in my direction, I stood up and bellowed "DONNA!" at the top of my voice, waving both arms like a flag in a stiff wind.

She saw me and smiled a huge smile and waved back. You never heard so many whistles. For just that second, I was in the spotlight with her.

"She's my sister," I announced so everybody sitting nearby in the bleachers heard.

The Hornet gathered the flags and Miss Williams and Miss Brennan took positions spotting the cheerleaders. They jumped into formation and began their chant.

The Hornets are back
And ready to sting!
The yellow and black
Are out to win!

And with that, they sashayed their short skirts, black with yellow inside the pleats. The place went wild. They went through half a dozen routines with more cheers they had made up themselves.

They saved the best for last, the flying cheers, and Donna and Kimmie were the only flying junior cheerleaders. They stood on shoulders to form the top of a pyramid, kicked one leg out for a second, and the whole formation dropped down like a tent collapsing.

It took my breath away.

The bleachers shook from shouting and stamping.

The cheerleaders ran out, waving and calling, "CU there! CU there!"

Donna waved at me again, and I stood a little taller waving back. I had meant to use my bragging rights as a form of flattery on Donna's behalf, but it raised my standing, too.

This past summer, when she had learned I'd be skipping a grade for the second time, Donna had said she was glad she didn't have to follow in my footsteps at school. She thought I'd be a tough act to follow. Ha! I could never follow her cheerleading act.

Come to think of it, sports teams and school clubs were pegs in their own ways, too, good ways. If Mrs. Richardson hadn't warned me before the school year started that extracurricular activities might be a bit much for me to handle for a while, I would have figured it out in this first week. They definitely were out of the question for the time being, but if I really wanted to fit into place as neatly as a puzzle piece, all the activities and clubs and teams were something to consider for the future. It wouldn't be cheerleading, though. That took a lot out of you.

I respected cheerleaders a lot more after the pep rally. People thought they were snobs, but only the best could make the cut on any sports team, and very few could make the cheerleading cut. It was obvious why it was practically the most exclusive team. The cheerleaders deserved their pride of place. And I could see that Donna was the best of the best.

She was in a class all her own.

In other words, her own peg.

Now that was the way to go.

But in the meantime, not a bad one to hang on.

CHAPTER 18

I MADE IT TO the weekend in one piece, although the week had taken a toll on me. I slept so late that it was almost lunchtime when I went downstairs. Homework would have to wait. Mom took Gabe and me over to the Meyers' owners' apartment on the top floor of the Arms. "It's a surprise," she said.

Carl and Frieda always had the coolest heads, but today they were jumping beans. They had bought a color television, brand new and top of the line. They moved furniture so it would fit under the biggest east-facing window, where Carl set up the most powerful antenna money could buy.

There was a reason for all the fuss. Dieter's qualifying trials were starting Sunday morning in New York City. We wouldn't be able to watch them—but the Tokyo games were going to be the first Olympics ever broadcast. They were over a month away, but Frieda and Carl were not going to leave the television reception to the last minute and find out it wasn't good. If Dieter qualified, they planned to see every second of his Olympic race.

If. That was the big word. Nobody wanted to say it, but you had to. Of course, we'd watch even if he didn't qualify, just like Dieter would himself. He'd see what he missed, and we'd see who he'd been up against, what the races were really like, and maybe there would be a peek of Japan.

If the network came in. Their old black and white television got about one and a half channels, when the weather was good.

"Drum roll," said Frieda.

We held our breath. Carl plugged the new television in and Frieda turned the knob on. *Mighty Mouse* appeared in a bright yellow and orange outfit. We cheered. Gabe pushed up and down on Mom's lap. He reached for the TV.

We laughed, but it was another network they were desperate to get, and Carl wasn't satisfied with the picture quality. We gave him feedback each time he shifted the antenna's position to improve the reception, which he said came from a broadcasting transmitter on a mountain in New Hampshire.

Frieda turned the channel knob, and sure enough, *Caspar* came on, picture perfect and clear as a bell. Whew. Gabe squirmed out of Mom's hold and crawled to the TV, and I jumped into action to keep him from smacking the screen.

I didn't go for ghosts at all, not even a supposedly friendly one in a cute cartoon, but the television was a distraction from thinking about Dieter competing in the trials. I had to admit, most of the time, school had been a big distraction. The TV wasn't enough to keep me from feeling nervous for his performance, though, and I knew I should pray instead. It's what Dieter would be doing.

After we left, Mom sprung another surprise on me: *Mary Poppins*. It was at the Bijou. Today, at least, I had another big distraction.

Gabe, feeling happy that I was at home, went down for his nap as usual. With Marcia and Donna to look after him, Mom took me to the matinee, just the two of us. That alone was special.

We had to wait in line, but it was a lot better than getting turned away after the show sold out. I went in and put her cardigan over the back of her seat to hold it while she got popcorn. When she came with a Coca-Cola too, I was as surprised as if it had been a dry martini.

"Coke settles the stomach," she said.

What with Tina and Janice, the PE episode, the change to my diet, and Dieter's trials, she knew my tummy needed settling.

"There's a girl at school who could use some," I said. "She throws up every morning."

"Oh, dear. Is she someone you know?"

"Sure. Brenda Pratt. She told me she hates school. Must be nerves."

"Mmm...it could be...or any number of things."

"Like what?"

In college, Mom had specialized in food and nutrition. She thought for a second. "There are many types of food allergies."

"That could make you throw up?"

"Nausea is a common indicator. I knew a family whose children were affected by the lactose in milk, but they'd been told milk was good for children, so the children drank it and were very sickly. When I finally convinced the parents there were other forms of the nutrients found in milk, the children's health improved almost immediately."

"Maybe that's it." I saw Brenda in the hot lunch line, and it was a wonder hot lunch didn't make more tummies upset.

The theater darkened and fell silent.

And for over two hours, I was thoroughly distracted. I wasn't the only one. The movie was wonderful. Mom and I took our time strolling Parker Street afterwards.

"I'll go see it again," I said, since everybody would be going, and it also cheered me up. A spoonful of sugar wasn't what you'd think it would be, but it was just what I needed to face the next week of school. For that matter, the pile of homework I still had to get done.

We stopped in at Putnam's Art & Photography and I bought yet another album. I already had one that was only for the photos of Gabe that I took every Sunday, and another one that was for everything else, but I planned to transfer the photos I had already taken of the Bowl & Grill lot into a separate album.

Then we went into a long entryway with window displays on both sides. On the left was Four Seasons Formals, and on the right was Four Seasons Fabrics, and at the end were separate doors for each shop.

We eyeballed the Formals display, which already had mannequins decked out in homecoming outfits, but Fabrics always had its own seasonal displays as well. Both sides were fun to window shop. After our fair share of oohs and aahs, we entered Fabrics.

I headed for the bargain section to pick out something for the Jiffy skirt I'd be making in Home Ec, but when we passed by the velvets, Mom said, "Wait, Ette. Aren't these beautiful?"

They sure were. I fingered a bolt. "It's as soft as a kitten."

"Yes. Velvet would drape well from a gathered waist."

I saw where she was headed. "But it's awfully expensive."

Mom shrugged. "Are you on a budget?"

"No, not unless you say so. Mrs. Spaulding said we could pick what wanted."

"I say the sky's the limit!" Mom smiled.

I guess this was my day for getting pampered.

Still, I hesitated. "I thought I would start with something inexpensive, in case I make a mistake."

"The pattern is very simple, but I understand. It's your choice."

We continued to the cottons. The skirt would need a few washings to soften up, but the material would be easy to work with for my first sewing project. I already knew what color I wanted.

"I like navy blue," I said. "As far as I can tell, everyone looks good in it."

"Yes, it's very versatile," said Mom.

On our way to the cash register, she stopped at the velvets again and ran her hand over a bolt as deep blue as sapphire.

"You like it, don't you?" she said.

"Sure, I like it the best."

"Then let me tell you Retail Rule Number One—"

I laughed.

"I'm serious. Helen taught me this rule when we were in college. Here it is. If you really like it, buy it."

"If you can afford it."

"Of course, and sometimes it's worth saving up for or putting on layaway. If you really like it, whatever it is, you will wear it or use it with pleasure over and over. Some things last a lifetime and are passed on."

Then again, some things didn't, like underwear, but Donna still took Retail Rule Number One seriously.

"So buying something you really like is just following the rule," I joked.

"*Absolument.* And I have been following all the rules."

"There are more?"

"Rule Two is the emergency rule. If you don't like something, don't buy it just because it's affordable, not unless it is necessary. It's usually not, but these things happen. Do you remember my heel?"

I did. We were going out to dinner in Montreal and Mom broke a heel in a sidewalk crack. We ducked into a shoe store and she bought an inexpensive pair of high heels she didn't like that much and doubted would wear well, but after all, we had a reservation time.

I was liking the Retail Rules. "Well, the velvet is really nice. I could wear it at Christmas."

"Or Thanksgiving or New Year's or your birthday."

In other words, any cool weather special occasion.

"Maybe I should think it over."

"Oh, no. Retail Rule Number Three is never walk away. As often as not, it won't be there when you go back. It is better to return something if you're undecided."

"Do they take back cut fabric?"

"I suppose this is an exception. Let's make it Rule Three A. Not all things can be returned—but in this case it doesn't matter. You can use this fabric after you are more confident. You'll make something out of it no matter what."

Which was just the retail version of *carpe diem.*

CHAPTER 19

DENIS CAME ALONGSIDE ME as soon as we left home room for English.

"May I carry your books?"

"Did you say, carry my books?"

"Yeah." He smiled down at me.

I thought about it. We were in general ed classes together, even the same study hall and lunch. Didn't he realize he would be carrying my books all day? What about walking with my girlfriends between classes? What if I went to the bathroom? Would he wait outside?

"What for?"

He looked surprised. He shrugged.

Too late I realized that Denis was not put off just because I vetoed Amber, but he did move to a seat across the room. Luc took the seat next to me that Denis would have taken.

"Okay, people," said Julian, clapping his hands together. "We have learned that all literature involves some type of conflict, perhaps more than one of the basic types. Now that you've read the entire play, as we work our way through it, we will identify the types. For now, let's identify the conflict that makes the play happen. The problem."

"Bert Cates read about evolution to his sophomore science class," said Luc.

"Very succinctly stated," said Julian. He liked to throw in a lot of vocabulary, since it was English class. "It is the problem that initiates the action of the play." He drew a triangle on the board and labeled the upslope *Rising Action.*

"But Bert didn't think what he did was wrong," said Tom. "He said teaching evolution isn't as simple as doing a bad thing. It's not good or bad, black or white."

Tom was spot on as well, not that I agreed with Bert Cates.

"Then why was doing so a problem?"

"It was against the law," said Alistair.

"Because?"

"People believed the Bible back then," said Tom.

As if they only believed it then.

"Yeah, instead of evolving from monkeys," said Luc defensively, but it was succinct.

"And what does the Bible say?"

I dove in. "The Bible says God created the heavens and the earth and everything in them in the beginning. They didn't evolve over time."

Exactly the opposite of what Bert Cates read.

"But it doesn't say when the beginning was," said Mary.

"Yeah, that could have happened millions of years ago," Tom backed her up.

"Bert says it could have been a long miracle, not just seven days," said Mary.

"The Bible says six days," I said. The play got seven wrong, too, but I let that fine point go. I was already butting heads, but I added, "If it meant millions of years, it would say so."

"Aha," said Julian. "In addition to the conflict of man versus society—in this case, the law—we find another conflict, between religious beliefs and science."

No, we don't, I thought. At least, I didn't. But then, this was the first time I ever heard anybody bring it up.

"Can't the Bible be scientific?" I asked.

"That is a central question played out in *Inherit the Wind.* Is the Bible sufficient for explaining our origins, or is evolution? The conflict over which one should be taught in schools is a courtroom drama, where sides must be taken. And that question is still being asked."

"If it's legal, then why bother to read the play or put it on?" asked Margaret.

"It remains illegal to teach evolution in Tennessee, which is where the Scopes trial took place, and it's also illegal in Arkansas and Mississippi. Other states have debated it. The issue is far from over."

"Evolution is in our biology books here," said Bucky. "I've seen it." He must have looked at his sister Roxanne's textbook. I made a note to check Donna's.

"Consolidated Union has adopted texts that advance the theory of evolution and we teach from that perspective. Vermont has always been in the vanguard of freedom. However, many people continue to question the theory, so it remains controversial. It is this enduring conflict between faith and facts that makes the play relevant today."

He did it again, made faith separate from facts. Like the Bible isn't true. Just like the play tries to make it.

And that bothered me, since I have faith in God. I felt different from the moment I was born again, and that's probably why I took God's Word so seriously from that moment, when I began reading it for the first time.

The problem that started the play was still a problem.

Mine.

CHAPTER 20

MATH AND GEOGRAPHY TOOK me into calmer waters, but lunch really put me back on an even keel.

Theresa and Margaret went with me into the school store. It was a small room off the cafeteria and only open during lunch since it was run by students. I picked out some sticky CUHS Hornets decals for my lunch box, the one with the domed lid Marcia was too embarrassed to use. It was perfect for me.

Being Mom and a nutritionist and menu developer, she not only planned my lunches based on what I liked that was in season, but she also calculated them based on the short lunch period, as well as on my schedule, mainly planning for little time to digest on PE days. She posted my own menu for the week on the kitchen cork board, "pending contingencies," she said, which was always the case. You never knew what a day might bring.

I also got milk money and a little extra for what-not. My first expense was the school stickers, and I was pressing them on when I informed Margaret and Theresa of my plan. I'd seen it work for Luc and for Marcia and Donna.

"I'm going to stay after school and take the late bus," I said. "I'd rather get more homework done before I go home, and this way, I won't be interrupting Gabe's nap."

I'd figured out that arriving home on the earlier bus was smack in the middle of his nap time. As long as he went down for his nap as usual, he'd just be waking up when I arrived on the late bus. He'd returned to his routine over the weekend, and I wanted to keep things that way. It was a win-win. He'd sleep, I'd work.

"I will, too," said Theresa, getting on board immediately. "Everybody seems to think I'm available to babysit the minute I walk through the door. I'm calling home right now." She got a hall pass and went out to the pay phone.

By the time Margaret pushed some peas into a blob of mashed potato on top of a chunk of meatloaf, she decided that was a clever idea. When Theresa returned, she said, "Be right back." She took a mouthful and left the table. Now there was a girl with a stomach of iron.

Although the plan was a good policy for both Gabe and me, I counted every second until I got home to him, but things were different for me than it was for my friends. Larry and Cathy Fortin were school age, but they still needed looking after when they got home, especially with Mrs. Fortin expecting. Debbie wouldn't like Margaret's new plan one bit. She'd have to pick up the slack. As for Theresa, over time I had discovered that she had eight nephews and one niece, and her family relied on her help. So I understood. We all had our own reasons.

The highlight of the day was Home Ec. It turned out the fabric I picked for my Jiffy skirt was easy to pin to the pattern, and it cut cleanly. Some other girls had picked stretchy material and had problems cutting, which was good to know for when I got around to using the sapphire velvet.

As soon as the final bell rang, Margaret said, "Let's leave our things here and roam the halls."

"I thought you needed to buckle down before you went home," I said.

"I do. But I haven't even seen Daddy's new room yet. This way, we'll really know our way around."

I had to agree. There were diagrams posted that pointed out *You Are Here* but there's nothing like figuring out the big picture personally.

"It's up to you. I can buckle down later."

"Are we allowed to wander around?" asked Theresa.

"Sure. It shows we've got school spirit," said Margaret. "Troublemakers would only stay late for detention."

We had the run of the place. We walked the halls without passes and ventured into senior high territory, including the drafting room and the biology and chemistry labs, where we stood behind Theresa, who took her time checking them out. We were easy to spot as junior high tourists, but one of the teachers asked, "Can I help you?"

"Not today," she said.

We looked into one room after another. I wanted to see the cafeteria kitchen, but it was off limits. The closest we got was a room so big it extended out from the building, but unlike during the school day, the gray metal doors to the Physical Plant were open. Behind a custodian's desk, it was stocked like Neston Farm & Hardware. We got a better look inside a janitor's closet, which was chock full of cleaning products and paper supplies and mops in buckets.

On our way to see Mr. Fortin, we hugged the wall where someone had swung by with a circulating buffer machine. The polish pattern would get scuffed come morning, but we had been raised to show respect for a freshly cleaned floor.

It was more than that, though. I think each of us developed an appreciation for all the hard work that went in to keeping the school running. It took a lot more than teachers. The Physical Plant employees constantly maintained the school, from keeping it spic and span inside to tending everything outdoors as well, especially the athletic fields.

Mr. Fortin was correcting papers, but he was happy to see us and showed off the up-to-date materials on his bulletin board. A poster of *United States History Timeline* was on the left, and *World History Timeline* was on the right. There you had it: junior and senior History classes in a nutshell.

We ran out of time to see the auditorium, but Julian said he would hold a class in there one day in order for us to understand how a play was written to fit on a stage, so we headed back to home room.

There was vim in our step. Margaret was right. We stayed late to buckle down, but getting the lay of the land was more important at the moment. Sometimes a good policy is just that, and it can be broken for other good purposes, like our perspective of high school, which was cut down to size now that we had navigated its whole world.

If I could have chosen people instead of a place for my Geography project, I would have had plenty to report on the daily changes I observed in my friends. As we'd found out in no time flat, some days could be a roller coaster.

The walkaround helped Theresa besides an hour less of babysitting. In her own way, she was just as enthusiastic as Margaret, but from the minute she'd stepped on the bus and been bullied, school had whittled down her enthusiasm.

But Margaret bent with the wind. A scorch here and overwatering there weren't about to blight her for good. Just being around her helped both Theresa and me. As we boarded the late bus, the wilt in our posture was corrected, at least for the moment.

Chapter 21

SOMEBODY MUST HAVE TOLD on Brenda Pratt because I almost walked smack into the head nurse escorting her out of the bathroom.

"See ya," said Brenda. "I'm outta here."

"Where are you going?"

"Private school."

"Come along, Brenda," said Nurse Gilbert.

Brenda had the last word. "You can say I said so."

I doubted anyone would ask me where she'd gone, but I hoped it was the kind of place Brenda could like. It's hard to learn when you hate school. Maybe they could straighten out her nerves and whatever food allergies were making her sick to her stomach as well.

It was difficult enough for me, and I loved learning. I also had Mom and Dad to talk to; plus, my first solo appointment with Mrs. Richardson was starting tomorrow; and I always had God. The nice thing was, I could talk to God any time, any where. I started my day talking to God first. My love for Jesus was still a baby love, but that was just as it ought to be. I was only a month-old Christian.

But since that day, one thing or another helped me grow. I came across an old devotional booklet, the kind for the taking at church. Mrs. Lacroix had put it with other odds and ends she found when she was cleaning. Call it chance, but in the passage that it was crumpled open to, God gave me the same advice that he gave the apostle Paul: "'*My grace is sufficient for you, for My power is perfected in weakness.*'"

I was interested to see how that would work out. More than once at school I felt like the time I was sitting next to Mom when the station wagon spun out of control on a snowy downhill. Talk about feeling weak. Mom turned in the same direction of the spin, and I screamed and braced myself for the crash—but it never came. After we straightened out and I calmed down, Mom explained it was the only way to regain control. Turning in the opposite direction would have only pulled us deeper into the spin.

I figured there would always be spinouts in life. Sooner or later, you had to get some traction. In the meantime, all you can do is keep turning to grace. Like turning in the direction of the spin, it's not a natural reaction, but I had to trust God that it worked.

Seeing Brenda being led away, I prayed in the moment, for her and for myself. I just knew this was the beginning of a spinout day. The conditions were already primed for it.

There had been no word from Dieter on Sunday or Monday about his qualifying tryouts. My hopes were as high as they could be, but the suspense was killing Frieda. She promised to let us know right after she and Carl heard from him, but the earliest I'd find out was after school.

"Okay, people." Julian clapped his hands once. He was in classic form.

So were JJ and Tom and Alistair, the most frequent discussion contributors. Tom brought up an example of man versus man conflict that rears its ugly head more than once in the play: Reverend Brown versus Rachel Brown.

"This example is particularly important because the title of the play is introduced in the context of the conflict between the father and daughter," said Julian, "although the title applies to the overall theme. Where does it first appear?"

"On the cover," said Denis.

Julian ignored him but the rest of us laughed while we found it in Act II, Scene I.

"*Inherit the Wind* is taken from the book of Proverbs, chapter eleven, verse twenty-nine in the Bible. 'He who brings trouble on his house will inherit the wind, and the fool will be servant to the wise of heart.' Here, only the first half is quoted. By whom?"

"The prosecutor," said Alistair.

"Proper names, please," said Julian.

"Matthew Harrison Brady," said Alistair.

"Yes, he's arguing the case against Bert Cates for breaking the law. To whom does he quote it?"

"Reverend Jeremiah Brown," said Tom.

"Yes, Hillsboro's minister. Why?"

"Because he tries to curse Rachel," he said disapprovingly.

"Why would he do that?"

"Because she tells him not to pray for Bert's damnation," said JJ, all smug over getting away with saying damnation.

"And?"

"And then Reverend Brown prays for it on her. He says—" JJ looked down at his book, "'Lord, we call down the same curse on those who ask grace for this sinner,' even though it's his daughter."

"So Brady quotes it to stop him," said Luc.

"He says Reverend Brown is overzealous," said Margaret.

"It's still wrong," said Tom, and the tide of indignation turned against Reverend Brown.

Of course it was wrong. Reverend Brown was completely out of line. Who ever heard of a minister cursing his daughter in public? Or another Christian, a famous one, calling him out for it?

And there was a bigger issue. Since when does a minister pray for grace *not* to be given to a sinner? The whole point of the Bible is grace from God. Especially when you're at your weakest.

"Okay, so we've set the stage for the proverb," said Julian.

Maybe so, but I was not on the same page as Julian.

Lord, what am I supposed to think of this?

CHAPTER 22

FAST-MOVING CLOUDS BROUGHT thunderstorms throughout the morning, so PE was held indoors. The girls' gym was set up for volleyball. Miss Williams and Miss Brennan opened with the rules and positions, and like before, had us do practice drills.

As we rotated through the positions, my size was an advantage when I was close to the net. I recovered a couple of shots that dropped right down next to it and popped them up for others to volley the ball over the net, but when it came time to serve, I failed to get the ball over the net three times.

"Let's try another style of service, shall we?" said Miss Brennan. "Many of you may prefer this style."

We shall.

After two more attempts, the ball curved high.

"Excellent!" she said, and the other team sprang into action.

Sophie gave me the thumbs-up, but not everyone was so sportsmanlike. Some things weren't going to change.

Social Studies was among them. I was as unprepared for the news as I had been for Vietnam.

Mr. Shaw started the class by saying, "It's time we look at some current events in addition to the conflict in southeast Asia."

At first, sighs of relief rippled through the room.

He paced, waving his glasses this way and that. "Some are non-violent, some are violent, some are deadly—" he stood stock still "—and *all* are taking place in the United States of America today. We have some catching up to do."

Like the first day of class, he had our complete attention.

"America was born out of revolution. Be it taxation without representation or individual rights, citizens have engaged in civil disobedience as a means of achieving freedoms when other methods fail. In a bid to achieve the longstanding goal of civil rights for all Americans, the United States are in the midst of a very active era of civil disobedience. Some, myself among them, consider the levels of present-day resistance and protest to be unique in our country's history, and likely to increase."

The only protest I knew about was what I'd seen on the Fourth of July, but even it had gotten a little violent.

He wrote 1964 on the board in the center of an arrow stretching left and right.

"As you know, events happen in context, and so the date of any event represents a moment in a continuum of time."

Check. Things can change a lot in a day.

"We will study the backgrounds leading up to our present predicaments. The major ones are as follows."

It had been a busy summer. It was supposed to be the Freedom Summer, three months of registering Negroes to vote—but the Ku Klux Klan had its own forms of resistance to that, including burning the car of some organizers, who weren't found until weeks later—shot and buried.

The Civil Rights Act of 1964 had been passed, but problems were far from solved. There had been race riots in Harlem and Rochester, and only days earlier, in Philadelphia. And they were just the most recent.

The predicaments came with their own vocabulary. On one hand, there were non-violent demonstrations, marches, pickets, rallies, boycotts, sit-ins, and the peace symbol. On the other, there were drive-by shootings, lynchings, assaults, arrests, arson, and Molotov cocktails.

"If you have not done so," he said, "*now* is the time to begin to come to grips with where you stand on these issues and more. Yet again, America is in a civil war. Its social landscape is increasingly marked by division, and its political landscape is sure to be affected in short order."

And here, I'd been swimming and biking all summer like everything was hunky-dory. All that time, I'd had no idea. It's a wonder there hadn't been a bigger protest at the parade, but then, unless you counted Chauncey Smith, who went about his civil disobedience as quietly as he could for as long as he could before he skipped town, Neston wasn't exactly a hotbed of resistance.

Mr. Shaw only gave us a snapshot of the situation, and already it was enough to make me want a big glass of Coke.

CHAPTER 23

I TILTED MY OPEN umbrella to dry in the breezeway. The house was quiet. Gabe was sticking to his nap.

I found Mom on the phone, her back to me.

Was it the call we'd been waiting for?

She heard me behind her and turned around. She'd been crying!

"Ette's home now." She paused to listen. "Yes, I will. Thank you, Carl."

Carl! That meant Frieda was too upset to talk.

Dieter hadn't made the cut.

I ran up to my room and hid my face in my pillow.

But Dieter worked so hard, God, and he always gives you the glory. He deserved to make the cut! Wouldn't you get more glory if he qualified?

I cried and cried. For Dieter, for Frieda and Carl, for myself, for the beaten and murdered victims of injustice. I couldn't hold back the avalanche of tears.

I heard Mom pass by my closed door to get Gabe; an hour later, when she tapped my door, I let her in. She relayed the whole story Carl had given her.

Dieter had been in the sixth out of eight heats for the 200-meter freestyle, so even with two more heats to go, he'd seen how tough the competition was, but he had gone into it feeling hopeful.

"He said to tell everyone he was pleased with his time. I wrote it down," she said. She kissed my forehead and left the note on my nightstand.

Dieter made 2 minutes, 4.5 seconds. In the final heat, last place came in at 2:3.9. And he was separated from first place by a whole three seconds. Only seconds and fractions of seconds divided Dieter from making it.

But he would never say that was all that kept him from going to Tokyo. I had to keep reminding myself of what Dieter had said to Old Mr. Tedeschi, to the reporters, and everyone else he talked to about competing. His job was to do his best, to pray, and to leave the outcome in God's hands.

I took a deep breath. He may not have qualified to compete in the Olympics, but I was sure he had come in first place in giving glory to God in everything he did and said during the tryouts.

I turned in the direction of the spinout and wrote *NO* in my prayer journal, in capital letters because it was such a big no. It wasn't mine personally, but I took it personally. I'd literally been at Dieter's side through a lot of hoopla over the summer, and I figured I had felt it more than everybody else. They hadn't been there.

Now I shared another thing in common with Dieter. Like him, I had to leave the outcome in God's hands by trusting that grace, and not a place on an Olympic team, was sufficient.

CHAPTER 24

A SULLEN BOY SAT opposite me in the Guidance Offices waiting room, his hair as greasy and black as a well-oiled cast iron skillet, but my appointment with Mrs. Richardson got underway as scheduled, so I didn't have to squirm too long.

She gave me her kind look. "I hope you have had the opportunity to see that what happened last week is not typical of high school, Etienne. It was very regrettable and an unexpectedly difficult start to the school year for you."

"For Theresa, too, and all the other girls, but things are a lot better now in gym class. Everybody likes Miss Williams, and especially Miss Brennan."

"Why do you think that is?"

"They're showing us how to do things, not just yelling at us."

She didn't say anything, so I went on.

"I'm still the Sharks softball captain. We're playing better, but so are the Giants."

"I'm glad to hear of these improvements. How about your other classes?"

"I thought things would be more fair."

"How so? Can you be more specific?"

"Well, the main problem is English. I love to read, but I wasn't expecting anything like that class."

"What were your expectations?"

After Miss Gendron, she must have wondered if I had my feelers out for unfairness.

"You mean, of the teacher?"

"The teacher..." She trailed off and spread her hands to show that it could mean more.

"I don't think I should have to compete just to get a word in edgewise in class."

"Do you feel that's what you have to do?"

"I know it. Do you remember when Theresa's brother said this was the Coliseum, not a school?"

"Yes."

Who could forget?

"Well, in English, Julian doesn't like us to raise our hands, so—"

"Pardon me for interrupting. Who is Julian?"

"The teacher. Mr. Picard."

"Oh. Yes. Go ahead."

"He makes us call him Julian. Anyway, you have to butt in just to say something."

"During open discussion time?"

"It's always open discussion time, and that's not fair either. Participation counts, and all the quiet kids just stay clammed up. Mostly girls. There are some quiet boys, but usually the boys are the ones who call out whatever they want to say. It's like asking girls to play tackle football against boys. They don't have much of a chance."

"Are you quiet in class?"

"I am in English, a lot more than I used to be. I know about giving all the kids a fair chance because I used to raise my hand so much at Neston Elementary that my teachers had to ignore me sometimes."

Mrs. Richardson smiled.

"Anyway, I'd definitely participate more if I liked the play. You know, the one the whole school has to read."

"Yes, I know it. However, you will be learning many things, and you will like some things better than others."

"I figured that, but the other big problem is the play isn't very nice toward people who believe in the Bible, and sometimes I think Julian only wants to hear that other side. I feel left out."

"I encourage you to participate as much as possible, Etienne. Your ideas are as important as anyone else's."

I let that sink in. "Okay."

She looked up at the clock. "Our time is about up. Unless you have something else that's important, we'll pick this up next week."

"No, that's all for now."

"Remember, if you have any significant difficulties, let me know."

What difficulty could possibly be as significant as the one that had already happened?

Well, there was another, but it was not anything Mrs. Richardson could help me with.

CHAPTER 25

BEFORE HE RETURNED TO Connecticut in August, Dieter had warned me that there might be some difficulties because of my faith. "The old dragon isn't very happy—"

"Dragon! What dragon?"

"The ancient dragon is a figurative name for Satan."

"The devil?"

"Satan, the devil, the dragon, the deceiver, the accuser, the adversary, he's called all of them and a lot more."

"Why would he care?"

"He cares very much. Jesus Christ is his enemy, so that makes every follower of Jesus his enemy. It's a spiritual battle. He does everything he can to prevent people from taking the path of righteousness, but once they set foot on it, the closer he'll nip at their heels."

"In Neston?"

"The dragon has his own followers, called demons, and they roam the whole earth looking to trip people up, especially believers."

"Well, I can't picture how that would happen to me, but since you warned me, I'll take your word for it. If it does, what should I do?"

"Always reach out to God. The Holy Spirit is called The Helper, and God hears his children when they call for help. It's important to resist the devil, but it's more important for you to

109

get to know God, and you can do both by spending time in the Word."

"You mean the Bible."

"Yes. Reading the Word is the way to hear from God, and prayer is communicating with God. They're the surest ways to grow in your faith."

"Okay."

"Do you have a Bible?"

"Two. The teachers used to read from the Bible at Neston Elementary, mostly the same things over and over, especially Joseph and Easter and Christmas, but they had to stop—there was some new law—and the school gave all its Bibles to the Meetinghouse. Rev. Bouchard said to help yourself, so I did."

"Great. I'll be interested to hear what you think. A lot of new believers start reading in the New Testament, but I was encouraged to start in Genesis. I was told I would understand the whole book better if I started at the beginning."

Of course you would, just like you'd read Chapter 1 if you wanted to understand Chapter 22 in any book.

"I don't want to overload you, but you also might want to try Proverbs. I read them a few times a year. There are thirty chapters, one for each day of the month."

"Like One A Day vitamins."

"Exactly."

In light of what he'd said, I had to wonder: was The Dragon of Neston nipping at my heels?

It couldn't be. Miss Gendron had ogled girls for over a decade. The whole school was reading *Inherit the Wind*. There wasn't any hue and cry about it, or Julian, for that matter. Besides, no one was picking on my faith. After I prayed with Dieter, the only other people I told I was born again were Mom and Dad, and they said they were happy for me.

All the same, I had more than one motivation to read and pray. First of all, I knew a thing or two about wanting to grow physically. As a spiritual baby, I wanted to keep growing in that area as well. I was on a journey, and I needed daily direction.

Dieter was right about one thing. Proverbs came in handy. That's where I got my second motivation. I'd read and thought about Proverbs 11:29 before it came up in English class. When I read it, I thought I would never want to bring trouble on the Durand house, and not just because I wanted to inherit a lot more than wind. My family was really important to me. And I certainly didn't want to be a fool. I wanted to be wise. Wisdom is one of the things I ask for every day. It's a good policy.

There was no doubt in my mind that *Inherit the Wind* looked at the proverb completely differently than I did. The people of Hillsboro are portrayed as the fools, yokels who are easily whipped up into a religious frenzy. So is Brady, the prosecutor, who's picked apart for his beliefs, making him also look foolish, making the Bible itself look foolish. But the evolutionists, who are educated and say they're on the side of science, are supposedly wise.

That was just the tip of the iceberg. Mrs. Richardson had said I wasn't going to like everything I learned, and that was definitely the case with the play.

Henry Drummond, the lawyer defending Bert Cates' right to teach evolution, denies that he wants to destroy everybody's belief in the Bible—although it looked that way to me. He says he's trying to stop Christian bigots and ignoramuses from controlling education.

Now that hurt.

I believe the Bible is the Word of God. That made me anything but intolerant or ignorant, about science or anything else, but the play didn't miss any chance to portray Christians that way.

And how long a day lasts gets poked fun at so that it could be anywhere from thirty hours to ten million years long, and then you could fit in evolution, but the Bible says each day of creation was made up of an evening and a morning, just like every day is now.

Since I had begun reading my way through the Word, I'd discovered that it says in many places that God created the heavens and the earth. Genesis is just the first place. It even says in the Ten Commandments that they were made in six days.

My fifth grade classroom at Neston Elementary still had the Ten Commandments on the wall, next to the American flag, but I didn't know that part about six days because it was cut out; the short version only says to "remember the Sabbath day, to keep it holy." So I only found out when I read the full-length Ten Commandments.

The tables sure had turned. Drummond got what he wanted. Creation was out, evolution was in. I had asked God what I was supposed to think, and I was getting the answers, over and over.

The only difficulty was, English class was going in the opposite direction. Even if The Dragon of Neston wasn't in on it, my motivation to get to know God better and grow in faith was woven into the predicaments I was experiencing in everyday life. Now, the next question was, *Lord, what should I do?*

If anyone else besides me was on the side of the Bible, I couldn't tell. Maybe Luc. Maybe Margaret. But they didn't come out in the open on the side of God.

If I was going to speak up as a Christian who believed in the Bible, I had to be prepared to get pegged. Was I ready for that?

If I turned out to be the only one, I'd be way outside the norm. Alone. Trying to fit in at the same time would be hard, and maybe my friends wouldn't like it. It would affect them. For all its benefits, pegging did that. There was a down side. I saw it.

Take Patrick. He was already pegged because he hardly talked. His peg: loser. That was the worst peg of all. And it was a real shame because they didn't understand that Patrick was probably bored stiff, thinking of other, more interesting things. In Study Hall, I saw him reading *Principles of Engineering.* For fun. He probably could have skipped half of elementary school.

Take Denis. He'd brought class clown on himself, but it also wasn't the whole picture. The company he kept said a lot about him. I doubted Patrick would suffer a fool as his best friend. Denis was like a court jester: funny covered up for clever and smart. He might not be up to Patrick's reading level, but while other boys snuck *The Adventures of Superman* comics into Study Hall, he read *Popular Mechanics.* They were like two sides of a scale: he was so outgoing, he made up for Patrick's bashfulness, and everything balanced out.

Take Adele. There's no denying she was the prettiest girl, but it was a shame to limit her to that peg, and the part about her being shy wasn't true at all. As Art class proved, she was quietly observing, just as her parents did for a living.

Take Theresa. She was well on the way to being misunderstood. The Princess, whose brothers brought her to the bus pickup location in late model Lincolns. The best dressed. Everyone knew her family owned the North Shore Restaurant and Marina, simply because everyone went there. She expected to be listened to and had plenty of practice with her brothers, whether it was over something small or something big, like when she had insisted that research be done on Sue. Hollering out answers in English class took away that opportunity, and after the PE episode, she had retreated into herself and closed her shell, but others didn't give her any leeway, so she was taken as a snob. I, too, needed to give her room to be serious because the only Theresa I knew up until this point was overflowing with *joie de vivre*.

For that matter, take me. Shrimp. Nobody said all pegging isn't true. It just depends how words are used. If Mom or Dad had called me shrimp, it would have meant I was deliciously cute. I would have felt the same if they called me peanut, and if Marcia had called me string bean, I would have taken it as a compliment; all the models she admired were string beans. People used food as terms of endearment all the time, but just trying calling Junior "cabbage" at school, and you might get a detention.

What if you wanted to change? Or it just so happened you did change? Who wanted to get pegged one way forever? People came to conclusions whether you wanted them to or not, and awfully fast, before they even really knew you. On the other hand, I think they were just desperate to fit in, and who could blame them?

Sophie and Luc had the right idea: change things up a bit, and maybe you could keep your peg options open. I'd just have to work harder with the other pegs. Anyone can try to make things work out better, although it's only up to you to a certain amount.

I decided that that when it came to pitting evolution against what God says many times about creation, I had to be willing to stand with God's Word no matter what. I would always want to be pegged a Christian, which just goes to show, some pegs really are good forever.

Yet I'd also clammed up throughout the discussions. They were one-sided, although the play supposedly opposed McCarthyism—accusing people unfairly when you don't like their ideas, and muffling their free speech. Yet Julian never tried to encourage an opposing view. I wouldn't have taken him as a person who stamped out students like gadgets, but so long as discussion rolled merrily along, he was satisfied.

I made a promise to God to stick with him, and I couldn't give in to my first test and turn traitor. I wasn't about to fly a white flag and surrender to evolution. Maybe there really was a tiny dragon nipping at my heels, trying to make me tuck my tail between my legs and slink away, but it didn't work.

I didn't believe for a minute that I evolved from a worm or blobs of jelly or a monkey. I was made. I was made a female. I was made in the image of God.

When you came down to it, I was in Bert Cates' shoes. We both had opposing views that rocked the boat, but he was the defendant for evolution and I was the defendant for creation. English class was my courtroom, and I, too, needed to put my hand on the Bible and swear to tell the truth, the whole truth, and nothing but the truth.

So, help me, God.

CHAPTER 26

GOD'S ANSWER TO MY prayer for help surprised me.

With the unit on *Inherit the Wind* coming to an end, I was constantly aware of time running out like the last grains of sand passing through an hourglass. Once it was turned over, the opportunity for me to open my mouth would be lost.

Our final and biggest homework assignment was an essay, and as I started on it, God opened my eyes that writing was another opportunity to speak out. What's more, I would have the floor all to myself.

Unlike elementary school, where we pretty much copied out whatever was in a book, Julian actually asked us to present our own ideas, and he explained how topic areas should relate to the thesis. Discussion might run amok, but when it came to writing, Julian was a stickler for clarity.

"Think of your introduction the way you would if you were introducing a person, but you are introducing an idea. Identify the main thing the reader needs to know, the idea that will govern the essay," he said. "And in the conclusion, I want to see you do something more than just repeat the thesis or summarize the points you made in the body of the essay. There are a variety of techniques to make conclusions interesting and effective. One way is to say something provocative. Another is to make a bold statement. Another is to ask a thoughtful question, something philosophical, something that requires more than a yes or no answer."

Now he was cooking with gas.

I decided to write my essay on Hillsboro, the town where *Inherit the Wind* takes place. Twice, the playwrights say the town is on trial. All I could think was, *for what?* I chose it to write about, first, to figure out the answer, and second, because we never talked about it in class. I doubted anybody else would pick that as a topic, which should at least make it unique.

I brainstormed.

Why is Hillsboro on trial?

I didn't mention it in the final essay I handed in, but to think this question through, I drew on my experience with turning Sammy in to the police last summer. Let's face it, charges weren't brought unless someone was suspected of committing a crime. But a town?

What are the charges? What is the evidence?

I got the evidence straight out of the book. Hillsboro is charged with being a sweltering buckle on the Bible belt, a small town of simple-minded clock-stoppers.

What is the verdict? Is Hillsboro innocent or guilty?

Guilty on all counts.

Maybe, just maybe, Hillsboro had to be found guilty because Bert Cates was found guilty. Maybe he'd have been found innocent somewhere else, a different place with different people on the jury, where there were different ideas and different beliefs. It has happened.

What is its sentence?

Hillsboro is already serving it. Every time *Inherit the Wind* is read or performed, Hillsboro is judged. But like Bert Cates, maybe Hillsboro would appeal its verdict—insist that it's really innocent, to give it another chance.

My approach was a little risky, since the essay would count for a lot of our grade, but I made my points clear, and my examples came right out the text, so it was fair play.

But I was certain the Lord also wanted me to speak up in class about my viewpoint, and I remembered over and over that Mrs. Richardson had said my ideas were important, too.

All week, I kept the pressure to express my view bottled inside. I needed to release it before I made myself sick over it— or blew up like Tony George, which I'd regret doing in front of the whole class. It had to be done the right way.

I certainly had plenty of opportunities. When it came to conflicts, *Inherit the Wind* was like the food groups: it had all four of them, a banquet big enough for Julian to keep going back to the buffet table over and over.

Yet I kept holding my cards close to my chest, even though we were in the final stretch, down to the wire.

Julian wrote *denouement* on the board.

"Denouement is a French word used to refer to a play's conclusion."

"So, it's the ending?" said Denis.

I smiled. I was wondering that myself.

"It's broader than ending. Denouement starts with the falling action after the climax."

Julian drew the drama triangle on the board. We'd been shown rising action on the upslope, the climax at the peak of the triangle, and now he labeled *Falling Action* to the downslope.

"Often, strands of the plot other than the main conflict are addressed. The ending is the final part of denouement."

"Capiche," said Denis.

Ditto.

"And in *Inherit the Wind*, the denouement includes a particular technique called the circular narrative. Something introduced early on is repeated at the end, forming a circle in the story, a loop connecting the end to the beginning."

Julian gave us his look of expectation.

It wasn't ringing any bells for the blurters, but I knew what he was referring to.

"The proverb," I said.

"Yes, the proverb that forms the title. In the rising action, only the first half is quoted, but in the denouement it is quoted in full. 'He who brings trouble on his house will inherit the wind, and the fool will be servant to the wise of heart.' We've seen how the title informs the play early on, and that a politician quoting the Bible to the clergy is an example of irony."

"By the way," he added, "we also have an example of word play in the use of the word *house*."

We'd already seen how *wind* was used several times.

"Reverend Brown loses his daughter from his house," said Julian, "but he also works in a house of worship, so the clergy's narrowmindedness brings wind to the church also, emptying it of scientific thought."

Is that so?

I played my hand.

"And Bert Cates is in a jail house."

Somebody snickered.

"He brought wind to his students."

Julian squinted. "In what way?"

"He taught evolution in a school house. So he brought trouble to it."

"How does evolution trouble schools?"

"Evolution is a controversial theory, but nowadays it's the only idea most schools teach about how we got here. Nothing from the Bible. So the schools are emptying classrooms of what the Bible says."

"And that's troubling?"

"It is if you don't believe man evolved from monkeys. It is if you believe, like I do, that I was created on purpose."

In the history of Julian Picard's English class, the room had never been so quiet.

"Intriguing discussion," said Julian eventually. He went to his desk and moved a piece of paper around.

"Now, where were we?"

I knew where I was. I was standing on the rock, closer to Jesus than ever.

"Ah, yes," said Julian. "Now we encounter the proverb in the denouement, where its repetition ties it to its initial use. Can someone locate it?"

Someone did.

The proverb gets quoted against prosecutor Matthew Harrison Brady, just as Brady had quoted it against Reverend Brown. Julian did not have to say anything for everyone in the class to see that it tied them together as fools who would inherit the wind. The circular use of the proverb was no better in the end than in the beginning.

I didn't air any disagreement during discussion, though. I'd made my point. I didn't want to dilute it. Better to be like Carl or Patrick, and speak sparingly. People are more likely to listen then.

CHAPTER 27

PAULA AND I TALKED on the phone, but it wasn't the same as spending time together like we would have every day, so we planned to get together. I could afford an afternoon out. It was the long Columbus Day weekend, followed by a teacher in-service day. I scrambled to get all my work done so I could have some time free and clear.

I would have been glued to the TV, since the Olympics were getting underway in Japan, but my plans to watch the swimmers changed. As it turned out, the broadcast wouldn't run until the wee hours. I would never stay awake. Frieda and Carl still planned to watch, though, and I knew Dieter would.

After Gabe went down for his nap, I crossed the common to the parsonage. Paula greeted me in the mud room with a hug almost as big as when we'd just finished bicycling the final stretch of Île de L'eau.

"I've been missing you something awful," she said.

It warmed the cockles of my heart. No question, we were still best friends.

"I miss you, too."

"Come on in, Ate," said Mrs. Bouchard. What with her accent, I'd always be Ate instead of Ette. I didn't mind. She sat me down for one of her mid-afternoon pick-me-ups.

"What may I get you to drink?" She opened the refrigerator door. "I've got sweet tea, Dr. Pepper—I'd offer you the TaB but Reverend Bouchard is reducing."

Was that Coca-Cola I spied?

"May I please have a Coke, Mrs. Bouchard?"

One minded one's manners in Mrs. Bouchard's presence.

"You surely may, darlin'. Coca-Cola originated in Georgia, you know."

"No, I didn't know that."

"Oh, yes."

"May I please have one too, Mother?"

Ditto for daughters.

"You certainly may, Paula."

I would have drunk it out of the green glass bottle, but in Mrs. Bouchard's world, that was uncivilized when at the table. But she had the next best thing: a set of shapely glasses with Coca-Cola written in its flamboyant script on them. Paula and I poured. More out of politeness than hunger I took a very small piece of peanut brittle from the platter she offered me.

"It seems like it's been a dog's year since I've seen you."

I'm sure she meant it kindly, but I recognized it as a coded message, which only took me a second to crack. It was the polite way of saying she had not seen me in church for many weeks. And I noticed that she didn't say "My, how you've grown," which was one of her standard lines to youngsters.

"Yes ma'am, it's been a while," I confessed. "I've been needing more sleep than usual. Dr. Lewis says I'll grow out of it, eventually. He said it's a phase a lot of kids go through."

"Oh, yes, Timothy is a bear to get up some days. Now, what have you young ladies planned for this glorious afternoon?"

Other than a heart-to-heart, I hadn't given it any thought, but I knew Paula would want to get out of the house, so I left it to her to answer.

"We're going for a walk," she said vaguely.

Good choice. She added the mandatory time of return, but it was also on the vague side.

"I'll be back before dinner."

"In that case, would you mind dropping off this letter at the post office?"

"Oh, I would, Mother, but we're not going in that direction."

Her answer startled Mrs. Bouchard—and me. The Theresa Effect had rubbed off onto Paula, only with the southern sweetness her mother had taught her.

"The foliage is very lovely around the lake," I said.

Mrs. Bouchard's expression returned to normal. "No harm done," she said, as polite as ever. "Do dress warmly. The wind off the water can be quite chilly."

We knew for ourselves just how much cooler the air over the broad lake could be, so with neck scarves for good measure, we flew the nest.

But it was more like Indian summer, and as soon as we crossed onto Lakeshore Drive, Paula untied her scarf and ran with it like she was hoisting a kite to take flight, and I followed her, the both of us running and laughing to the shoreline, where we took off our windbreakers and tied them around our waists. We strolled to the end of the beach, watching a boat scurry toward the south shore.

"I wish I was out there," she said.

"Me, too. We'll probably go out again. Theresa and I are getting to be good friends. Margaret, too—she changed from Peggy."

"I know all about that. Debbie says she's sick and tired of hearing her go on and on about you and Theresa. You know how she only wanted the three of us."

"Yeah, I know. I tried to talk to her, but she said to apologize, and I couldn't think of anything I had to apologize for. She wouldn't make up."

"Don't count on it now. She just hates how you and Margaret are friends. And get this. As soon as school started she got chummy with me, like nothing happened."

"Debbie's friends with you again?"

"When it suits her. She picks and chooses. She's says sixth grade is like being a senior, which is true, but she says we're the top of the heap and she acts like it. If you think she was bad over the summer, you ought to see her now. She's got an attitude a mile long, and nobody likes her bossing them around. It's the only reason she tried to get me back."

"You're kidding."

"No. Isn't that awful? She's so fickle, I don't trust her. I know better than to count on a fair weather friend."

"So what did you do?"

"I just said 'no thanks' every time she asked to do something, until she gave up."

"She must be friends with somebody. Who's she play with?"

"Valerie."

"Poor Val."

"I know. She's too sweet to say no to Debbie. I've been making friends with Francine."

"Francine's nice," I said.

"And Jeffrey."

"Jeffrey Scott?"

"Only a little. I'm up to the box step in dance class, and he's one of my partners. The best—and those blue eyes."

That meant she saw them up close, slow dancing. Mrs. Bouchard had enrolled Paula at Stages Dance Studio at the earliest age allowed, and since then Paula had been working her way through all the stages. Tap, ballet, you name it.

"Well, that makes sense," I said. It sounded more interesting than a crush on Ringo.

"I wish we were still in the same grade."

"Thanks." I couldn't really say I wished I were at Neston Elementary, though. Even after such a rough start to seventh grade, I didn't want to go back. I'd already made a big investment, and I didn't want to lose it. I'd gone through the door of no return. Anyway, there were problems to deal with on both sides.

"You could skip," I joked.

"Hah. Is it awfully hard for you?"

"Some things are."

"Like what?"

"Social Studies is pretty tough, but that's partly because of current events. The riots and all."

"Oh I know. It's practically another Civil War."

"That's what the teacher says."

"It was bound to happen. Who knows what it will be like the next time we go back to Georgia. Mother says we might have to put it off next year. Our family gets along just fine with Coloreds, and it's high time they stood up for their rights, but Mother says all the hullaballoo wouldn't make for much of a vacation."

Paula had traveled many times to Georgia, where her mother was from and the rest of her mother's family still lived.

"Have you ever seen segregation there?"

"I couldn't miss it if I tried. It's the way of life."

"Still? In schools?"

"Especially schools. Coloreds have their own schools, and Whites have theirs. Just like water fountains and lunch counters."

"How do you know which is which?"

"It's all marked with signs. *Colored. White. No Negroes. Colored Only, No Whites Allowed. Negroes in the Back.*"

"Really?"

"Don't look so surprised. What did you think the fuss is all about?"

"I guess I just didn't realize what segregation is really like, how much there was."

"Everything is segregated. Negroes have their own part of town, and Whites have theirs. The signs are just for areas where Whites and Coloreds mix in public."

It sounded like another world, although I knew school segregation was still being battled as far north as Pennsylvania and New York. Problems weren't just in the south.

What if they came to Neston?

In particular, after all I had learned about the racial divide, I was afraid for a man who worked at the Arms. Would somebody go after him when he left work at night?

CHAPTER 28

MR. GILBERT SAID THE number one form of personal risk prevention was to avoid sketchy situations, but if you couldn't, the next best thing was to be in a group. There was safety in numbers. That made sense, but I hadn't given a lot of thought about how practical it was until I put myself in Mr. Franklin's shoes. Other Negroes worked at the Arms from time to time, but they had moved on, and now Mr. Franklin had no one to come and go with. There were no numbers for his safety—not until he got home.

He and his family stuck together with other Negroes in Neston. I had to admit, that meant they were segregated, but lots of places were that way. In Montreal, the Chinese had Chinatown, and the Italians had their own Little Italy. I suppose there were times and places you wouldn't want to be in an area where you weren't one of them, but there weren't *Italians Only* signs posted, and the nation wasn't being ripped apart when a Chinese person went into an Italian restaurant. They were simply neighborhoods.

It wasn't so obvious in Neston, but the more I observed, the more I noticed that people tended to group together. Groups formed for lots of reasons. The Greeks were split between those in the general population and the Georges, who created their own clan, but they shared customs. We all did. The Wards had a tight circle that took more than money to crack into. On the other side of the coin, hard work and low pay were all it took for people to get into the Sawmill Apartments, no matter where they came from.

But unlike the others, Negroes sticking together only made them stick out more because of their color. That might make them easy targets for people who didn't want to get along with them, didn't want to see any more mixing here than in Alabama or Georgia.

Would trouble makers try to hurt Mr. Franklin's wife and children? What about the other Negro families? It might give me a stomach ache as bad as Brenda got, but I wanted to find out.

I asked Dad if I could interview him.

"Why?"

"For school. Mr. Shaw said we could interview someone to learn about cultural differences. He said conflicts weren't just about land but involved culture clashes, too. Theresa's going to interview her grandparents. It's only for extra credit, and at first, I wasn't planning on doing it, but I'd like to hear what Mr. Franklin says about civil rights."

"His perspective might be very interesting," said Dad, which is exactly what I thought. "I've known William a long time," he added, looking away like he was looking into the past.

"I know," I said.

"Ask him. You can tell him I said it was fine with me for him to use one of his breaks for a change, but if he says yes, don't take up too much of his time, Ette."

"I won't. We're supposed to keep it under twenty minutes." Although Theresa would probably go way over the limit.

William Franklin stood out, and not just because he was the color of dark Swiss chocolate. The top of Dad's head reached Carl's eyebrows, and the top of Carl's head reached Mr. Franklin's chin. He stood out in other ways as well.

The service hallway between the kitchen and back rooms was lined with photographs of the staff over the years. There was a section for people who had worked for five, ten, and fifteen years, and a few who had been at the beginning.

Another section showed the people in the Kitchen Brigade—the pecking order of positions. The Neston Arms wasn't a huge hotel, so Dad and Carl switched back and forth as Executive Chefs—managers who oversee every aspect of foodservice, and as *Chefs de Cuisine*—Head Chefs, who oversee cooking. Theirs were the first pictures in the lineup.

Next came the *Sous-Chef*—Deputy Chef. It's a lot like *Chef de Cuisine*, except more hands-on, and in fact the *Sous-Chef* became the *Chef de Cuisine* when both Dad and Carl weren't there. That was Mr. Franklin's job.

There were a dozen pictures of him posing with Dad and Carl and the *Chefs de Partie*—Station Chefs with more specialized responsibilities, like butchering, fish, sauces, cold foods, breads, pastries, or desserts. Most of them had been at the Arms the longest, and they reported to Mr. Franklin. The Kitchen Brigade was one part of the big picture of The Neston Arms, which was a well-oiled machine.

I held off until the staff were taking their meal break before dinner service to ask him. The wait staff was thoroughly trained in menu and wine tasting before they ever worked the floor, but daily specials samples were always provided for them so they'd be personally familiar with the dishes when taking diners' orders, and everyone else ate whatever service meal was whipped up for them. They had a break area next to banquet storage, but Mom and Gabe and I sat at the corner table in the kitchen. We were on such good terms with the staff that whoever had the privilege of eating there on any particular day didn't mind sharing with us, but they gave up their seats for Dad to sit with us for ten minutes. When he left, like always, Mr. Franklin came over to say hi.

"Good afternoon, Isabelle," he said.

I could remember when he only called her Mrs. Durand. It had taken that long for Mom and Dad to convince him to call her by her first name.

"Good afternoon, William."

He was always William, never Bill.

"Look at that fine young man," he said, referring to Gabe. "He's growing faster than a radish."

"They grow fast?" I asked.

"They do, Miss Ette."

Miss Ette was my name at the Arms. Mr. Michaud had started it, and with his French accent, it came out as Meez Ette, only quickly like it was one word, and Meezette caught on, too. Ate, Miss Ette, Meezette, I liked and answered to them all.

"How is school coming?" he asked.

"It's okay," I said. I dove in. "I was wondering if I could interview you for Social Studies class."

"Interview me?!"

"It would only take fifteen minutes."

"Oh, Miss Ette," he hesitated, not wanting to turn me down but not very comfortable with the idea, either.

"It's for extra credit."

He shifted his toque on his forehead. "Well, in that case."

"I'll leave you two," said Mom. She got up with Gabe. "Have a seat, William."

"Thank you, Isabelle."

I pulled out some paper I had folded and put in my pocket, so it wouldn't look too obvious that I'd expected him to say yes, and I grabbed a pencil from the empty ricotta container that held pencils point down in raw rice. I had practiced my introduction so it wouldn't show that I got upset about what I'd learned, especially the people who'd been killed. Mr. Shaw said to focus on open-ended questions.

"We started out with Vietnam in Social Studies, but Mr. Shaw said we had to back up because of the Freedom Summer and Civil Rights Act, and I didn't know anything about them or how Negroes were treated, but ever since then, we've been keeping track of things, and I watch the news all the time now, so I was wondering what life is like for Negroes here in Neston."

I took a breath.

Mr. Franklin took a breath.

"Life isn't perfect for anyone, Miss Ette, but it's better here than many other places, and that goes for all sorts of people, not only Negroes."

Well.

"Can you tell me about your background?"

"My family descends from slaves who escaped to Canada on the Underground Railroad, and some of them returned to Vermont because it was a free state. Neston was growing, and there was more opportunity, so we joined our family and moved here. My father had a job as a cook, and when I wasn't in school, I worked the back of the house, doing dishes and cleaning. I watched him, though, and at home I learned my way around a stove from my mother and grandmother. We were the last of the Franklins to move to Wortham County. The rest have been citizens for some time, born here. We are the newest Americans, but still, French Canadian-Americans."

Negro French Canadian-American. Just like Mom, who was White French Canadian-American. Just like a lot of Neston.

"Dad said you were in the service, a cook like he and Carl were. What was it like?"

"Now, I think what you want to know is, was there a lot of prejudice?"

I nodded. "And segregation."

"Yes, both. Negroes had their own units."

No surprise to me now. "Was it dangerous?"

"If you strayed, but I understood all the unspoken rules and forbidden places, and I kept out of trouble."

"Did people call you bad names?"

"Oh, I've heard them. So did the Italians and the Germans during World War Two. Nowadays it's the Russians. As far as I can tell, Miss Ette, everybody gets called names sometime in their life. Maybe not for the same reason, but it's universal."

What he saw, and the way he personally took it in stride, made a deep impression on me.

"So, you came back to Neston."

"In due time. I made a choice to learn as much as I could, and after I was discharged from military service, I stayed on in New

Orleans to master Creole and Cajun cuisine. You see, God had given me the perfect background. I paid my dues with many long hours of on-the-job training, and it was worth it. I got hired on in good places, high volume restaurants in the French Quarter."

I was all ears.

"They call it the Big Easy, but it wasn't for me, or for most of my people. I found out what they suffered, what they suffer to this day. If it weren't for the Lord Jesus, I don't know how anyone would get by."

"I believe in Jesus!"

"Then you'll do fine, Miss Ette. But sometimes God wants us to grow through our tribulations. I wanted to leave, but I felt the Lord telling me to tarry, and because I did I met my precious wife, Monique, a Creole herself. In time, we prayed again, and we agreed that this time the Lord said yes. I heard from my family that Durands and Meyers opened the Arms, and I sent my qualifications to your father and Carl. They wanted me as soon as I could get here, and Monique and I took the step of faith and moved to Neston. I came here to the Arms for the interview, which included a night on the line. They put me on sauté, and they hired me at the end of the shift. I started in charcuterie and worked my way through cold and hot, on and off the line."

"*Chef de Tournant,* right?"

"You know it, Miss Ette. Prepping, cooking, cleaning, the bakery, the stations, the line, I worked it all."

According to the pictures in the hallway, Mr. Franklin was *Sous-Chef* two years after he started, a fraction of the time it usually took anyone to reach the top. It wasn't just that he could bake as well as he could cook, which few people could do, he also knew how to run things, got along with everyone, and kept an immaculate kitchen. It's no wonder Dad and Carl thought Mr. Franklin was the best; he was talented and trustworthy, and you don't get that every day of the week.

We were running out of time, so I asked a closed question.

"Do you think Negroes are treated fairly in Neston?"

"There's no color line, Miss Ette. Unlike many places, on November third, we will stand with our neighbors just as we have before. Here, it's the vote that counts, not the color of the person casting it. Neston is a fine place to put down deep roots."

So much for the kids who were itching to leave. I was glad to hear somebody else felt the same way I did about Neston.

"Thank you very much, Mr. Franklin."

"You are most welcome, Miss Ette. I hope you get the extra credit."

CHAPTER 29

WHAT MR. FRANKLIN SAID was not like the race riots the news reported, but he'd had troubles enough. The pot had been percolating right along, and it boiled over. It was the same way in Vietnam. It was the same with a lot of things.

Something he said rang a bell. It couldn't have been easy for Frieda or Carl during World War Two. Her maiden name was Norden, and Carl was a Meyer, both German names.

I went upstairs to talk to her.

"Did people ever give you a hard time during the war because you're German?" I asked.

"Not so much before I got married."

"Because people didn't know?"

"No, everyone knew."

"So how come they didn't bother you?"

"I didn't say they never did."

She wasn't being mean toward me for assuming; Frieda would never do that. She said it in a quiet way that showed me they did bother her, sometimes. Mr. Franklin was right. We all did, some time, some way.

"Then what?"

"Sooner or later, they would come to realize that it was not in their best interest. You see, Ette, Norden Real Estate isn't just one company, it's the parent company of a portfolio."

"I didn't know that. I've seen portfolios at Putnam's Art & Photography."

"In that case, you know a portfolio can hold several pieces of art. To Norden Real Estate, it means our company handles more than buyer and seller representation. We have many types of real estate holdings."

"It's your company, too?"

"Yes. Albert holds down the fort at our main office in Connecticut, but I have my say."

"What kind of holdings?"

"We have what's called a diversified portfolio. In other words, holdings in various sectors. Land, industrial and commercial businesses, residential property. We lease as well as buy and sell our own properties. A good chunk of our market share is in the metropolitan New York area, but as we've grown, we've spread out. Various holdings across geographic areas reduce risk if one sector or region takes a downturn."

I didn't expect to get a business lesson. It reminded me of the advice Mom had given me when I was losing at Monopoly, except it was real life—and another discovery about Frieda.

"So...that's why..."

"So it helped people think twice before insulting a Norden in any shape or form."

"They wouldn't dare."

"A few tried."

I was on pins and needles to know what happened, but I waited, like Mr. Shaw said to do.

"Real estate can be very complex," she said. "Not every transaction makes it to completion."

She didn't need to explain. I got it.

I wondered if what Carl had to say would be as interesting.

"What about Carl?"

"You'll have to ask him."

"Do you think he'll let me interview him?"

"You can try."

He came up to bathe and rest before the dinner service, so there wasn't time for anywhere near a twenty-minute interview, but it was a *carpe diem* moment too valuable to give up.

"Carl, could I just ask you a quick question about World War Two? It's for school."

I could see his reluctance, but I rushed on, "Did people call you names during the war, like they call Negroes names?"

He sat down and carefully untied one shoelace. "It was a difficult time for those of us with common German names." He paused. "Meyer is also a Jewish name."

He answered my question, but raised another one, a huge one. Was Carl a German Jew? Millions of Jews were killed. It wasn't the time or place to prompt or push him, not that it would work with Carl anyway, so once again I stayed silent and waited.

He slowly loosened the other shoelace. "In the service, at first, a lot of the recruits ribbed one another. It was the usual tough guy competition. One's too fat, one's too skinny, big noses, Polack jokes. They got over it pretty quickly."

He paused. I waited.

"They had each other's backs in the war. That's what comrades in arms do," he continued. "Now they're all friends at the VFW. In any event, I was spared that."

"Because you were stationed in Greenland?"

He smiled. "That's right. When it's thirty-five below zero, and you've got to pair up just to get from the mess hall to the barracks, you don't call your buddy a name."

Of course not, just like you wouldn't insult the buddy who's got your back during combat.

"But you put up the Meyer flag," I said, "and the Norden flag," referring to the coats of arms flags that flew in a row outside the entrance to the Arms: Durand, Benoit, Norden, and Meyer—with the American flag in the middle.

"We've had calls asking about our names or if we allow certain people to stay here. The staff is trained to handle them. Not all business is good business."

Which is pretty much what Frieda said.

I was surprised about all I had learned.

It didn't change that pots were boiling over all across the country, but the interviews showed me that prejudice simmered along everywhere, in all sorts of people.

When I read my extra credit report aloud, from time to time I looked up, like Mr. Shaw did, for emphasis.

"One's got too many pimples, one's too short," I threw in among the examples from Carl.

I couldn't accuse anyone of being a name caller, but I could make a point for everyone to think about, so I turned it into a provocative conclusion like Julian said to do in our essays.

At the very end, when I read, "Every time people point a finger at someone else, like calling them a name, just remember, their own four fingers are pointing right back at themselves," I happened to glance straight into Tina Henry's eyes.

Big mistake.

CHAPTER 30

WE MAY HAVE MOVED on from *Inherit the Wind* in class, but you could say it had a long denouement: weeks later, the Theater Department held tryouts for the performance.

Denis turned around in home room and said, "I made it on the set crew."

"Congratulations," I said, although I wished it were for a different play.

"We're building the courthouse square this week."

"That's great." As far as I was concerned, it was the scene of the crime, but set construction wasn't to blame, and it was right up Denis's alley. He loved Shop.

"You are going...aren't you?"

After my classroom drama, I could see why he'd ask. I still wanted to see the performance, not because I liked the play and not because it was required; it was purely optional. Like Julian said, a play is meant to be performed, and I thought theater arts in action might be interesting. I wanted to see how the students played the roles and how the audience reacted, including Mom and Dad.

"Yes."

"I'd ask you to go with me, but I'll be switching the sets during scene changes," said Denis. "The crew wears black, and the lights are dimmed but there has to be enough to see where to move the set pieces, so you'll be able tell who it is."

"Are you sure?"

"Yeah. You'll see me on stage. Which performance?"

"The second Friday," I said. The show ran two weekends in a row, and I wanted to go right away, but Mom suggested tickets for the next-to-last night.

"My mom said, if there were any problems, they'd be ironed out by then."

"That's true. And the cast won't have their feet out the door, thinking about the party after the final performance."

He turned around, and the bell rang.

Speaking of feet out the door, he was on my heels. "Do you want to go with me to the cast and crew party?"

Denis just didn't give up. When he had asked to carry my books, I couldn't imagine why he'd want to, but afterwards, I saw it pegged boys and girls as "together," whether they dated or not. You knew they broke up when the girls went back to carrying their own books or a new boy did. You'd think students would have more important things to tend to than the book toting business. I was glad I hadn't fallen into that trap, but I hadn't told Denis the real reason why nobody would be carrying my books.

My age. And even if I were older, a cast and crew party was out of the question. The official party, with the directors, was one thing, but kids always found a way to carry on. Certain places off the beaten path were known for it.

Faced for the first time with an actual request for a date, I had to scramble for an answer that wouldn't hurt Denis. He was always so nice to me, and I liked him, but I also didn't think we could be friends. Denis was too interested in me—and he was an item. Not many girls would be turning down dates with him. I could tell him I didn't want to go to the party, which was true, but given his persistence, he'd just try to find something I did like doing and ask me out for that.

"No," I answered him, "but it's not you. I don't plan on dating for a long time."

"Like, how long?"

"Really long. Years."

"What are we talking? Freshman year? Sophomore?"

"No."

"Junior?"

"Probably not."

"Because of your parents?"

Marcia and Donna dated, and Donna had progressed to going steady with Peter Jarvis, so I doubted if Mom and Dad would mind.

"No. I made a decision not to date anyone unless we both were interested enough in each other to consider getting married some day." It was an idea I learned from Dieter, and I liked it.

Denis was speechless.

"Or at least thought we might. So that wouldn't be until after high school or maybe college."

"You're kidding, right?"

I shook my head.

So did he, but he didn't mean No.

What I didn't say was that I believed true love could come along at any time. You never know. These things happen.

We got to English, and I could feel his eyes burning into my back from his seat at the rear door. I wondered if he would repeat what I said. He was the only person besides Mom and Dad that I told, so if word got out, I'd know who started it.

But I didn't care if he did. I was relieved to have it off my chest. Learning to say no gracefully was good practice. It would be easier the next time, if there was a next time. The good part was, I wouldn't have to be rude and tell someone "I don't want to go out with you," or make up lame excuses. I guessed I'd have some other talking to do, though. It would just be a matter of time before Denis asked me why I made that decision.

CHAPTER 31

WORLD'S FAIR POSTCARDS HAD been popping up everywhere since Dieter returned from the Olympic trials in New York City.

The first one I saw was on the bus, where Mr. Ted had tucked it into the crevice above the bus windshield. It was a picture of a tire, except the tire was really a tall Ferris wheel. The kids got a kick out of it.

Frieda and Carl's postcards, which were lined up on their mantelpiece, included one about a machine called a computer, which Dieter wrote would one day make Frieda's accounting a breeze, and another one of the Top of the Fair restaurant. It was set on pillars high off the ground because its roof was a helipad, which was probably anything but a breeze for a restaurant manager. Carl agreed. He said that restaurants in skyscrapers offered great views, but getting food and supplies in and out added to the challenges of high volume foodservice.

On the bulletin board next to the time clock, staff tacked postcards of the pavilions Dieter had eaten at. From dishwasher to housecleaner to waiter to cook, he had something personal to say to each individual. It got to be a sport to search cookbooks for kimchi, momos, falafel, tandoori chicken, shawarma, and nasi kuning, and if the ingredients weren't expensive or too difficult to find, and the recipe wasn't too complicated to make, a few staff meals provided before service featured some of the dishes.

To us at home, he sent postcards of the Japan Pavilion, which had two restaurants. He'd eaten sukiyaki and shirataki noodles, as well as a dish that was prepared tableside. La Terrasse wasn't likely to serve that dish of bean curd with beef and vegetables in a hot pot, but he knew we'd especially get a kick out of it. All summer, he had been the king of the *gueridon*—a special cart for tableside preparation in the dining room.

But there was another dish that he highly recommended for our Sunday brunch. It was the most popular dish at the entire World's Fair: Bel Gem Waffles. Waffle makers were already on the station setup for brunch at La Terrasse, and like omelets, were custom cooked to order. A bestselling menu item was right up our alley, and Mom immediately researched and tested recipes that would replicate the yeasty taste he described. She also worked on a few of the other dishes for us at home. My Guinea pig duties went far beyond waffles.

A couple of postcards were pictures of the Billy Graham Pavilion, which had eight sides. On the first one, Dieter wrote he had watched a film called *Man in the Fifth Dimension* on a gigantic wrap-around screen. On the second one, he wrote, *It was moving to see people who wanted to receive Christ as their savior. I got some info about a discipleship group on the Yale campus, which I'll look into next fall. In the meantime, keep me in your prayers? You all are in mine.*

That second postcard was the only one of several he sent that didn't spark immediate discussion. Everybody just had a thoughtful expression.

The postcards sat against the kitchen table napkin holder for a few days, until another one arrived. I figured Donna was completely over Dieter, or she would have taken them. I put them in the front flap of my prayer journal notebook, and like photos, they reminded me to pray for him. I wrote him a letter and said so. I enclosed a recent photo of Gabe, as well as one of the Bowl & Grill when it was pasture and one of how it looked now. I ended with *P.S. I'm sorry you lost.*

He wrote a whole letter back to me personally.

Dear Etienne:

   I feel such joy every time I look at the photos from the picnic—and the most recent ones you sent. The summer in Neston continues to feed me in so many ways, and your pictures keep everyone ever closer in my thoughts and prayers. Thank you!

   Here's one for you. That's my nephew, Sydney, Jr. sitting next to me. He calls me Uncle Dieter now, and I'm holding the two day-old addition to the family, my niece. Stefanie and Sydney named her Suzanne, which means lily or rose, and she is a perfect little rose bud. Seeing how much Gabe has grown has made me realize that I need to get out to Long Island more often than I did after Sydney, Jr. was born.

   I will be meeting with an advisor soon to plan the proposal of my senior thesis for approval. When you and I looked at the postcards of Neston in its earlier days and you said that you live in the baby pictures, your comment made an impression on me, and it echoed over and over when I saw the photos you enclosed of the pasture-turned-construction lot. My interest in how towns can preserve their history while moving forward in the present and planning for the future has grown because of your perspective, and it has helped me firm up my proposal concept.

   Taking a cue from your new hobby, I plan to take photos of a handful of nearby architectural landmarks and compare and contrast them with postcards of the past. If postcards are currently made of those places, I will also include them, since it is unlikely they will look like any photos I take. As valuable as they are as primary sources, postcards tend to make things look more ideal than they really are. I hope my project will provide real insights that I can continue exploring during my architectural studies at Yale.

   As for the Olympic trials, please don't feel sorry for me. At home, my bedroom wall is covered with shelves full of trophies and shadow boxes of medals and ribbons. I haven't placed worse than third since my sophomore year, and now I've competed with the best in the country. Winning is a blessing but there are many blessings other than the winner's circle, and whatever happens moving forward, I have been blessed greatly. I may not have won, but I definitely did not lose.

My classes are better than they've ever been, but more importantly, are yours as interesting as you hoped they would be?

Your brother in Christ, D

Most of my classes were interesting enough, although, as I told Mom, "Some things aren't ironing out very smoothly."

I said the same thing to Mrs. Richardson. "It's not that the material is hard, not all of it, anyway," I added. "It's the way it's explained."

"Can you give me any examples?"

"Well, Mr. Reilly said subtracting a negative number from another negative number was just adding a negative to a negative. We were all confused, and I asked him how can you subtract if you're adding, and finally, he showed us on the number line and then we understood."

Mrs. Richardson nodded. "Good. Asking for clarification is the best first step."

"I tried that in English, too, but the answer wasn't very clear. In the book we're reading now, nobody could figure out who the hero is. It turns out the hero is an anti-hero. That's like adding to subtract. The good guy isn't supposed to be the bad guy, but anyway, we're supposed to call him the protagonist instead. And the antagonist doesn't even have to be a person. It took a while for the class to catch on, but it would be a lot better if it was explained first. I don't think I'm the only one who gets confused."

"Some of the challenge of new material is not the content, but rather, that it is not quickly or easily resolved."

"Well, I'll have to remember that, but math is still one of my favorite subjects because there's always one right answer. Mrs. Meyer—she's the accountant at the Arms—she shows me things with numbers."

"Such as?"

"So far, only income and expense from our restaurant."

"What's your impression of business math?"

"I like it a lot. The numbers are connected to things, and that makes a different way of looking at them. They make sense."

She only smiled.

Without her saying a word, I saw her point. I'd just have to take it with me back to class.

Knowing where we stood in those bookkeeping categories made a real difference in our lives, as Mrs. Lacroix's housekeeping service and sapphire velvet proved. As far as I was concerned, you could have your Wonder Woman. Frieda was Number Woman.

"But Mr. Shaw's Social Studies class is really tough. Sometimes I think he forgets he's not teaching juniors and seniors any more. I think he must've picked the new textbook."

"Would you say you have to stay on your toes?"

"You sure do." I paused. The challenge was both the content and the fact that it definitely was not easily resolved. "In more ways than one."

Besides the textbook assignments, each of us had a subscription to a current events magazine, which was more serious than *My Weekly Reader.* On top of them, Mr. Shaw encouraged us to read the newspapers and magazines that reported world events. We weren't held responsible for them, but we had weekly tests on the other readings.

"It's all new material to me, I guess for almost everybody." I sighed. "I'm not sure if I'd call it interesting, but it's important. And Mr. Shaw is very fair."

"That is a positive note to end on, Etienne. At some point, after things iron out a bit more, what would you say to talking about what's going well?" asked Mrs. Richardson.

"Okay." I could do that.

"One more thing. I need to move next week's appointment. Would you mind adjusting your study hall and taking a later lunch?"

"I'd like that." Not that I didn't want to be with my friends. Lunch was way too early.

CHAPTER 32

NO SOONER HAD I taken Mrs. Richardson's advice to heart than the next issue of the current events subscription magazine tipped me off that we were about to study something that actually would be resolved soon, and reasonably, if not easily.

"With the elections approaching on November third, we will be shifting gears to civics for the next several weeks," said Mr. Shaw. "Civics comprises the rights and duties of citizens, and, I would argue, the duty to vote is among the most important. We will continue to note developments in southeast Asia and the arena of civil rights, but our focus will turn to politics, beginning with a broad look at the three branches of government."

He flipped the map to *United States Government: Executive, Legislative, Judicial Branches* and discussed the responsibilities of each.

It seemed this would be a less disturbing unit, but elections also riled people up, so there was no telling if they would turn out as violent as riots and war. Mr. Shaw had made it clear that those things affected each other.

"On the federal level, elections will be held for members of the Senate and House of Representatives."

He flipped the map to *Bicameral Legislature.*

"In order to understand how voting works in the presidential race, we will examine the Electoral College, which is not a place but a process. Moreover, at the state level the gubernatorial race is open—that is, for the governor. As we study, think about who you would vote for, and why you would vote for them, or not vote for them. You will have the opportunity to learn how to exercise your civic duty. A school-wide mock election will be held in the gymnasium."

Everyone liked that idea, especially because he said we'd be part of the whole process. Everyone would have to register to vote, Shop classes would build and set up voter booths, and volunteers would be needed to act as clerks to check people off the voter checklist so they wouldn't vote "early and often."

"It is not merely the current electorate that must be informed of issues, but you as well. The oft-quoted saying, 'the children are our future,' is especially used by politicians during an election, and entirely applicable, so you also must be aware of the events and ideas influencing American society. They play significant roles in how people vote. Indeed, they are changing our culture."

Now I could write to Dieter and wholeheartedly say that I was learning something both new and interesting to me. It also had practical use for the future. Supposedly, everything we studied was valuable, but some things were more practical than others.

I had not known it as civics, but it so happened that Margaret had already gotten some of us engaged in our rights and duties as citizens.

"Let's write a letter to the police about the left turn problem," Margaret said at lunch one day after the issue came up again.

It came up often because The Traffic Group—the name stuck—made sure it did. Patrick and Denis had taken to timing how long the Hinton bus took to turn onto Neston Avenue, and most mornings they'd come to Geography class and report it to Bucky, which, of course, they could have done long before Geography started, especially since the class was well past discussing the observations we made our first day in the field, but their conversation before each class kept the pot simmering.

Mr. Shaw said that in war, strategy is partly based on knowing your enemy, and it seemed that's what The Traffic Group was aiming to find out. With JJ leading the opposition party, they learned exactly what the enemy thought. The opposition reacted to The Traffic Group's daily chitchat with everything from "What's three minutes?" to "They just ought to change how long the red light lasts," to "Why don't you give it a rest?"

"If you think a letter we write would actually get them to do something," Theresa said pessimistically. Her confidence was at low tide.

"Of course they will. I wouldn't bother asking if I didn't think so," said Margaret the eternal optimist.

"I think so too, if we tell them how a traffic cop would help the drivers, like Adele said," I added. Now that we all knew that her father was a border agent, a special kind of police officer, it was clear why she'd made that suggestion.

Margaret scooped a spoonful of Chili Con Carne, unclicked her binder, and took out a piece of loose-leaf paper. "Yeah, she should be in on the letter," she said after swallowing.

She flew over to Adele and flew back. "She said she could stay after school."

"Good," I said.

"First, we have to find out exactly who it should go to." Margaret scribbled *research* where the address block went. "The Chief of Police, but maybe some other people should get it, in case he doesn't pay attention to it."

"I'll work on that," said Theresa. "Papa and my brothers go to a lot of meetings at the municipal center. All the offices are there."

"Okay, you can be the leader in that area," Margaret decided unanimously. "Now, the introduction."

We blasted out notes on the W's: what the problem was, when it happened, where it happened, and how it so happened we seventh graders were writing.

My job was to put the pieces together later so it flowed correctly. "Just so you know," I said, "I won't be putting all those details in there at the beginning, only what they need to know to get the picture. Like a real introduction to a person, except it's a problem."

"Right," said Margaret. "I'll hang on to our brainstorming ideas in case you want them."

"But we should say we've seen some problems and we're writing because a police officer directing traffic would help," said Theresa.

"Check. Then we can be more specific about the observations to make them see the problems."

"Alright, then," said Margaret. "The Traffic Group can work on that part."

She flew over to their table and flew back a whole three minutes later. Theresa and I just stared.

"Good news. They're doing traffic for their individual observation projects."

"That explains why they're always talking about it," said Theresa, "but aren't they still working together, too?"

"No—well, sort of, but not really—" but just that moment, Denis came over and sat down at the hole in our lunch table.

"Patrick says we should wait for more data," he said in a low voice.

"What's daytah?"

"Information, statistics."

"We already decided to meet after school to work on it."

"Where?"

"The library."

"We'll be there."

———◄O►———

Margaret, Theresa, Adele, and I sat on one side of a table behind low bookshelves with plants on top, and Denis, Bucky, and Patrick sat on the other.

Luc, who came in to do his after-school studying, stopped and said, "Did I miss a group assignment?"

So much for camouflage.

"No," said Margaret.

Nobody chimed in.

"Just off-limits, is that it?"

"We've done a lot of work already," said Denis.

"Let me guess. Traffic?"

"You could call it a personal civics project."

"That's okay, I'm too busy anyway," said Luc.

If he wondered why we girls were getting involved with The Traffic Group on a personal project, he made a smart move acting like he didn't care. It showed he wasn't jealous of Denis; the two of them took turns sitting next to me in English. Luc came to our lunch table once in a while, so I guess he figured he'd find out what we were up to sooner or later.

He went to another corner to study, but it was clear that we stuck out like a sore thumb. We kept our voices low and our books open to look in them whenever somebody went by.

"What's wrong with writing the letter now?" asked Margaret.

"The letter is a really good idea," said Patrick slowly, avoiding our eyes. "If you want a traffic cop, it's fine to write it now. But if you want more than someone to direct traffic, say, something that involves other departments, the police chief won't make the decision by himself."

Adele nodded. "Other people would have to get involved."

"I'm thinking it could be several departments," said Patrick. "It'll probably end up with the selectmen."

"Like they did with the Bowl & Grill," I said.

"That took a while," said Theresa. "There was a lot of debate."

"So what's this big idea?" said Margaret.

The boys checked both ways and leaned in.

We girls looked at each other as if that was a bit much, but our fearless leader Margaret leaned in for an honest to goodness tête-à-tête, so the rest of us followed suit.

"We might ought to—" Patrick finished in a whisper.

You could have knocked us over with a feather.

"That's brilliant," I said.

Patrick didn't react. Of course it was.

"But the letter was your idea," said Denis.

"Margaret's," Theresa and I said.

"You agreed to work on it," she credited us.

"We want to join forces," said Bucky.

"Why?" said Adele.

"You've already got the ball rolling. We're still working on the data."

"Our observations for Mr. Swenson's class are supposed to be individual," said Adele. "Aren't you cheating?"

"No," said Bucky, "we are doing separate work. You'll see when we give our presentations."

"We're just getting double duty out of combining them for the letter," said Denis.

"Scientists do it all the time," said Patrick.

"Really," said Theresa, the wheels in her head spinning.

Patrick nodded. "On big projects, they do independent research, but they work together and combine their data to publish the results in different places."

"And we could use some help putting the ideas together the right way," said Denis.

"You mean in writing," I said.

"Yeah."

I suspected help with writing was the real reason why they wanted to join forces. It explained their willingness to reveal Patrick's secret to us. Well, we each have our own strengths, and sharing them would make us better students.

Margaret removed the sheet of chicken scratch from her binder and ruthlessly drew lines through some of the brainstorm notes. "We can keep some of this, but what you're talking about will take a lot more work, and there's no deal if you don't cough up this data."

"We will," said Patrick. "Deal."

"Deal," we echoed.

We didn't spit and shake, but we meant business, and we got down to it. I had no idea if the secret solution that Patrick proposed would be accepted, but I was willing to take the risk.

Traffic had changed Neston to the point that it had its first regular traffic jam. It was easy to join forces to try and help solve the problem we all personally experienced, and the idea that others might come on board who could actually fix the problem was a lot more appealing than just getting a grade.

As I saw it, there was more than traffic at stake. City people who visited Neston often said how they liked the slow pace of life here. They didn't mean they liked getting slowed down because of traffic snarls. They already had that.

The bottom line was, we had to speed up left turns at the town's main intersection if we wanted to keep our slow pace of life.

CHAPTER 33

AS PLANNED, I MET with Mrs. Richardson at a later time than usual.

"I'm doing okay," I said in a tone that indicated I was only fair, not really okay. I had buckled down and gotten the hang of math and steady homework, but a different challenge reared up.

"I still like learning new things, but a lot of it isn't exactly interesting—or it is, but it's so sad. I need a spoonful of sugar."

She understood. "Perhaps more incentive to study serious subjects?"

"Mmm, I don't know," I said doubtfully. I always thought learning was incentive enough all by itself, but she wasn't entirely off, either. For the first time, I was discouraged by some things I was learning.

"As I recall, you've said you've come to find geography inspiring."

It wasn't a sad subject, but geography continued to surprise me as being more appealing than I ever guessed it would be. I had told her I'd been enjoying the long unit on maps, although I found it dry at first. Then Mr. Swenson had us make topographical maps, and I discovered there was so much more to cartography than roads from point A to point B. After that, he took us over the hump of contour lines to see that physical features and the natural resources within them had everything to do with population and economics. From then on, it was much easier to appreciate the world's geography.

"I see what you're saying. Mr. Swenson makes the subject more interesting, and I guess it's the way he teaches that motivates me to learn more."

She said nothing.

"But sometimes the teacher isn't enough. Mr. Shaw makes Social Studies class very interesting, but the things we cover usually aren't inspiring. Especially war. I hate it."

"Yes," said Mrs. Richardson empathetically. "Hating war is understandable."

Of course. Who didn't hate war?

"And I like math but, well, not Mr. Reilly so much. I guess the teachers can help you feel inspired about a subject, but it's not all up to them. Sometimes it's just inside you already."

Like health. I had a great personal interest in food labels, weight management, and avoiding contamination, but the unit on nutrition did nothing to inspire interest in the other kids. Some of it definitely had to come from yourself.

"True, yet the opportunity to be inspired can only come when we learn about the subjects, including serious ones. Give them time."

"Okay. Thanks, Mrs. Richardson," I said more dutifully than gratefully as our appointment came to a close.

My stomach growled as I headed to the cafeteria. Switching our appointment put me in the latest lunch period, and I didn't mind being hungry for a change, but the hollowness came as much from disappointment.

I knew already that Mrs. Richardson would fix what she could, like Miss Gendron, and she would help me all she could, but she wasn't going to give me the answers to everything that ailed me. She couldn't. Her comment to give serious subjects time reminded me of Mom saying on the first day of school that things would iron out.

But since that day, for every little thing that ironed out, two wrinkles appeared. I felt like I'd stepped onto an active earthquake zone. The ground was constantly shifting, and when it cracked, as it often did, I saw the wreckage.

The best I'd done in pinning down the problem was to realize that I'd always thought of America a certain way—the postcard way, but it didn't look as ideal to me any more. I couldn't find my way to amber waves of grain without going through ghettoes, or scale purple mountains without glimpsing soldiers on the other side of the shining sea.

At the cafeteria, I figured Donna would let me sit at her lunch table, but before I had a chance to look for her, I had to pass by Marcia to get into line. All I wanted was milk. She was sitting at a table crowded with one other girl and three boys. Talk about changing things up. I knew them all by name except the one I recognized as the sullen troublemaker I'd seen in the waiting room of the Guidance Offices. Alice Dubuque was nowhere to be seen. They were laughing to beat the band. Senioritis, I guess.

"Ette! Are you lost?" Marcia called out to me, as if she cared, and without waiting for an answer, said to the crowd at her table, "You remember my kid sister, the girl wonder, child prodigy, forgetful genius."

They laughed again.

I stopped. "I'm not forgetful." Prodigies were in a whole other league.

"Randy, get her a seat," Marcia ordered.

Randy squeezed me in.

I was going to tell her I was looking for Donna, but she grabbed my lunchbox out of my hand before I could react. For a second, I thought I might just stand up to her, but I looked down at her lunch tray. No solid foods.

"Three chocolate milks?" I said in disbelief. She wanted hot lunch, and here she was, throwing money down the drain.

"I traded, and don't get righteous on me. Your precious Donna trades for red Jell-O."

"Fine." There was no point in arguing, although I felt sad to know that Donna was just as wasteful. They didn't want hot lunch because they liked it or to spare Mom. They just wanted to trade.

And the boys were gulping down what Marcia practically gave away.

The clock was ticking, so I sat down.

She opened my lunch box. "Let's see what's on the menu."

I'd play the game. "I'll take the turkey sandwich," I said. "*If you don't mind.*"

"Oooh," the table chorused.

"I like what you've done with my lunch box," she said, handing the sandwich to me.

"*My* lunch box," I corrected her.

"What, only a sandwich, a bag of peanuts, and an apple? No soup?"

"Not enough time to eat that much," I said between bites, reached to her tray and stole one of her chocolate milks.

"She scores!" crowed Lance.

"Okay, smarty pants," said Marcia, "let's match wits."

I chewed and shrugged.

"We'll draw straws." She blew the paper off two unused straws, turned her back, tore them into pieces, and offered them. One by one, the others at the table drew a piece out of her fist.

"Chuck, you got the short straw. Topic and question."

Sullen announced the topic. "Current events."

So, his name was Chuck. He looked like a tyrant king. Chuck the Sullen. Instantly my conscience pricked me for unkindly name calling. *Sorry, Lord.*

They eyeballed me. I realized they were waiting. As if I could challenge the subject, not that I would. I was up on it.

"Ready."

"Who's the leader of The Merry Pranksters?" asked Chuck.

"The Merry Pranksters? That's not a real current events question."

"Oh, but 'tis, my little pretty. I've met them, I've met the man, I've seen the bus."

"What bus?"

"*Further.*"

"That's its name?"

"'Tis."

"Shouldn't it be *Farther*?"

"Not where they're going," said Randy.

"What do you mean?"

"Further into the mind," said Chuck.

"You're cold," I said, to blame his clue as useless.

"On LSD," said Chuck.

"You're getting colder."

"Psychedelics," said Lance.

"Freezing."

"Psychedlics are drugs that induce hallucinations," said Marcia matter-of-factly. "Is that getting warm enough for you?"

"Like sniffing glue?"

"That's kid stuff," said Chuck, "not a real high like LSD."

"Hallucinations," said Lance in a wavy voice.

"Visions in living color," said Chuck. "Better than the NBC peacock."

That did not sound merry to me. Hallucinations could get you put away. And weren't pranksters mischief makers?

"So, some pranksters are on a bus called *Further* to take drugs that make them see things that aren't there?"

"Sometimes they're there," said Marcia.

"How do you know?"

"Hearsay."

From Chuck, I figured. At the very least. I didn't want to know.

"Yeah, well, I think the prank is on them. I wouldn't want to be on that bus."

"I think it might be—what's that you're always saying? Interesting."

Marcia would never admit that to me if it was as bad as it sounded. It couldn't be, if she was willing to try it. She was snide but she wasn't stupid.

"It sounds pretty far outside the norm," I said, using a saying I picked up from her.

"Nothing wrong with that."

"Maybe, maybe not. It depends."

"You still haven't answered the question," said Chuck. "Who's the leader of The Merry Pranksters?"

And I never could have if Sylvie hadn't said, "Let's give her a hint."

Randy held up a paperback book. I recognized it as what they were reading in senior English class. *One Flew Over the Cuckoo's Nest.* The author had to be the leader of The Merry Pranksters.

"Ken Kesey."

"She scores again!" said Lance.

"You made it too easy for her," complained Chuck.

No, no they hadn't.

"I've got to go," I said, but the ground trembled so bad I could hardly stand up and walk away.

CHAPTER 34

THE BUZZ IN THE school bus rose to a swarm. The *Neston News* had run front page pictures of the Bowl & Grill sign installation the day before, but the real thing was something to behold.

A bowling ball as big and bright as the moon was placed between two tall posts sticking out of the ground at angles. It had finger holes on the bottom, *Bowl & Grill* in the middle, and a crossed spoon and fork at the top. A bowling pin attached to one of the posts had BOWL written on the vertical, like the Leaning Tower of Pisa, tilted toward the building, with an arrow on top. The ball and pin and BOWL and GRILL were outlined in neon.

A triangular sign for changeable messages fit into the V of the angled posts below the ball.

GRAND OPENING FRIDAY
20 LANES!!!
Noon to Midnight!!
Six Days a Week!

There was no need to say what day it would be closed, since everything was closed on Sunday. According to Theresa, who got it from her father and brothers, one of the restrictions the B&G had been slapped with was not advertising the bar as a bar, at least not on the road sign—but the marquee over the entrance made it clear—and its double sized letters certainly could be read clear across the enormous parking lot: *LOUNGE!* She and I knew the tilted martini glass on one side and beer mug on the other indicated the bar was fully licensed. The rest of the marquee said *Parties! Adult and Youth Winter Leagues Forming! Tournaments! Pinball and Pool!*

While we waited behind the Billington Springs bus to turn onto the school grounds, everybody twisted around to get another good look at the sign. It dwarfed the CUHS sign in front of the school, but both signs looked the same coming and going.

"Youth leagues?" said Margaret. "I can't wait to learn how to play. It'll be so much fun. Don't you think?"

"No time," said Theresa dryly. Clearly not much interest either, but Sophie said, "I'll sign up for a youth league. Want to join together?"

Was there a sport Sophie didn't like?

"Yeah! What about you, Ette?"

"I haven't got the hands for it like you do," I said. It was true, although I couldn't see myself joining a league; it would be as time-consuming as any other extracurricular activity.

"You two can come watch," said Margaret.

"Maybe," said Theresa, and who could blame her?

No doubt the North Shore Restaurant's diners would check out a new place that served up heaps of onion rings, flame-grilled burgers, and their choice of cold foamy on tap or Coke over crushed ice.

She changed the subject. "The fence was another thing they had to agree to," she said to me.

"It won't help that much," I said.

"Not much," she agreed.

The tall privacy fence between the parking lot and school was intended to prevent students from being distracted. It was made of wood, so it was supposed to look natural, although the permanent chain link fence that ran the rest of the perimeter looked industrial. The entrance and exit were on each side of the sign, so nobody would be sneaking in; however, we could still get distracted.

Admittedly, from the ground, a good chunk of the bowling alley was hidden by the wooden fence. But the track and field bleachers were on the other side of the fence, and its top seats were higher than the top of the fence. And the second-floor classroom windows on that side of the school overlooked the building's flat roof. From Study Hall, a side service area with trash cans and crates next to delivery doors were visible.

We'd watched the progress from there, including delivery trucks for the past week leading up to the grand opening. They couldn't get around us being disrupted by that, or when the trash truck came, and the metal can lids got tossed aside and the cans clunked when they were heaved onto the side of the truck and dumped. I wouldn't be surprised if the study hall got moved to a different room. This room would be perfect for Julian.

Maybe I was the only one who noticed or cared, but by mid-afternoon, the fence would block the setting sun from shining on the bleachers facing the track and field. On frosty days, the warm sun on your back ought to be part of the fun. And it would not be able to hide the sound of traffic into and out of the bowling alley lot any time of day, especially during Friday night football. It would always be a distraction.

The opening was just in the nick of time for my Geography observation project. The presentations were in a couple of weeks. I'd photographed the Bowl & Grill from the beginning, during the long middle, and on this day, after school, I took the ending: the parking lot crammed to capacity.

CHAPTER 35

I HAD BETTER FISH to fry than joining the crowds at the B&G opening weekend. Gabe's birthday was Saturday, and I asked Theresa and Margaret and Paula over to help manage Gabe's guests. I don't think anyone remembers their first birthday party, but it's too big a milestone not to make a to-do over, and I planned to take plenty of photos of him and of my friends.

It would have been a hard sell for Theresa except she had to babysit anyway, and the first person on the list was her nephew, Jason George. Barely two months younger than Gabe, he was the baby who didn't quite make it as Neston's first of 1964. They'd be in school together. Jason might be the next best thing to a brother to Gabe.

Theresa gave me the scoop on another baby to invite, one who in time would also be Gabe and Jason's classmate. Nancy Bedard was the baby who beat out Jason. Both Lina George and Joanne Bedard had been at the hospital to deliver their firstborns at the same time, and each had hoped their baby would be Neston's first of 1964. The couples became fast friends, often spending time at each other's houses. The Bedards knew and trusted Theresa, and so did baby Nancy.

Naturally, new parents of ten month-olds, starved for their first night out in who knows how long, and faced with the offer of babysitting with a party thrown in, took it.

Paula informed me that Gabe needed another girl as his guest to balance the sexes. Under the circumstances, boy-girl-boy-girl seemed ridiculous, but she should know. Mrs. Bouchard insisted that her children learn the social graces from a young age. She had been born and bred a hostess, and Paula had been following in her footsteps, whether they entertained in the parsonage or at church. She had chipped in at breakfasts, luncheons, teas, bridal and baby showers, even small wedding receptions. Paula once said the only thing she liked about church was weddings, but lately she'd been enjoying helping out at just about all of those events. She learned how to be a great guest, too, always picking the perfect gift, so she was invited to more birthday parties than you could shake a stick at.

Paula's idea only partially came from being groomed by Mrs. Bouchard. She was very keen on her latest dance lessons, the paired ones. Boy-girl was on her mind more than usual. In any event, I had every reason to trust her. Paula knew a thing or two about putting on any sort of get-together.

If Mrs. Fortin's next child was a girl, she might join the guest list in the future, but in the meantime, another George child fit the bill: Gregory and Doris's youngest, Phoebe. She was two, and the only girl Theresa's brothers and sisters-in-law had out of the nine children between them. Twins ran in the family, but Gregory and Doris must have been willing to risk a second set in the hope of having a girl, and they got her. Not only would Phoebe even things out for Gabe's party, she'd have another girl to play with for a change. I figured they'd all like to have playmates their own age, and even if, at two, Phoebe was double the age of the others, it probably wouldn't matter. It was close enough.

They'd be getting plenty acquainted in time anyway. With names beginning with B, D, and G, three of the four would probably spend kindergarten through twelfth grade seated near each other.

Theresa and I agreed that the party had to be held from 4:00 to 7:00. That time frame, after nap and before bed, prevented crankiness, and it included dinner. I wrote up the menu:

Gabe's First Birthday

Scrambled Eggs
Puree of Squash
Choice of Cream of Rice or Oatmeal
Banana Pudding
Milk and Apple Juice

The choices were only backups in case somebody was fussy. The pudding was Mom's idea. Bananas provided natural sweetness without triggering cravings for sugar at an early age, and she hadn't met a kid yet who didn't like them. The rest of us were having sandwiches, mainly because we'd be busy keeping the kids corralled—and were we ever.

Phoebe was a true toddler. Gabe didn't have enough balance yet for walking very far on his own, but he was an advanced crawler who tried to match her speed. Nancy and Jason gave them a run for their money, scooting across the rug to chase balls and burst soap bubbles. They showed equal expertise at knocking over blocks with their own favorite teddy bears they'd brought and mooing and quacking to *Old MacDonald Had a Farm*. I expected more tears and tussles than there actually were.

Gabe's birthday was so much more precious because my friends were with me to celebrate it. They were real troopers to put in so much effort, but we were rewarded in more ways than one. Theresa got out of the house and had some fun. Margaret, who was gearing up for a baby in her own house, was as energetic as the kids. Paula saw for herself how much more relaxing and fun it was to be around Margaret instead of Debbie. The four of us fit together as neatly as the last pieces of a thousand-piece puzzle slipping into place.

I had to agree with Paula. What was little early start? Gabe's first birthday was, including himself, his first paired party, and a dinner party at that. It was a fine debut on the Neston social scene, even if it was a low-key affair. Other than a few balloons, we didn't do anything in the way of decorating, and I was the one who blew out Gabe's 1 candle—with a prayer instead of a wish.

CHAPTER 36

SCHOOL STAYED NOSE TO the grindstone for me. We started a book in English that took the Lord's name in vain so many times, I stopped counting. Math got harder. The elections had come and gone and the sky hadn't fallen, so in Social Studies we were learning about lame ducks, a new congress, and the names of our new leaders come inauguration day.

I was looking forward to Thanksgiving break. At least for a few days, I could put things behind me, although I would miss my meeting with Mrs. Richardson, since school was on recess from Wednesday on.

We were all excited with plans. The Fortins were having fourteen at the table on Thanksgiving; the three table leaves would be in. They always went for the traditional cooking and celebrating at home. So did the Bouchards, who were only having ten this year.

For as long as I could remember, mentioning the number of people you'd have at your table was a popular form of bragging that often turned into gossip.

Word got around last year after Mrs. Fred Ward, Sr. just so happened to need to make a trip to the A&P her very own self for something the cook forgot, where she let drop that she was having twenty-two.

The Durands would be serving dozens of people who were happy to let someone else do all the work. Our effort was their comfort. It was a big day for La Terrasse. The Arms had been fully booked for months, and putting out the *NO VACANCY* sign was one of Frieda's favorite chores.

The Georges also would be working. It was a huge day for business at the North Shore Restaurant as well. Our families would still have our own celebrations with all the fixings, though. We'd just get takeout from our own restaurants.

I was two days away from food and fun and a lot of napkin folding.

Denis, however, was looking back in time. As soon as he sat down in home room, he turned to me and asked, "What did you think?"

Of the play, of course. He'd kept track of when I said I'd go with Mom and Dad.

"It was a good production," I said.

"Yeah?" he fished.

"The students played their characters really well, and the way the lighting changed added a lot of mood."

He nodded, hanging on.

I got to what he was waiting to hear. "The set was great, and the crew worked fast."

He smiled from ear to ear. Yes, I'd seen him.

"Even the snacks at intermission were good." The proceeds went toward class trips. "There was a lot of school spirit all around."

Which I would have missed if I hadn't gone. The students manning the food tables and the ushers and the actors and the crew gave me a new and different enthusiasm for school.

Denis was satisfied, and I couldn't blame him for wanting a little more recognition after the applause faded. I was glad that I was able to give him a positive answer while being honest at the same time. In fact, it wasn't my original saying.

After the final curtain closed, I'd asked Mom and Dad what they thought of the play.

"It was a good production," said Mom. Dad agreed.

When it came to saying something nice or nothing at all, Mom was the perfect example. Her polite answer was just right. It gave credit where credit was due.

It reminded me of the old saying, hate the sin, love the sinner. *Inherit the Wind* was like that. I hated the play but loved theater arts. I simply followed Mom's good example, adding the details.

CHAPTER 37

INSTEAD OF REGULAR GEOGRAPHY classes, Mr. Swenson had scheduled our individual observation presentations, which added to the holiday atmosphere. We'd signed up for when we wanted to present, and except for one person having to present on Monday when he wanted Tuesday, it worked out just fine. Some people wanted to get it out of the way as soon as possible. Others of us, including the members of The Traffic Group, signed up for Tuesday.

JJ led off with his observations about the Connecticut River shoreline behind the Sawmill Apartments. True to its name, the apartments had been built to house saw mill workers back in the day, and still does; his father was one of them. With the river in his back yard, JJ had been fishing there for years, and recently he had noticed that the shoreline was exposed more than usual due to low rainfall. I found his observation interesting since I also detected every little change in Stony Brook where it ran through my family's property.

Depending on what was observed, we could make recommendations based on our information if we wanted, and JJ's made perfect sense. The junk exposed on the riverbank needed cleaning up. He got our applause, and not just out of politeness. We'd learned that President Johnson had just released a report on pollution of the environment.

Adele followed JJ. During nesting season in the spring, some Canadian geese had taken over a popular skating pond on the edge of the town park in Keenan. They pooped all over and charged at pedestrians who walked near their goslings. After they migrated north, the town cleared out the nests and let the grass grow tall, which was supposed to discourage them from returning, but there were complaints from the walkers. Then the pleasure skaters and ice hockey players insisted the grass get mowed before the pond froze. The town planted evergreen trees around the pond, but when the weather turned cool, the geese had been winning again, and would be until the trees grew enough to interrupt them from landing. The nesting area was the perfect staging stop since it was on the trip south. Worse, kids took to feeding the geese, so *Do Not Feed* signs were posted. Without at least a fence, it might be years before people got the upper hand again, so a storm had been brewing all during the migration south over other ways of getting rid of the geese. More than one person threatened to bag a Christmas goose, but as far as Adele and others had observed, the entire geese population had safely survived their stopover in Keenan. She practically got a standing ovation.

Adele was a tough act to follow, but Alistair was up to the task. He talked about how his back yard got landscaped. It had a slope, so the family never spent much time out there, but over the past months, landscapers had leveled out the top for a stone patio and gardens. When the work wrapped up just recently, the yard had changed from natural slope to three broad flat ledges, and as far as the family was concerned, the manmade change was all for the better. They got a whole new yard, and next year, after the grass grew in on the lower ledges, they'd have level grounds for croquet and badminton. I sniffed a little envy in the air, but our restaurant, La Terrasse, got its name from its terraces, which had been formed the same way his back yard had, so I applauded him more enthusiastically than anyone.

I kept an open mind during Janice and Tina's presentations.

A white birch tree in Janice's yard had died, and her father had planted a red maple. She documented how quickly the sapling was growing and the ways it was changing. She didn't have any conclusion to make other than the fact that unlike garden plants, whose life cycle most of us witnessed year in and year out, it was unusual to watch a tree growing before your eyes. She had a point. She also did something unexpected. She asked Adele why Keenan didn't plant red maples around the pond, since they grew fast and were pretty, especially in the fall. Adele didn't know, but Mr. Swenson said it was likely because evergreens planted near a pond used for skating would keep it free of leaves while still providing barriers against the geese. Plus, they made good wind barriers and provided color all year.

Tina also reported on birds, except she said she wanted to attract them. She had put a bird feeder in her back yard and listed how many different kinds of birds showed up, and many that she either rarely saw, or saw less of, were regulars now. She observed that some birds ate from the feeder, but others ate from the ground, which led to an interesting spin. Her cat also liked to observe the birds, and one day she found him eating a dove. "Oh!" said some girls, but she also got laughs. It was a good presentation.

CHAPTER 38

I KICKED OFF TUESDAY'S presentations with my photos of the Bowl & Grill lot, from the first picture I took even before school started to the day the B&G opened. Everyone had to get up to look at them. I'd chosen the best pictures out of my album and attached them with corner mounts onto stiff poster boards, which Mr. Swenson clipped to the bulletin board. Week by week, the changes unfolded.

I let the pictures do most of the talking, and instead of making a recommendation, I asked some questions. They included one yes or no answer, but I thought it was still open-ended enough for a maybe.

"How soon will every lot in the New District be gobbled up?"

"Will all the greenery be gone forever?"

And, according to our personal civics group's prearrangement, I tied my last question to the next presentation.

"What will all the growth do to traffic?"

It primed the pump. One by one, Patrick and Denis presented clear evidence that the left turn issue was a problem. In sparsely populated Hinton, less traffic fed onto the River Road, so the bus easily turned left onto it, but in Neston, where more local traffic fed onto the River Road, there was a wait at the light to turn onto Neston Avenue. Bucky's observations showed the same traffic problem on the weekend; sometimes it was worse because people not at work were out and about.

Patrick indirectly attacked JJ's previous comment that the wait was only three minutes. As long as there were no vehicles turning left, traffic sailed through the intersection, but as soon as there were, they held up all the traffic behind them. The Hinton bus might be stuck through two or three red lights, in which case, both the students and everyone else traveling through the intersection were set back to the tune, on average, of four minutes.

"That's only an average," he said. "It could be much longer. Just think if you had to wait that long in the lunch line."

Next he attacked the comment made about changing the red light timing. He said it could be changed to give drivers traveling north more time to get through the intersection, which would mean those turning left would have to wait less, but it would mean that those traveling south would have to wait longer, so the problem would just happen in reverse, but not quite as much.

"And it wouldn't solve the safety problem. Drivers turning left have to squeeze in their turns, and I saw drivers from both directions screech to a halt to avoid head-on collisions."

Nobody challenged him, and he concluded with another effective device: doom.

"Changing the signal timing isn't the best solution, but it might work. For a while. With traffic increasing on Neston Avenue, things are going get worse."

"Wouldn't a three way stop work here?" said JJ.

"Traffic would be backed up more than it is now," said Patrick. "More than one vehicle at a time needs to get through the intersection to keep the traffic flow moving."

Theresa followed them with the final slot, and it wasn't because she was shy about public speaking. She'd rushed to the sign-up sheet to get it. It was part of our plan.

"I also observed traffic," she said, which initially drew groans from a certain quarter, but proving that introductions can be just as provocative as conclusions, she went on confidently, "and my results are the opposite of what the others found, although it was a left turn on a busy road."

She had our ears.

"Every afternoon on the bus, I observed how much time the left turn onto Lakeshore Drive takes. It was always less than a minute. I conclude there are four reasons why traffic does not back up."

And she proved that you didn't need to drag things out to make a point.

"One. When Neston Avenue was widened, both turns onto Lakeshore Drive were also widened with additional lanes for turns, one on each side of the Sherburne River bridge. Two. Blinking yellow lights were added in both directions. Three. Lower speed limit signs were posted. And four. *School Bus Turn Ahead* warning signs also were posted."

She paused for effect.

"In closing, the bus has plenty of room to get into position to turn left because of the extra lane, and with the signs and lights, drivers slow down or stop if needed, so it has the time it needs. The turn is safe and efficient for everyone."

The scientist in Theresa was showing, and unlike English, where she had to fight for a word in edgewise, once you gave that girl a soap box, she'd deliver. I suppose Patrick's reasons for clamming up were different from Theresa's, but like her, when you gave him a soap box, he opened up just as much.

JJ didn't say anything, but from his look, his gloves were on. All the same, it was a happy ending, which was another one of Patrick's ideas. He'd recommended the order of our presentations, especially the last one. Like Julian said, beginnings and endings tended to make the strongest impacts, and people remembered the longest what you said last—another reason for a strong conclusion.

Everything was going according to plan. Part One of our civic duty started with joining forces; Part Two, the presentations, were behind us now; and Part Three, the last phase of work, would begin this weekend.

I'd reserved the fish bowl room in Ward Memorial Library, where we could work in private. The others in the group had never been in the room, but they were familiar with it, and it held the same fascination for them as it had for me. Adele dropped out of the group; she lived the farthest away and couldn't promise to make our meeting, but she provided some important information we could use, and everybody else was all in. Denis did not hide his excitement over seeing me during the holiday break.

"I asked for a bunch of annual reports," I said. "They'll have them waiting for us."

They liked that. So did I. If Miss Harrison, one of the librarians, hadn't known I'd looked at primary documents with Dieter in the fish bowl room, I'm not sure I would have asked, but let's face it, a kid asking for annual reports is not likely to be goofing off.

"What if somebody sees us?" said Margaret.

"Everybody will," I said. "If you mean, kids from school, they won't be allowed in to talk to us while we're in the room. Only our names are on the reservation, so remember to tell the librarian at the circulation desk who you are and that you're signed up to use Meeting Room 1A."

"What if somebody asks later on?"

"Yeah, we all need to say the same thing," said Patrick.

"Say what I told Luc, that it's a personal civics project," said Denis.

"This is different. What if they get nosey?"

"Say you'll tell after we're done."

The clock to Thanksgiving vacation was ticking. All I had to get through were PE and Social Studies.

CHAPTER 39

THE DAY WE STARTED the unit, Miss Williams had said, "Basketball is a game that requires a lot of close teamwork."

We'd had a taste of close teamwork with volleyball, but the addition of running back and forth across the court required us to pull together more than ever. What's more, once we got the basics down, our team positions had been chosen based on our traits and abilities.

Naturally, that meant center went to the tallest players. Tina hustled on the court and scored plenty. Sophie was a power forward. No matter how fast she ran the court, she never tired out, and she led in rebounds.

I was a point guard. I'd been told there were short basketball players in the NBA. I was no NBA player, but I wasn't a total washout either. I frustrated blocks with my low dribble and passes—and I passed the ball like a bullet. I did have one thing in common with them, though: taking a tumble on the court. Now, basketball isn't meant to be a contact sport, but you'd have thought this was rugby.

The first time Tina bumped me, even before Miss Williams blew her whistle, she raised her arm and called "foul," really apologetically, and shook her head like she was a disapproving spectator, not the perpetrator. She bounced the ball to Miss Williams, who pursed her lips and cocked her head at her. "I should say so," she said.

I was allowed a free throw, which, lo and behold, went in.

Next class, Tina fouled me so hard that Miss Williams and Miss Brennan blew their whistles as long as a locomotive at a crossing.

"UN-necessary contact! Flagrant roughness!" barked Miss Brennan.

While Miss Williams checked to see if I was okay, Miss Brennan fumed. "And unsportsmanlike!"

Tina hung her head but Miss Brennan wasn't done.

"Off the court," she said in the most disgusted voice.

Tina's jaw dropped. "It wasn't on purpose," she said.

"It looked that way from where I was standing. You are sidelined for the rest of the game, young lady."

"That is not fair."

"You just earned yourself a detention."

Tina defiantly put her hands on her hips.

"Make that two," said Miss Brennan.

Tina stomped over to the bleachers.

The girls stood frozen like it was a scene in a scary movie. It would have been surprising enough to see an interaction like that between any teacher and student, but when it's by a teacher as nice and well-liked as Miss Brennan, it's downright shocking.

She came over to make sure I was alright before she and Miss Williams helped me up.

"Does anything hurt?"

"No. It stung at first, but I'm okay."

Thankfully, I'd skidded on my forearm instead of taking a direct hit to my elbow. The scrape was pink but it hadn't broken the skin. A light abrasion, they called it.

Accidents happened. This one wasn't. I was shaken but I was in one piece. I got another free throw. That one missed.

Naturally, Mom and Dad noticed the abrasion above my wrist. I would have told them anyway. Since it might be part of the ongoing Eddie saga, I had to explain who fouled me, and tell Mrs. Richardson, too. I'd said I just wanted to put it behind me. What I didn't say was that I figured Tina had been put in her place like Miss Gendron had been—finally. I thought, mistakenly thought, that had taken place at the bus stop on the first day of school, but I was certain it had with this episode. My job was to forgive her and let it go.

In fact, I completely got over her hurting me in any way, shape, or form. Tina would be on her best behavior, and not just because of the detentions. If she wasn't, no other girls would ever want anything to do with her. Her reputation was suffering.

Today, like always, we started with drills, and with Thanksgiving holiday vacation starting in mere hours, we had a little extra vim in our step.

"Watch your footwork," said Miss Brennan. "Basketball is ballet."

We had found out from Sophie that Miss Brennan used to be a *corps de ballet* dancer—one of the ballerinas who dances as part of a group. It explained why she was so light on her feet. And ballerinas don't have sloppy footwork.

"The better you play, the more fun you have," said Miss Williams, sounding just like Dieter when he told me that consistent swim strokes improve speed. Just as we had advanced in softball, both teams were playing the best basketball ever, including me.

I caught the ball and dribbled and pivoted to pass to Sophie for the bank shot and—

Chapter 40

I CAN'T HOLD IT in any more. Hot urine streams out.

I'm sorry Mom. I haven't wet the bed since I was six.

I wait to hear her say, "It's okay, sweetheart, these things happen."

Instead, she changes my diaper.

Someone is helping her. A woman. My eyes are too heavy to open, and I don't recognize her voice.

I reach out to be picked up, but I can't move my left arm.

I try my right. My hand hits a bed rail.

"Ouch!"

"Ette!"

I put my free hand over my eyes.

"Ette, can you hear me?"

But Mom, I don't need the bed rails any more.

I am too tired to figure it out.

Turn out the reading light, Mom. I can't sleep with it on. I want to go to sleep.

A hulk is hovering over me. I can tell by the shadow on my eyelids. A thumb tugs on each eyelid—then a flash of light in each eye.

I twist my head. *Cut it out!*

"...thank goodness..." Dad.

"...so afraid..." Mom.

What do you mean? Is Gabe okay?
"...constant observation..."
Mr. Swenson?
"...how long..." Dad.
"...hospital..."
What's going on? Where's Gabe?
But no one answers.

Mom and Diaper Helper are changing me again.
"There, Ette. Fresh and dry. You always liked being a clean baby, did I ever tell you that?"
Yes.
"Oh, sweetheart."
"Isabelle, come to bed." Dad.
Sigh. Mom.
"I'll wake you if there's any change." Diaper Helper.
You'll wake me? I don't want to wake up, I want to go to sleep! Turn off the light.
A kiss on my forehead. Shalimar.
Another. Moustache whiskers and Old Spice.
Gone.
Diaper Helper stays.
Click. Static. Whine. Tune. Music.
Turn it down, will you? How do you expect me to sleep?
"And you just heard *Chances Are* on the Nightlight Show on WBZ. That Johnny Mathis is pretty groovy. This is Dick Summer with you on Radio 103. And did you write us to get your copy of the booklet by Theopolous Q. Waterhouse, 'How to Give Mouth to Mouth Resuscitation Without Getting Emotionally Involved'?"
"Hah!" Diaper Helper laughs aloud.
It was pretty funny.
More music.
Coffee comes in.
"How is she?" Donna!
Speak up, Diaper Helper, I can't hear you.
Donna takes my pulse.

"It's normal."

Diaper Helper double-checks it.

"How long do think this will last?" Donna.

Well?

More music.

I doze under the light.

Footsteps.

More coffee arrives. Not Donna, another woman. She and Diaper Helper change my diaper again.

Diaper Helper leaves. More Coffee stays.

Too hot. More Coffee blows on it. Just right. She is sitting in my chair.

Yoo-hoo, I could go for some coffee. How about it? I won't tell.

Fine. Be that way.

The least you could do is unchain me from the bed.

Click. Volume.

"Dick Summer with you on Radio 103. And it's time now for the award that most people have been waiting for. It's the award known as"—drum roll—"The Nightlight Top Crumb Award. As you know by now, it was the Duke of Shrewsbury who invented a couple of slices of bread with something succulent in between. That invention was stolen by the Earl of Sandwich and called a sandwich. Actually, it should be called a shrewsbury and we've been trying for some time now to get that name changed, and the campaign has been coming along very well, thanks to your help. Each and every night we have the Top Crumb Award and we award it to the person who has done the most for the cause of shrewsburyism in the past day or so. Just call or write the station and let me know about it."

"Ah ha ha ha!" I cough from laughing.

"Etienne?"

What?

"Etienne, can you talk to me?"

"Mmmpf." Angry. *Don't turn off the radio! It's just getting good. Turn off the light.*

I wait and wait.
Nothing doing.

The hulk is back. Eyelid Lifter does his business again. I squirm.
"Good, good."
Eyelid Lifter talks to Mom and Dad in the hallway.
Footsteps.
"That poor darling girl."
Mrs. Bouchard! Tell Paula I miss her.
"Let us pray." Reverend Bouchard.
Silence.
Diaper Helper is back.
Jean Naté. Donna.
"Wake up, Ette. It's almost Thanksgiving."
Well, I would, but the lights have been on so long I'm really tired.
Tabu. Marcia.
Old Spice, Shalimar.
Isn't anybody working? Where's Gabe?
More Coffee is still here.
Always coffee.
And not a drop to drink.

Hot wet again. *I'm sorry, Mom. I'm so ashamed.*
More Coffee and Diaper Helper lift me up like I'm Snoozie
Thumbelina. But my left arm stays glued to the rail.
Roses.
Brussels sprouts.
*But you know I like green beans with the turkey, and I'm hungry,
and I want to get out of bed.*
I flap my right hand like Gabe. *Where's Gabe? I want to see
Gabe.* I hit it hard against the rail.
"Oooouwww."
"She's awake!"
"Ette, wake up, honey."

"Unngh." But I'm stuck on the yellow brick road and I fall sound asleep in the field of poppies.

"Heavenly Father—"

Dieter!

But it couldn't be. He would have said if he was driving up for Thanksgiving.

"—we come before you to intercede on Ette's behalf."

But it must be. It's his voice. And his smell. Citrus, and that other ingredient I can never remember.

God, are you there? It's me, Ette, remember?

"'The LORD is my shepherd; I shall not want.'" Not Dieter.

But I hear Dieter chime in with Mom and Dad and Donna.

"'He makes me lie down in green pastures; He leads me beside quiet waters.

'He restores my soul; He guides me in the paths of righteousness for the sake of His name.

'Even though I walk through the valley of the shadow of death, I will fear no evil, for You are with me;'"

You are with me—you do remember me!

"'Your rod and Your staff, they comfort me.

'You prepare a table before me in the presence of my enemies.

'You anoint my head with oil; my cup overflows.

'Surely goodness and mercy will follow me all the days of my life, and I will dwell in the house of the LORD forever.'"

And goodness and mercy will follow me all the days of my life. Thank you, God.

And God prepared a table before me but it was in the presence of my friends. Turkey, sage and onion and celery in the stuffing, green beans and carrots and corn, the yeast of the Parker House rolls. I can picture the Duchess potatoes. I just can't eat.

But no one is.

Isn't anyone going to say grace?

The food just sits.

It's getting cold, you know.

"And coming right up..." Frieda.

I salivate at the garlic, shrimp, wine, lemon juice right under my nose. Shrimp Scampi on Thanksgiving?

Or is Thanksgiving over? *If I could just wake up, God.*

"Apple, pumpkin, mince, pecan," Donna sing-songs, and the pies parade by and sit on the sidelines.

Coffee gets takers.

"Or tea if you'd like." Donna. "We've got black and Earl Grey."

Earl Grey tea. That's it! The ingredient in Dieter's aftershave. Not the tea, the thing that gives Earl Grey its smell: bergamot. Citrus and bergamot aftershave. I figured it out!

"I'd like to try one more thing." Not Dieter.

"I hope you will let me join you." More Coffee.

"Please, do." Dieter.

"But I'm holding the weapon of last resort." Frieda.

Laughter.

Weapon. I must be dreaming. *Why was that funny?*

Clattering. Tabu leaves.

"'Is any one of you suffering? He should pray. Is anyone cheerful? He should sing praises.'" Not Dieter.

"'Is any one of you sick?'" Dieter. "'He should call the elders of the church to pray over him and anoint him with oil in the name of the Lord. And the prayer offered in faith will restore the one who is sick. The Lord will raise him up. If he has sinned, he will be forgiven.'"

A warm oily cotton ball on my forehead.

"Amen." Dieter and Mom and Dad and Donna and Not Dieter and More Coffee. I can almost say it out loud. *Amen.*

Crying in the hall. Crying, coming closer.

I take a breath.

"Gabe."

"Stay with us, Ette." Dad.

"Open your eyes, sweetheart." Mom.

"I can't. They're stuck shut." Worse than every time I slept like a log.

Immediately a warm wet face cloth was put over them, and I rubbed them with my free hand until my eyes unglued, but I covered them again.

"The light's in my eyes."

Finally, my reading lamp is switched off.

Mom and Dad.

"Hi."

Sniffling and laughing.

"Hi to you," said Dad.

I looked around. Donna, Frieda. More Coffee? Not Dieter? And Dieter! It was enough to make me wonder if I was hallucinating.

"I'll go call Dr. Lewis," said More Coffee.

"I want Gabe."

Marcia entered the room holding him out.

"Welcome back," she said.

"Thanks."

She handed him over to Mom.

I held up my right hand for him to grab.

"Ahh."

"Baby Gaby. I'm almost as stinky as you."

Everybody laughed.

"I'll change his diaper," said Donna.

"See you later, alligator," I said, "as soon as I get cleaned up, too."

"After Dr. Lewis looks at you," said Mom.

"If it's okay, may we come back later?" said Dieter.

"You have my permission," I said, at least as well as Audrey Hepburn did in *Roman Holiday.*

Everybody laughed again, and he left with Not Dieter and Frieda.

CHAPTER 41

DR. LEWIS ARRIVED WITH Diaper Helper and slowly, they shifted me to full upright.

He put a big Band-Aid on as soon as More Coffee removed the saline fluid IV from my left arm. She unwound the Ace bandage from the rail, where it had been held secure to keep in the needle. The IV was the culprit behind all that peeing in bed, but as it turned out, there was a rubber mat covered by layers of sheets, so I didn't really wet the bed. I never knew there were such big diapers.

He lifted my eyelids again and flashed a light over my pupils. "Good, good."

He and Diaper Helper moved my legs over the side of the bed and he pinged my knees with a tiny rubber hammer. Like always, my feet swung forward. He checked for bruises. There was only one, on my left shoulder, another reason my arm was pinned to the bed rail. With a flashlight, he carefully felt through my hair. My head had also taken the fall, but as he put it, my skull had stayed closed, which was the nice way of saying I hadn't cracked my head open. The whole time, he asked one question after another. Did this hurt, could I do that?

After I finally passed muster, he said, "The injury affected your brain, not seriously enough for a coma, but deeply enough for a brief spell of unconsciousness, and according to our observations, semi-consciousness returned fairly quickly, although it lasted longer than I would have liked."

Of course it wasn't Mr. Swenson who ordered constant observation, it was Dr. Lewis.

"That sounds about right."

"Do you remember anything about how you were injured?"

"The last thing I remember is playing basketball. Then I was here in my room."

"Yes, yes, you were brought home after one of the players knocked you to the ground."

I didn't need to ask who. "A foul?"

"To put it mildly. Let's put that aside for later. What else do you remember?"

"At first I thought I was dreaming, but everything sounded real."

"So, you heard us?"

"Only a few things at first, and the radio, and then I started hearing more, all the people coming in and out, and right before I woke up, I heard everybody praying, but mostly I smelled a lot, all along."

"That's good, very good. The stimulation was deliberate."

"It sure worked."

"Mmm hmm," said Dr. Lewis, to sounds of agreement from Mom and Dad.

"I'd like to see her put on some weight," he said to them. "She's under the recommended guidelines, and at this point, she needs energy reserves."

I felt bad for Mom. It was anything but her fault. It was lunch period. No matter how much thought she put into my lunch, I wasn't a fast eater, and I simply ran out of time to eat much. Most days, I properly digested a sandwich but didn't have the piece of fruit until after school for a snack.

"Give it to me plain, Doctor," I said as precociously as Shirley Temple.

"You will need to give your body time to recover."

"You mean I'm not recovered now?"

"Yes, yes, partly. But not entirely. You won't be returning to the basketball court this season."

Playing sports wasn't at the top of my list, but it meant I'd be good to go otherwise.

"I expect a full recovery," he said.

Big smiles, heaves of relief.

"Just remember one thing."

"I promise."

"One step at a time. Take each one slowly."

Step one was walking. Step two was getting cleaned up.

Diaper Helper and More Coffee, practical nurses whose name tags identified them as Sharon Lemieux and Joyce Yandow, had actually done their best to keep me clean, but there was only so much they could do.

Hands under my bent elbows, they helped me stay upright as I walked to the bathroom, and into the tub. Mom stayed with me while I bathed, and the nurses changed the sheets and then settled me back in bed. Diaper Helper—I mean, Miss Lemieux, stayed on. If I was better by the time Miss Yandow returned to relieve her in the morning, another step would be to see if I could use the bathroom alone. It was strictly a "see how it goes" situation.

The next steps had to be drinking and eating. I drank some milk through a bendy straw, but Doctor Lewis said nausea sometimes accompanies concussion, so I had to take food gradually. I started with the same puréed carrots Gabe had for Thanksgiving. I was reduced to sippy cup and baby food—and it was a step forward.

"If you keep this down, the second course will be turkey with mashed potatoes and green beans," said Mom.

"Oh, goody."

"Small portions, but you'll feel full quickly. Let's give the carrots half an hour."

"Okay. I'm really hungry. Who brought the roses?"

"Carl. He sends his love."

It was a lot of love.

After I brushed my teeth and spit into a curved pink bin Mom held under my chin, Donna and Dieter and Not Dieter and Frieda returned. They were real, all right, and Dieter was a sight for sore eyes.

The nurses had set up some folding chairs. With Mom and Dad sticking around as well, my room looked like a contest for how many people could fit into a phone booth.

"Hi again," I said. "Sorry I couldn't dress for the occasion."

They laughed.

"You haven't lost your sense of humor," said Frieda.

"No, but I mean it. I was supposed to finish a dress."

"This one?" Donna held up the sapphire velvet.

"What?"

"Marcia finished it," said Mom.

Never mind what Marcia had said me about looking like an Old Timer in long skirts, she had cut the dress to fall below my knees—and sleeves to reach my wrists on the top side, but from the elbow on down, the bottom of the sleeve flared out in a point all the way to the hem, just like a medieval queen's gown. Even on a padded satin hanger, the dress was gorgeous.

"Oh my goodness." My eyes filled with tears.

Not Dieter stood up as if to leave, but I said, "Don't go. I'll be okay." Better than okay.

I dabbed my eyes and blew my nose and looked at Not Dieter and said, "I guess you know who I am."

He bowed. "Andrew Patterson, at your service."

I smiled.

"Drew is my roommate at Avon," said Dieter.

Drew was about the same height as Dieter, but he was lankier. I'd seen his brown eyes and hair and well-defined eyebrows before.

"Anna's brother?"

"So that's how I'm known."

I smiled. "Anna and Andrew. They sound so much alike, did you ever get your names mixed up?"

"Not unless we wanted to pull jokes on my parents. There was a method to their madness. They named us for people in the New Testament, but my nickname's been Drew all along."

"I think Andrew was an apostle, but I don't know who Anna was. I haven't come across her yet."

"You're right, Andrew and Peter were the first apostles that Jesus called to follow him. Anna only makes one appearance, but it's an important one. She was a prophetess and the first woman to recognize Jesus as the Messiah when he was brought to the temple after he was born."

With names as meaningful as Paula and Timothy, Anna and Andrew had a lot to live up to.

"Are you going to Yale next year, too?"

"That's the plan."

"Maybe you'll get to stay roommates."

"No, the Dieter and Drew duo will be breaking up. Dorms at Yale are assigned by academic departments. I'm Near Eastern studies, Dieter's Architecture, so we'll be in different buildings."

"We'll see each other frequently, though," said Dieter, "at the very least Sunday Chapel and discipleship group."

"That's good." They'd still be two peas in a pod.

"There are hundreds of people praying for you," said Drew. "We got on the horn right away."

"How did you find out I was sick?"

"I called Albert," said Frieda, referring to her brother, who is Dieter's father.

Now that must have thrown a wrench in the Connecticut Nordens' Thanksgiving plans. I had the impression it wasn't a family dinner but an important social event, you know, all the best people, and Dieter's absence would leave a huge hole in their table.

"And he let you leave?" I asked Dieter.

"I said life is more important than food," said Dieter.

"Really?"

"Really." He shrugged.

I was amazed. Dieter believed so much in honoring his parents. But I guess there comes a time to spread your wings, and he was right on time.

"They drove up and prayed all night for you," said Donna.

"All night? After driving for hours?"

"Mrs. Bouchard started the Meetinghouse prayer chain as well," said Dad.

"Will you tell her I said thanks?"

Mom nodded. "I'll call her. Everyone wants to know how you are doing."

"You can tell them I said their prayers were answered."

"That they were," said Dieter. "Praise God."

"I'm sorry I ruined your Thanksgiving break," I said to him and Drew. "You must be really tired."

"Nah," said Drew. "We have a good amount of experience pulling all-nighters, and anyway, we split the driving so we both got some sleep on the way up."

"And Drew anointed you for healing," said Donna.

The oil on my forehead.

"You can do that?"

"Strictly speaking, it's a job for the elders of the church," said Drew. "But we were here."

"And Drew's preparing for the ministry," said Dieter. "It was done in faith and good conscience."

"Rev. Bouchard only does visitation," said Frieda.

"Oh," I said, but I'd never heard of anybody getting anointed nowadays anyhow.

"I remember hearing him and Mrs. Bouchard, for a few seconds, since I was still pretty out of it then. But I remember all the food."

"Just a variation on the old smelling salts treatment," said Frieda.

"We were trying to think of every possible way to stimulate you," said Dad.

"You sure did." It explained all the perfume. Who knows what would have happened if they had brought in Gabe sooner, messy diaper or not?

"Whose idea was the Shrimp Scampi?"

"Frieda's!" said the chorus.

"I cannot tell a lie. It was Carl's idea," she said. "He thought of the brussels sprouts, too. He said something you don't like would work as well as something you do, so we went with both."

"He was right." And he made up for the brussels sprouts with the roses. "I heard you say something about a weapon, and I got scared. Was that it? Or the coffee? It smelled so good." I like coffee a lot, and I never got more than a glass creamer's worth at a time. Coffee was a good temptation to wake me up.

"Neither one. The coffee was just to stay awake," said Frieda.

All these people had given up hours of sleep to pray for me and sit by my side.

She picked up an oversized pepper mill sitting on the windowsill, one of the style we used at La Terrasse for tableside service. "Now this I can take credit for. If it came down to the wire and nothing woke you up and you'd have to be shipped off to the hospital, then I planned to sneeze you awake."

Laughter is the best medicine.

"Duty calls, my dear. Don't sleep too tight. Tah tah!" Frieda blew me a kiss and left.

Donna got up, but she stopped at the door. "I'm glad you're okay. I was really scared."

I teared up but I smiled.

On second thought, laughter is good medicine, but love is the best.

"I guess you have to go," I said to Dieter and Drew.

"We weren't planning on it," said Dieter. "But if it will tire you out too much—"

"No. I've got a million things to talk to you about."

"If time operated the same for us humans as it does for God, we'd have enough time to talk about everything. With the Lord, a thousand years is like a watch in the night, but all we've got is the watch in the night."

"Okay, I was exaggerating, but I do have some."

"Have at it," said Drew. "I'm hitting the sack. Whenever you're ready, I'll take the first shift behind the wheel."

He turned to me and bowed again. "It was a pleasure meeting you. 'The LORD bless you and keep you.'"

"'And make his face shine upon you,'" I quoted back.

"He just has," he said with a grin and left.

Mom and Dad also stood to leave.

"How about if you two catch up?" said Dad.

Everyone except Miss Lemieux left.

"Miss Lemieux?" said Mom.

"Oh, I didn't realize—" she said as she went to the door.

"They'll be fine," I overheard Mom say as Miss Lemieux preceded her out. "They have a special bond."

CHAPTER 42

DIETER MOVED OVER TO my reading chair. In the waning hours of daylight, the lamp had been turned on again. As he moved it back and adjusted the lampshade so the light tilted away and wouldn't bother my eyes, I asked him, "How's your senior thesis coming along?"

"It's off to a good start. My proposal was accepted, and I've been to sites I have postcards of that are still standing. The site work is a lot of fun."

"Can I read it when you're done?"

"I'd be honored."

"Thanks. Listen, I know you said not to feel sorry for you because you didn't make it to the Olympics, but weren't you even a little disappointed?"

"Yes. Naturally, I wanted to make the cut, but it was special just being there. I met people from all over."

"Will you try again?"

"The Lord willing, I'd like to. I learned a lot, which helps to know what to expect next time, and I've got plenty of moral support for another attempt to qualify."

"What did you like best?"

"The swimming itself is always the high point for me in any competition, but afterwards, when I didn't make the cut, I received a tremendous amount of praise and encouragement. I really appreciated that."

"Have you seen Carl and Frieda's TV?"

He laughed. "Have I! They think I deserved to make it to the podium in Tokyo, but I watched the events, and it's clear that if I'd made the cut, it's unlikely I'd have taken any medal."

"How come?"

"The competition was fierce. Olympic records were broken in all of the events, and world records were broken in ten of them."

"Wow."

"Exactly. So that's another reason why I'm satisfied with my performance as a qualifier."

"Yeah, I can see why now."

We fell silent for a few moments.

"Thanks for all the World's Fair postcards."

"I really enjoyed writing them. What a place. The World's Fair was unlike anything I've ever seen, and the Billy Graham Pavilion wasn't like any of the other pavilions. Just knowing people were praying with counselors to receive Christ as their savior while I was there really touched my heart. The Holy Spirit was moving. I actually felt the holiness."

"I wish I could have gone."

"I think you would have liked it."

He took a sip of coffee.

"Can I have some?"

"Coffee?"

He chuckled. "No, I don't think so. At least not from me. Hang on."

He went out and left his cup and saucer on the hallway table.

"We've used up enough of our watch on me," he said when he returned. "What's foremost on your mind?"

"Bible questions for one, just things I didn't understand when I was reading. I figured out some of them, but I still need a lot of help."

"Did you try calling? I never got any messages."

"No. I didn't want to bother you."

"Ette, you could never bother me. Here, this is one of my father's business cards." He turned it over and wrote. "I'll give you my home number and our dorm suite. And Stefanie and

Sydney's home number, in case I'm on Long Island. You can always get a hold of me. Leave a message with Drew if I'm not in the dorm. I'll get it." He tucked the card into the upper left corner of my desk blotter, in plain sight.

"Thanks."

"So, Bible questions."

"They are on my mind, but they can wait. I'm writing them down. I have a question about what happened, how I got the concussion."

"I can see why. I heard the girl who ran into you had given you a hard time. Is that true?"

"Yeah. Tina. And another girl, Janice. They picked on me. I thought it was over, but it wasn't."

"I can't imagine it will continue now."

"Me neither, but it bothers me. Tina had also fouled me before so I had a skinned arm and she got detentions for it and for lipping off to the teacher. Now this. I feel mad at her, and I feel sad that it happened. What about the bulwark? I know it was there, for a while, and then it was gone."

"It's still there. God spared you."

"Yeah, but I got hurt anyway. I didn't even have a chance to call out to The Helper."

"Why do *you* think it happened?"

"Tina's mean. I know it didn't really have anything to do with me. I didn't do anything to her. It's her problems, inside her, eating at her."

"I think your insights are very mature, Ette."

"I've had practice."

"You have?"

"Debbie."

"You haven't made up?"

"I tried. It looks like it's going to take time. But I still don't understand what happened to the bulwark. You said God protects us. Considering that people I thought were my friends have hurt me, it makes less sense to me now than I thought it did."

"All martyrs are protected, but that doesn't mean they never suffer or get killed. The bulwark never leaves. The real protection is in the security of the soul."

"Well, you didn't tell me that."

"I thought you knew."

"Anyway, I'm not a martyr."

"Maybe not in the classic sense, but all of us who have had to stand up for our faith have experienced what it feels like to suffer for the cause of Christ."

"I was only playing basketball, not standing up for my faith. Although...now that you mention it..."

"What?"

"There is one thing."

"A time when you defended your faith?"

"Yeah, in English class. Not just once. I felt like the teacher was against me, and maybe some of my classmates were because I stood up for God."

"Including Tina?"

"Yes."

"Were you opposed?"

"Yes." I told him about Julian and the play.

"I know how you feel. We read it at school, too."

"Were you the only Christian?"

"Probably not, but most of my classmates are in the same shoes I was before I trusted in Christ. They think going to church makes them a Christian, so they don't have a solid foundation of faith and don't know enough of the Bible to look at the play from its viewpoint. They have a sense of fairness, though, and after I brought up the fact that it takes as much faith to believe in the theory of evolution as it does to believe in the Bible's account of God's six days of creation, we had some good discussions in class, and outside of it as well. Even so, Drew and I know what it is to be the outsiders."

"I guess I am, but I'm trying not to go too far outside. If I do that, then my friends will feel like we don't have anything in common any more. I'll stick with God if it comes down to a choice between God and them, but I hope it doesn't come down to that.

I like them, and I want for them to learn about Jesus, too, but I don't want to scare them off. You know what I mean?"

"I do. It will come naturally if you just let them see that your love of God hasn't changed because of the foul. And you can be sure that neither foul nor concussion separates the love of God from you."

"I'll keep that in mind."

"I'm not surprised this happened to you."

"What! How can you say that?"

"It goes back to the issue of suffering for the sake of Christ. You stood up for God in class, and there is every possibility you are being persecuted for your faith."

"Teachers are supposed to make sure things are fair. I don't think Julian was, and I told my guidance counselor so. Anyway, this happened in Phys Ed, not English."

"Resistance can come from any direction. You know as well as I do that the sneak attack is most effective. Have you considered that you may be the only person Julian has ever heard defend the Bible's view of creation?"

"Come on. He knows what it says."

"Intellectually, yes, but how many students do you think Julian has encountered who believe in it, heart and soul?"

"Who knows."

"And your classmates did, too. You said none of them stood up for six days of creation. We live in a fallen world now, but God's engineering design at creation was perfect. Evolution is a mindless string of events that have absolutely no probability of ending with a complex universe. You were courageous to stand alone for the truth. That's a privilege, Ette."

"I don't think of it that way."

"It is. God is using you."

"But it's junior high."

"It was the church and state for Bonhoeffer and Luther. You're a witness for Christ, maybe the only witness to some of them. It won't go to waste."

"I hope not. I definitely felt opposed. I mean, I really was."

"The ancient dragon still influences people."

"The Dragon of Neston."

"Of everywhere. Satan admits to prowling the earth, and the apostle Peter warns us of it. He says, 'Your adversary the devil prowls around like a roaring lion, seeking someone to devour.'"

"Kids?"

"To the devil, anyone is fair play. A seed of faith has been planted in you. Satan's first strategy is to take it away."

"Nip it in the bud."

"Exactly. But when it's too late, like it is with you, he has Plan B and Plan C. Whenever he can't succeed, he tries to stunt the growth or smother it."

"So I'll give up."

Dieter nodded. "I've seen it before, kids who are born again and growing in faith, on their way to becoming strong adult Christians. Satan will do anything to keep their seeds from growing and bearing fruit."

"Hmm. I guess it's starting to make sense. I read in Genesis about the serpent in the garden of Eden, but I don't have the big picture like you do."

"How far have you read?"

"Second Kings."

"Since August?"

"Yes."

"That's terrific progress."

"I would have made more progress, but all those names took a long time to get through. And there's a lot of surprising stuff. I had no idea. You could have warned me."

"I'll say this much. You'll meet the dragon more often in your reading soon, and the picture will get clearer. By the end of the Bible, you'll find out what happens to him."

"I hope it's a happy ending."

"You haven't peeked?"

"No. I'm sticking to the reading order. Except Proverbs. And I added Psalms. I like how David wrote some things down when he was in trouble. I know how he felt."

"Etienne, I think God is refining you. You are growing so strong in grace."

"I've been getting practice with that, too. Anyway, when Drew anointed me and everyone was reading that part in Psalm 23 where it says 'You are with me,' that's when I started to wake up all the way. I guess the bulwark really is with me."

"Now you understand. Remember, nothing can separate you from God's love."

Miss Lemieux knocked, although the door was wide open.

"Come in."

"Sorry to interrupt," she said. "I need to take Ette's vitals."

She took care of business. Once she was out of earshot, Dieter said, "I don't know if you were aware of it, but Miss Yandow asked to be here when Drew anointed you with oil. She said her whole church was fasting and praying for you."

"Wow. Did she say where she went to church?"

"Drew asked her. Groveton Chapel."

"Groveton is in New Hampshire, but it's not that far, it's only across the Connecticut River. And Rev. Bouchard came right over, and Mrs. Bouchard got the whole Meetinghouse praying, too." I was amazed by how much people cared for me.

"You see, Ette, there are believers all around. You just don't always know it."

"Can we pray before you go?"

And on that happy note, our watch in the night ended.

After Dieter left, Mom and Dad came in. They asked how I felt and I said I was tired, but they lingered. I could tell they didn't want me to go to sleep again, but I said I was okay.

My soul was secure.

Chapter 43

AN UNEXPECTED RESULT OF the concussion was that I caught up on enough sleep to go to church. But there was no Dieter to attend with, and because I was very early in the recuperation stage, going alone was out of the question, even if it was only across the common.

For the first time since before Gabe was born, Mom and Dad went to church. It was his very first time.

Mr. and Mrs. Pecor were on greeter and bulletin duty along with some prayer chain ladies, who went all aflutter over my return to civilization standing upright in one piece. It was nice. I thanked them for praying for me and said it meant everything to me, although that seemed to surprise them. Pretty much everybody eyeballed me. Now I understood how Dieter felt: on stage, exposed, all the time.

Everyone said welcome back and good to see you to Mom and Dad, in a kind way, so they wouldn't feel bad about not attending for so long, and Gabe got a year's backlog of oohs and aahs.

We arrived early enough that seats were available in the rear, and if we bumped somebody who usually sat there, well, too bad. We were far enough away for the volume of the organ and piano not to be too loud for Gabe—or for me. The deal was, if he was as quiet in church as he was in La Terrasse, he could stay with us in the pew, but just like the dining room, if he started to fuss, Mom would vamoose with him to the nursery until the service ended.

No need to worry. From the choir filing in to the first note of "Come, Ye Thankful People, Come," he was as fascinated with church as with the Meyers' color television set. He started waving along with the choir director! I added conductor as a new possibility for his habit of flapping his arms. But that wasn't all. He sang along—the way he always said "ahh," but he just kept going, stretching it out. Mom made no attempt to stop him, and people all around us smiled.

The song ended, and in the silence, he let loose with one more long "ahh." The congregation laughed and clapped.

"Indeed," said Rev. Bouchard, who'd weathered worse interruptions during the service, "as Psalm 8 tells us, 'From the mouths of children and infants You have ordained praise.'"

Somebody said "Amen."

"Mmm," hummed from pulpit to pew.

Atta boy, Gabe. I hoped he would always have such zeal for worshiping the Lord, but it wasn't to be today.

My battery ran down in no time flat. I expected to bounce back completely once I was on my feet, but Dr. Lewis and everyone else saw it differently. "It's going to take some time," they all warned. I gave Mom and Dad a shake of the head, my signal that I was fading.

We left during the song before the sermon. I was sorry we didn't get to stay for it, but from the sermon title, Rev. Bouchard would be launching the congregation into the Christmas season. I had a pretty good idea of what he would say.

As we passed by the Fortins, I looked aside to smile at Margaret and then at Debbie. Margaret wouldn't mind, and it might help Debbie thaw a little. There's nothing like an injury to get sympathy.

Mr. Pecor was standing at the back and followed us into the vestibule, and when Dad said I wasn't up to snuff quite yet, he gave us a ride home, all several hundred feet of it.

CHAPTER 44

ON MONDAY MORNING, MR. Gaudet called and informed us that Tina was suspended for the week. I was relieved, not because I hated her. It was a matter of justice. She fouled me deliberately, and there were a lot of witnesses to prove it. She injured me. Dr. Lewis said it might have been worse, in which case she'd be looking at more than suspension. She deserved the suspension, although returning to school next week would be lot harder on her than it would for me.

But the work cut out for me would take longer. I already had my Social Studies book, so I buckled down with reading, which I discovered I could only handle a little at a time. A regular assignment took twice as long. Never mind what everybody said, I needed a quick recovery.

I had more visitors than you could shake a stick at. Rev. and Mrs. Bouchard came over during the day. After school let out, Mr. Fortin helped Margaret lug my other books and assignments and homework. The teachers had to prepare all the work in advance, so I had a week's worth. Margaret promised to stop by every day. I not only looked forward to that, I needed it.

Most people would say it isn't very nice to compare a person to a dog, and usually it's not, but it described Margaret to a T. She was like a dog that was happy to see you even if you left the house and had to go back in ten seconds later because you forgot something. The dog would be there, panting and wagging its tail as happily as if you'd been gone so long it got lonesome.

That was the part of Margaret's personality I appreciated most. She must have her problems, but day in and day out, she tackled everything head-on. There's a proverb that says "a joyful heart is good medicine," and there were plenty of times when she was the spoonful of sugar I needed, none more than now.

She left me with a homemade get well card that everybody signed. Well, almost everybody. Most just wrote *Get Well Soon*, but there was one ditty surrounded by a border that looked awfully familiar—the same as the embroidery on one of my Peter Pan collars.

Carnations are red,
Forget-Me-Nots are blue,
Branches are amber,
And we miss you.

Denis! That rascal. He didn't need to put his name; the amber was a dead giveaway. It was sweet.

It was one of many cards, including one from the entire sixth grade of Neston Elementary School, and notes and flower deliveries, several of which came from the Arms. We were warmed by how much people cared, how many people said they were praying for me. Many were strangers, but that wasn't surprising. Word got out fast.

The school superintendent had to be notified immediately, followed by the board members. Tales of student injuries always went the rounds, and in my case, a concussion that left me semiconscious was serious news that went home to every hamlet and village on the high school bus routes before the day of the accident was out. It was followed quickly by the prayer chain, which spread the news to all the church members. And the *Neston News* did the rest.

The phone rang so much Dad said to take it off the hook when Gabe or I were resting. Newspaper reporters called at least once a day. Mom and Dad didn't particularly want to tell them any details, but once half of Wortham County knew anyway, it was better to let the press know that until I woke up, I had professional round-the-clock care, and I was recuperating under my doctor's supervision.

My friends told me everyone in PE who witnessed the accident had to see a guidance counselor. "How had the situation been handled?" "Were they feeling any anxiety?" they'd been asked.

I learned that our teachers had handled the situation properly, both the sports side and the emergency care side. Miss Williams and Miss Brennan had acted swiftly and wisely, Mr. Gaudet told the newspaper. The superintendent said the board members who investigated the school's policies and procedures agreed, although he said the next in-service would include a thorough review of safety protocols. I would have read all the articles, but I was barely keeping my head above water with assignments. Mom clipped the news articles for me to read later.

I wouldn't recommend a concussion for the opportunity, but if I hadn't been home, I would have missed a couple of priceless events. On Tuesday, Gabe walked for the first time! Really walked, not just a few steps. On Wednesday, he said "bub bye" for the first time when Dad left for work.

"Show Daddy what you mean," said Mom—and then he waved and said it again!

Besides Margaret and Theresa and Paula coming over after school, Adele surprised me with her mom, who had come into town for art supplies.

Denis, Bucky, and Patrick had kept the appointment with Margaret and Theresa in Meeting Room 1A over the break.

"We got a lot done," Margaret told me.

She also said they had no end of enjoyment in using the fish bowl room, although, of course, they really did work. We'd pick up our personal civics project again during the break between Christmas and New Year's.

I tried to look on the bright side. Sure, I'd been through the wringer, but the main thing was to keep looking up, and that included being grateful for who's on your side down here on the ground.

Late Thursday afternoon, Mom called up the stairs, "Ette, you have a visitor!"

She didn't say who, so I slowly went down the stairs, holding the banister like Dr. Lewis said to do, looking forward to another good surprise.

Lo and behold, there was Janice, standing inside the kitchen doorway.

CHAPTER 45

I DIDN'T SAY A word.

Mom picked up Gabe and left.

"Hi, Ette, I'm sorry you got hurt—" She ran out of air.

I knew exactly how she felt. I could hardly breathe when I had to ask Norman Levesque for forgiveness.

The ball was still in her court, but I minded my manners.

"Have a seat," I said.

I got us glasses of water. She took a gulp before she spoke.

"I never wanted you to get hurt. Honest, I didn't know Tina was going to push you. I would have told her not to."

She took another gulp.

"But when she started calling you Eddie, I know, I sided with her, so I'm not saying it's her fault. I picked on you every time she did."

She was coming clean, hard as it was.

"Why did you do that? Call me Eddie? And snub me on the playground. You knew those things hurt me. I tried to talk to you."

"Tina said we could get back at you."

"For what?"

"Don't you know?"

"What did I ever do to you?"

"Nothing."

"You called me Eddie for no reason?"

"No, it was because, because of my father. He almost got fired. So did hers."

"From the Arms."

"Yeah."

"What's that got to do with me?"

"Nothing. I just, I thought it would make me feel better."

"Did it?"

"No. And I told Tina I didn't want to keep it up. I never thought it would go so far."

"So now what?"

"So...I'm sorry."

She teared up, just the way I had when I asked Norman to forgive me, and he had forgiven me immediately. Now the shoe was on my foot to do the same.

"Okay." I paused. It took me longer to say than Norman had taken, but I said it. "I forgive you."

Janice took a breath and sat up straighter. It looked like the weight of the world fell off her shoulders.

"I won't pal around with Tina any more. All she wants to do is gossip."

"Are you sure? I mean, you don't have to do that for me. I won't be hurt if you stay friends. She'll be pretty lonely without you. After all, she's your neighbor."

"It's too late. I told her fouling you was completely wrong. She told me to like it or lump it. I said it was wrong to call you Eddie, too, and I didn't want to hear it—and I won't call you that again, honest, never again. She picked a fight with me and called me a two-faced traitor, so I told her I wouldn't bring any of her homework over when she's on suspension. I'm not sure where it will get me if I try to get along with her. Look where it got you."

Good point. "What are you going to do?"

"As far as I'm concerned, she's just someone who sits next to me, like some boy I'd never talk to. I'll avoid her."

"Like I avoid you two?"

"Oh, Ette, I'm so sorry. You've been nicer than I deserve—the way you encouraged me during softball, and you even clapped at my Geography presentation. Yours was a lot better, and I just sat there when everybody else clapped."

"Well, that hurt too, but it's behind us now. Water under the bridge, and I like it that way. I'm glad you came over."

"Me, too. I feel a lot better."

Cleansed, I thought, like I had been after I asked Norman for forgiveness, but surprisingly, I felt cleansed doing the forgiving, too.

"Do you think we could have a fresh start?" she asked.

I nodded. "Fresh start."

Supposing Janice and Tina did not see each other in the meantime, come Monday, Episode Two of Showdown at the School Bus Stop would play out. They were not only neighbors, they'd been peas in a pod just like Paula and Debbie and I had been. If Tina refused to make up with Janice, it would be just like Debbie cutting off from Paula and me. I didn't want to see the breakup of another long friendship.

On the other hand, there is a proverb that says those who walk with the wise will become wise, but the companion of fools will be destroyed. Janice didn't have to suffer Tina's foolish nastiness as the cost of friendship. Paula had figured that out with Debbie. With some distance between them, Janice would be better off without Tina's bad influence—and maybe literally safer.

As I wrote a *thank you* in my prayer journal, I thought of what a different kind of Thanks-giving this one had been. The return of Janice's friendship was a bittersweet answer to prayer. It had come the hard way, but still, it had been one of my biggest prayer requests. One down, two to go—Debbie and Tina. But the total remained three prayer requests because Janice stayed on the list. She might not feel it yet, but her friendship with Tina went way back, and the loss of the parts that had been good would hurt.

CHAPTER 46

GETTING THE ROYAL TREATMENT had to be the last thing Tina wanted for me, but from the moment she fouled me, that's exactly what I'd been getting.

As living proof of God's healing, I'd expected to be the center of attention when I went to the Meetinghouse, but I had not expected it when I was taking my baby steps to get my strength back. From the produce man and grocery stockers to the women shopping, people surrounded me during a trip I made to the Giant Store with Mom. Strangers stopped me on the street when I went for walks with Dad. And when I went through the break room at the Arms, some housekeepers cried.

I should have expected the attention. I had told Mom and Dad I was willing to let the *Neston News* run my fifth grade picture, under the condition that they print my statement with it, which the paper did: *I am grateful for all your prayers that I get well soon. God has heard and answered them.*

We figured it would go in the back section where kids get their pictures in for something or other, like a blue ribbon or valedictorian or Eagle Scout, but it was on the front page, although it was below the fold. I wasn't looking for the attention, but handling it provided dress rehearsals for returning to school.

As soon as I got to the bus stop, Alice Dubuque said, "It's nice to see you back."

"Thank you. It's nice to be back."

Tina arrived.

She didn't say anything to me, didn't even look my way.

Janice, not far behind, made a beeline for me, but Tina hissed her name as she passed her.

For a second, Janice looked confused, and no wonder. It was weird, Tina speaking to her like she was spitting at her. Janice ignored her and said, "Hi, Etienne. You look all better."

"Pretty much, but I have to take things slowly and be careful."

Donna joined us. "Come here," she whispered. She drew us aside. "Tina is calling you a name."

"She's just using my name in a nasty way," said Janice.

"Yes, but there's more to it. Janus was a two-faced god. His name is spelled J-a-n-u-s, and it sounds so much like your name that you wouldn't hear the difference."

"Are you sure?" I asked.

"We learned about Janus in English when we read *The Merchant of Venice* last year."

"Yeah, but Tina wouldn't know that," I whispered.

"I'm just saying, it seems that way to me," said Donna. She looked at Janice. "It's just too bad you can't prove she meant anything other than saying your name."

The ugly truth dawned on Janice. "She knows. She called me a two-faced traitor once before."

Now it definitely made sense. Janus was another insult, another Eddie, another wrong label. How Tina found out about Janus didn't matter. The proof was in the pudding. She used it in a way that showed she knew what it meant—the first time she accused Janice of two-timing.

"Because of me," I said.

"It's not your fault," said Janice.

"I know it's not my fault. It's not yours either. It's all her own."

The bus pulled up.

"Fresh start," I said.

Janice held back the tears rimming her eyes. "Fresh start."

I went to the front of the line to get on the bus. I figured I could get away with Queen for a Day. Maybe more.

"Morning, morning. Good to see you," said Mr. Ted, not mentioning me by name, although I suspected his comment was especially directed to me.

We passed Margaret and I smiled and said, "We're sitting back there."

Without my having told her, Margaret saw for herself. She understood. The others, who eyeballed us, figured it out too.

Tina got on last, and every kid sitting alone, including Margaret, moved to the aisle edge to block her from sitting with them—except for Martin Smith, the pimple-faced boy who always had a hole at his seat until the last minute.

Janice caught me up on school chitchat until we got there.

"Walk to home room together?" I asked her.

"Okay."

Denis was waiting outside the bus.

"May I carry your books?"

"Just this once," I said.

Donna handed off the extra she was lugging for me, since I had more than usual. He would have taken what I had, too, but I said, "I can handle these."

"Just let me know if you need a hand."

"I won't forget," I said. "You know Janice, right?"

Of course he did.

"Hi, Janice," he said.

"Hi." Her expression said she felt out of place, and she was. Janice by my side announced the break-up of the Tina and Janice duo.

Denis fell in on my other side.

"What was it like?" he asked.

Theresa and Margaret, who had asked me that already, kept in formation behind us, since a little crowd came up and echoed, "Yeah, what was it like?"

"It was like trying to wake up out of a deep sleep, you know what I mean?"

They nodded.

"But then I did."

Denis plunged through the group like a plow in a blizzard, and we went inside. Every step I took, I was noticed. I'd had some time to get used to the spotlight, but Janice was a little overwhelmed by sharing it with me.

Mr. Shaw nodded at me when I went in to home room. The nod from Mr. Shaw was as meaningful as the raised eyebrow, only in a good way.

The bell rang, and Margaret picked up the drill immediately.

"Walk to English with me?" she asked Janice.

And then it was Adele to Math and Theresa to Geography and Janice filling the hole at our lunch table.

That hole was turning out to be a blessing of musical chairs. God saw fit to bring who he wanted when he wanted. The O in hole was Opportunity to get to know others better.

I hadn't done much of that in the past, not even with my best friends. We just flowed merrily down the stream. I got away with it in elementary school, but over the summer, I saw there was more to them than met the eye. I discovered I had taken a lot of things for granted. Now, it seemed every day revealed something new about who a person was and where they were heading.

Lunch was another fresh start for Janice, but Tina was headed toward a dead end. Only Mary Halloran sat with her. Their table had two Opportunities. In the halls as well, people avoided Tina.

It didn't have to be that way. Sure, she'd gotten suspended, but she'd had a week to apologize to me. She made her position clear at the bus stop. Tina dug her own grave, but I hoped she learned her lesson before she spent her whole high school career alone.

After lunch, instead of Study Hall, I went to the Infirmary, better known as the nurse's office. I had to promise to take a nap for the first few weeks back at school, which meant no PE for me, either. I needed the time for studying, but rest was prescribed. Actually, there were several things I had to promise: if I got a headache or dizzy or nauseous or lost my balance or was still tired after the nap time, I would have to take a step backward for anything that needed more time. Dr. Lewis had impressed on me that doing so would bring my recovery faster than if I ignored those warning signs.

If the doctor hadn't ordered the siesta, I would have needed it anyway. I was tuckered. Besides adjusting to the routine again, I was not used to talking so much. It wore me out just paying attention to everyone—and to myself, to make sure I didn't mess up.

In the hallways, teachers smiled and nodded. Kids I knew said, "Hi, Ette." Kids I didn't know said, "Hi, Etienne," and if I had time, I said, "Hi! What's your name?" In the case of the farm kids I recognized, I said, "You're from Canfield Farm, right?" or whatever their farm name was, and they were so happy I remembered them.

I couldn't help but see that a gift had been handed to me; even if it had been the hard way, it was still a gift to have my every move watched. More than ever, it was important to let people see Jesus in me. If I messed up, he'd take the hit. Even if I was tired of talking, I wasn't excused from being Miss Congeniality.

A few kids were cautious, as if a concussion could be catching, but they were few and far between and shy types to start with, but most threw caution to the wind. All week, two or three kids squeezed their chairs up to our lunch table to interrogate me. Most just wanted to know what it was like, and I had already answered that, so I kept to it. What I wasn't prepared for were the curious.

"Was it spooky being in a coma?"

"No."

That wasn't enough. They wanted the dirt.

"I wasn't in a coma, I was sort of half-asleep a lot, but it wasn't spooky. People were with me all the time."

"Did you see a white light, like when people almost die but they don't and come back?"

"Just my reading lamp. That bothered me, but the doctor said a concussion can cause sensitivity to light."

"What about God?"

"What do you mean?"

"Did you see God?"

"I didn't see God, but when my friends were praying 'The Lord is My Shepherd' and they got to the part where it says 'you are with me,' God's words reached inside me and I started to wake up, so I guess you could say I heard God speak to me. But that can happen a lot, when you believe in Jesus."

"God talks to you?"

"When I read his words he does. That's the whole idea of the Bible, him talking to us, only in writing."

I wanted Janice to have more of a chance to talk; instead, she and Margaret and Theresa were great sports, although Margaret did put her foot down and say to give me a chance to eat. They also took an interest in what I was asked and what I answered. What's more, they could chuckle or snort at questions, but I had to take the interviews seriously. Traffic dwindled as the week wore on, and by Friday we knew practically every kid in the seventh and eighth grades by name. It was a real peg changer, for them and for me. We were definitely mixing it up.

The Infirmary was a relief. I nodded off quickly and was just coming out of my forty winks when Nurse Gilbert shook my arm before the bell rang for my next class. I wouldn't have gotten through the day without it.

CHAPTER 47

"WOULD YOU SAY IT hurt your feelings?"

It wasn't like Mrs. Richardson to ask me that kind of question, but I guess she had to get right down to the matter of whether I had a chip on my shoulder because Tina whacked me on purpose. I'd had an x-ray, which ruled it out, but we've all met people who carry chips on their shoulders from old injuries.

"Yes, it hurt my feelings," I said.

"How are you handling those feelings?"

Funny she should ask.

"They don't hurt so bad now. I keep clear of Tina, as much as I can. Almost everybody is. Things are a lot harder for her than they are for me. I'm not saying her problems are what's making me feel better. In a way, Tina did me a favor."

It also wasn't like Mrs. Richardson to look surprised, so I had some explaining to do.

"I've gotten really popular. Not just with my classmates, the whole school. I have a few friends, but I wasn't popular before, not like my sister Donna is. Nowadays, all the kids know who I am. They're always saying hi and asking me questions. And they're friendly. Well, some people just stare at me like I'm in the circus, but that happens everywhere I go, not just school. As soon as I started getting out and about, people would come right up to me and say, 'You're that girl, aren't you?'"

Mrs. Richardson nodded and remained silent. She often gave me time to think. As I sorted things out, I'd talk my way through, and then she'd ask more questions.

The conversation Dieter and I had did a lot to help me understand what happened, but since then so did that verse I found in the devotional. I tacked the page on my bulletin board. I read it so often I memorized it. "'My grace is sufficient for you, for My power is perfected in weakness.'"

If weakness from a concussion counted, the shoe definitely fit. I didn't ask for weakness but it found me. All I did was get hurt. You'd think God would want you to be strong, but I can see how that might get in the way if God wants to show his power in you. I thought he was, since I also didn't do anything to recover. I just woke up. Dr. Lewis said the process of recovery was helped by my being young and healthy—and following his directions. I know that's a natural part of how God brings about healing, but only because everything is under God's care. It's not just nature that does the healing.

"I don't think I ever told you this, but this summer I invited Jesus into my heart. I figured life might be a bumpy road, and I needed a hand to pick me up when I fell. That's not the only reason, but the way I look at it, grace is the only thing you can count on when you've got to turn into the direction of the spinouts, like when you're driving in snow and lose control, you know what I mean? There are a lot of situations like that.

"It seems to me that what Tina did was just a really big spinout. All I could do was ask for more grace from God—and since school started, I've been asking for Jesus to pick me up a lot. But I never expected I'd literally get picked up off the floor."

Mrs. Richardson tried not to smile too much.

"So, that's really what's making me feel better. But still, I honestly can't think of anything I could have done on my own to get this much attention. Now, I can't *not* get noticed anymore. It's taking some getting used to, but first it took some thinking over. I wasn't sure I wanted to be center stage in the spotlight, but once I saw I didn't have much of a choice, I thought, now what?"

The only real choice was whether I would be a reluctant witness to the grace of God, like Jonah, and we all know what happened to him, or an obedient follower and friend. I'd stuck with God in English class, and I could stick with God everywhere else.

However, I'd need The Helper more than ever.

"Being watched all the time is a big responsibility, but I have to take it. I don't think the attention will last very long, but as long as it's here, it keeps me on my toes. I actually don't have as much time to feel hurt. What with people talking to me so much, I've got new things to think about."

It wasn't like the bell to ring before Mrs. Richardson said that our time was about up and did I have anything else important to mention, but there we had it.

CHAPTER 48

IT WAS MY TWELFTH birthday, and the day had started very well with a complete surprise: a new bicycle, and not just any bike, a Schwinn Ladies' Varsity Tourist in Sky Blue, as hot off the line as a Mustang. Ten speeds!

I couldn't take it out yet because of the snow, but Dad lowered the seat all the way to check the fit, and I could reach the pedals with a little stretch. Next summer, I would be whizzing around Île de L'eau.

At lunch, Margaret and Theresa also surprised me with a gift. Actually, the gift itself was not too surprising. They had chipped in and bought me film.

"Thanks! I can never have enough film."

After school, I went to watch Sophie and Margaret practice for a girls youth league at the Bowl & Grill. They'd asked me more than once. I wasn't planning on joining their league. I wasn't interested enough in the sport to invest in a custom-made bowling ball, which I would need to play at all, but I was happy to cheer them on. Plus, I'd finally see the inside.

The B&G was the funnest place around—if you didn't mind commotion, and they didn't. Me, not so much. Eating next to the commercial dishwashers at the Arms would be quieter. Bowling balls thudded onto hardwood, whooshed down the alleys, smacked into pins, and balls and pins crashed into pits.

I could see how others liked it, though. There wasn't a lot of entertainment in Neston, and the B&G offered excitement, especially for teenagers, Sophie and Margaret included, and Sophie lived for sports competitions. To each her own. After all, Dieter lived for God, but competitive swimming came in second. I cheered them on, but after twenty minutes of the commotion, my head was pounding, too.

"I'm getting a headache," I said.

"Oh, no," said Margaret.

Ditto. I hadn't had one yet, and I didn't want one today, of all days. "I'm going to look around," I said. I could while away the time before Mr. Fortin picked us up.

The roar of the alleys was behind me but didn't entirely go away, and instead of bowling balls, cue sticks cracked pool ball formations apart. Pinballs clacked and pinged and dropped. And music blared out of every corner.

Besides a variety of entertainment, the B&G offered plenty of employment, too, from desk clerks, cleaners, mechanics who kept the bowling machinery running, line cooks, waitresses, bartenders, to kids old enough bus tables. Jobs are always valuable in a town the size of Neston.

In addition to the sit-down dining area, which spread out from the grill, customers could pick up their own food and tote it to tables set up behind the scoring seats at the alleys. Mountains of French fries with molten Velveeta seemed to be a hit. The Georges had tried them, along with everything else, and Theresa reported they were good, considering the fries were frozen, not cut fresh in-house, but of course the oil had been its freshest after opening. Only time would tell if it was changed often enough.

The Bowl & Grill made the most of Velveeta. Their signature bowl was chili, your choice of all meat, all bean, or a combo. You could get it drizzled with melted Velveeta, which also came on hot dogs and hamburgers, which also came with or without chili. Their other signature bowl was the sundae bowl; it was almost as big as the baseball cap they sold, which had Bowl & Grill monogrammed on it. I guess the lounge made up for what went down the drain on sundaes, since you couldn't make a profit on a dish four people probably couldn't finish.

The place was packed, and no wonder. Entertainment and employment were nothing to sneeze at. In no time flat, bowling fever had taken over Neston and beyond. You really must like your hobby if you'd be willing to drive home to Notch Gore in the dark in the dead of winter. But like they say, live and let live. Bowling was up Sophie and Margaret's alley, marine biology was up Theresa's alley, and food—and Gabe—was up mine.

I passed the hostess desk guarding the lounge at one end of the lobby and went into the retail shop at the other end, where the monogrammed baseball caps were sold, as well as shoes, balls, and cue sticks with their own cases. It was quieter, so I took my time. I was poking through the odds and ends, like tiny felt bowling balls on strings to hang over your rear view mirror, when they found me.

"I got my first strike!" said Margaret.

"Congratulations," I said.

"She's a natural," said Sophie, who was as natural as they got.

"Not until I coordinated my swing with my steps," said Margaret. "Then everything clicked and it was simple."

"Yeah, that makes sense," I said.

We went out to wait for Mr. Fortin, and they talked over their swings. It wasn't any different from how Dieter talked about strokes.

Thankfully, the cool and quiet air outdoors brought me back to normal. Lesson learned, and just in the nick of time.

I did not want to ruin my appetite for dinner. I'd be feasting on my own bowl tonight, every bit as fattening as cheese fries: cassoulet, a dish made with white beans cooked low and slow in broth with duck and pork and sausages, with breadcrumbs to soak up all their fats. It was so rich Mom only made the classic version once a year. And come Saturday, for my birthday dinner at La Terrasse, I'd have another rich meal off the grill: *Steak Frites*—a nice ribeye with French fries. I like a golden salty fry as much as the next person. For dessert, Opera Cake, and if I could swing it, half a cup of coffee.

I'd be wearing my sapphire velvet dress for the first time. I'd tried it on several times. Not only did I look taller, I realized Marcia made it long so I could wear it for a couple of years while I grew into it. I felt more grown up already.

Chapter 49

I WAS GETTING INTO the groove of being back at school, but that was just the problem. I was in a rut, since it took me so much longer to read assignments. Dr. Lewis said to give my brain a lot of rest stops. I was taking baby steps like the doctor ordered, but teenager steps were needed to keep up, so instead of the progress I had been making in getting assignments done B.C.—Before the Concussion—it was as if I'd started seventh grade all over. The last thing I needed was another spinout, but I got one anyway, and where I least expected it: Health class.

Mr. Gilbert's dental hygiene class focused on the importance of proper brushing technique. He actually demonstrated. Not sideways. Up and down. At a slight angle under the gum. Gently. I thought there would be a revolt when we each got a toothbrush, but he said our homework was to brush correctly.

We also got a handout with directions and a red pill about the size of a SweeTART called a disclosing tablet, which we were supposed to chew. If any red dye was left on our teeth afterwards, it meant we weren't brushing those spots as well as we should, and improper brushing could cause anything from bad breath to yellow teeth to gum and tooth decay.

I know dental hygiene is important, but a whole class on brushing? After Mr. Gilbert emphasized chewing the tablet thoroughly, Denis tried to make some sport of it. He raised his hand and said sweetly, "Mr. Gilbert, sir, will you please demonstrate the disclosing tablet?"

He got a few snorts but mostly looks like we couldn't believe he said that, but Mr. Gilbert was more on the ball than we expected.

"No, Denis," he said firmly, "no more than you would."

The only thing that turned red after that was Denis's face.

"No sir, no thank you," he said, very sincerely, and hung his head.

Denis looked truly apologetic, and he was silent for the rest of the day. I'd never heard him embarrass another person to get a laugh, but at least he showed that he knew his request was not the innocent thing he tried to make it out to be.

It wasn't my spinout, but I felt as bad for Denis as if I had been in his shoes. There was more to making a stupid mistake than being embarrassed. The stakes were always so high now. Patrick and Bucky would stick with Denis, but who knew if he'd get ribbed on the bus or how he'd be treated around school after this?

I'd had my moment in fifth grade. I had learned for myself that the conscience is a kind of disclosing tablet. There's only so long you can ignore the stain, which I had tried to do, but coming clean with Norman was one of the best things I've ever done. It's too bad disclosing tablets don't work in other ways. They could come in handy for revealing a lot of things in life.

I went home hoping I had mail to cheer me up. Receiving mail is on my list of my favorite things. It's a small thing, and I suppose it's different for grownups, who get a lot of bills, but for me all mail is a spoonful of sugar. Dieter sent postcards of Old Mystic and the Nathan Hale Homestead to me after he returned home, so I looked forward to mail more than ever. I had begun sending SASEs—self-addressed stamped envelopes, for free samples just so I could get more mail. I had received seeds and coloring books, and I was expecting stickers, book marks, and a brochure on animal tracks that folded to fit in your pocket.

I also had my own subscription to *Highlights* magazine. I was almost too old for it, and Gabe was too young for it, but I thought it would be a good idea to keep up the subscription. There was always some drawing I could show him and tell him the name of, like fox or penguin. He'd know what a hamster was before he picked one out to bring home, but the best drawings were things he could experience now, like snowflakes. Since their arrival this year, Gabe had gotten to know snowflakes very well. It was snowing again, and another back yard romp with him would really move me out of the doldrums.

I checked the box in case Mom or Dad hadn't gotten the mail, but it was empty. The *Neston News* was on the kitchen table, where it stayed most of the day, but whatever else wasn't theirs was left on the downstairs hall table, and just as I hoped, an oversized brochure was waiting for me.

Pine Tree Camp sure looked nice. Sophie had already sent me a postcard, just as she had promised to send one to Theresa. I suppose she sent one to Margaret, too. All she wrote on the message side was *You'll love it here! Sophie.* Whoever got the mail that day couldn't have missed it, since it took no longer to read than to figure out that it was addressed to me. With the brochure, the cat was out of the bag. I was planning to go to Maine for camp next summer.

I flopped on my bed and looked at the photographs, which were enough to sell anyone on going: smiling girls everywhere, sailing, hiking, horseback riding, circling camp fires, bunking. I started to think I ought to ask Mom and Dad if I could apply. It would give me something to look forward to, a reward for making it through seventh grade alive and in one piece.

Yet at the same time I felt as reluctant as when Sophie asked me if I wanted a brochure. It's not that I didn't want to enjoy myself with her and Margaret and Theresa. I hoped Paula would go, too. All of us together would be great. It's just that Sophie didn't mention until later that the sessions lasted two weeks. The longest overnight camping I'd done was one week.

I wasn't worried about being homesick, but by the second week, I was sure to be Gabesick. I suppose I needed to get over that hurdle sooner or later, but I'd rather it was later. Two weeks was too long to be away from him. He'd be scooting and talking a blue streak by then, and every day would be full of firsts that I wanted to be there for.

Besides, suppose Gabe got Ettesick? After all, if he wouldn't take his nap just because I started school, wouldn't he feel I deserted him if I was gone for fourteen days? Everybody knew the case of Lon Kovac. He was orphaned too young to remember it, but he kept saying how he knew he didn't fit, even though he resembled the rest of his family, so he went to see one of the guidance counselors, and eventually his parents told him he had been adopted. I suppose Gabe might recover after I returned home from camp and forget I'd ever been gone, but then again, he might feel like Lon that he'd been abandoned. He might be scarred for life.

Anyway, I also didn't want to miss a couple of weeks away when Dieter would be here.

I figured Theresa and Margaret got their brochures, too, and now, instead of feeling better about the mail, I felt worse. I'd have some explaining to do when they brought up Pine Tree Camp at lunch.

CHAPTER 50

WHAT WITH SCHOOL CLOSING at the end of the year because of Christmas and New Year's vacation, I wanted to wrap up old business. It was as good a time as any to talk to Mrs. Richardson about what was going well.

"A big thing is, Mr. Shaw put my Geography project posters on his bulletin board so his other classes could see history in action. They've been up since I gave my presentation, but I'm taking them home today."

"What an honor," she said.

"Mom and Dad said so, too. It was kind of a trade. He let me keep my camera in his desk."

"You've had a long showing, like a museum exhibit on loan."

"Yeah. I didn't think of that way, but I guess it is." It was still my turn to talk, so I continued. "I'm liking Art a lot. It has the most amount of guesswork, but nothing is ever actually wrong. Still, you have to take the assignments seriously and show you're learning the techniques."

Even if you weren't Mary Cassatt or Rembrandt, it was real work. Mrs. Casey also let us sit where we wanted, and we chitchatted quietly a little if we wanted, but it was not a free-for-all. There were due dates certain things had to be done by to show progress, so you really did have to pace yourself. It was a win-win.

"I drew my baby brother Gabe for the lesson on proportion. I take a photo of him every week to watch how he's growing."

"Every week?"

"Yeah, he's growing fast, and it's interesting."

"How old is he?"

"He was a year old in November. I'm really close to him."

"How so?"

"Before he was born, I used to put my ear and hand on Mom's stomach. I felt him move, especially when I talked to him, just like Mom did. We got to know each other. I can tell when something's wrong with him, and I think he can tell with me, too. I can't wait to get home to see him every day. He gets upset if I'm not on time."

"I see."

"Anyway, Mrs. Casey's class is like a pressure valve," I said. "I can let off steam, but in a good way."

"What kinds of pressures are you experiencing?"

It wasn't about what was going well, but I might as well mention one thing.

"Competition. Some girls act like every class is Phys Ed. They've got to beat you at everything. That's why I like Art. It's one class where I don't have to compete. It's more fun."

"Many people turn to enjoyable hobbies and interests as means of letting go of frustrations, and they can be very effective pressure valves, so long as the root causes of the pressures are handled."

I thought of Dieter. I'd probably never meet anyone more competitive than him. From that perspective, I saw how competition could be a pleasurable interest, so long as the right attitude, like he had, was in it. Sophie always had that right attitude, and so did Margaret. I saw it in PE and at the B&G.

"I'm trying my best. I guess that's why I like Home Ec so much. Cooking is a big interest of mine, so it's fun even if some of the girls in the class think I'm trying to outdo them because my family has a restaurant. I'm really not. It's too bad they can't just enjoy themselves."

"Competition is a natural part of human development. As we grow, the capacity for competition varies from individual to individual, and it's not unusual for high school to bring out the competitive nature strongly in adolescents. That may account for some behaviors you are encountering. And keep in mind, Etienne, you are on the same footing as classmates two years older than you. It's possible that also may account for some behavior."

"I'm really glad you explained. That helps a lot."

They were root causes I had not considered, and it was good to get another angle on human development. I kept her advice in mind. I never would have figured out that one reason they were competing with me was specifically because they saw me as competing against them, even though I wasn't. Once again, it seemed some problems weren't about me personally; in this case, it just came with the territory of skipping grades. I suspected this was another piece of the Debbie puzzle.

CHAPTER 51

CHRISTMAS THROUGH NEW YEAR'S was one of the busiest times for the Arms, and I was as happy helping out by folding napkins at Carl and Frieda's as I was looking after Gabe. On Saturdays, I combined them.

Some kids develop a sweet tooth. Gabe had a taste for TV. I had a feeling it wasn't any better for him, but it was easy to keep an eye on him while he was glued to *Porky Pig* or *Bugs Bunny*. I'd fold. He'd watch.

It was much harder at home, where he wanted to grab the tree, lights and tinsel and all. He threw a tantrum when he wasn't allowed to swat the gift boxes under the tree. After all, the floor was his territory. So it was a bit of a surprise to him when he was allowed to rip open his own gifts on Christmas morning, and of course, he offered to help us with ours.

Mom took him and me to church on Sunday, and he was as fascinated as ever by the special service, although this time he went into the good hands of the ladies working in the nursery so we could listen to the sermon. Gabe really helped me picture Jesus as a child, and in turn, after the service, we showed him the outdoor crèche up close. It was another important first.

"See, that's baby Jesus," I said, pointing, "just like baby Gaby, and there's his mom and dad, and look, there's a little lamb. Remember the little lamb? Baa?"

"Baa, baa, baa!" he roared.

He had baa down just fine, and if it had been up to him, he would have gone into the crèche and grabbed the manger so he could see baby Jesus up close.

Speaking of which, Neston's first baby of 1965 was not going to be a Fortin. Mrs. Fortin went into labor sooner than expected, so they would miss out on the free diaper delivery service for a year, but they wouldn't go without by a long shot. Mom, who had gone, said the Meetinghouse threw a splendid shower.

I prayed for a safe delivery and healthy baby, and both prayers were answered. It was a boy, Kenneth, Kenny for short. Margaret was excited, and not because the girls wouldn't have to add another bed to their room, which Debbie had been dreading. Margaret never had a preference for a boy or a girl. It was simple: she had a baby brother. I knew exactly how she felt. Hopefully, Kenny and Gabe would be pals.

Jason and Phoebe George, Nancy Bedard, and Gabe were already on their way. The Georges and Bedards held Jason and Nancy's combined first birthday parties after the first of the year. Mom and I took Gabe, and right away he recognized the guests he'd had at his own party. Their party was held at Tony and Maria's house, Theresa's oldest brother and sister-in-law.

From the day that I'd discovered that the George clan had four houses on the waterfront at Mallard's Head, I'd wanted to see inside all of them. From the outside, they were the same. Until now, I'd only been in Theresa's. Referred to as Papa and Mama's house, Theresa's ancient grandparents also lived there. It was chock full of nautical items and looked like you stepped right into Greece.

Other than framed nautical charts lining the hallway, the interior of Tony and Maria's looked nothing like Papa and Mama's. With five children, they had a rumpus room that took up their entire finished basement, so it was Grand Central for all the other George kids, too, by choice as much as convenience, since it had everything a child could want. I also went into their kitchen and looked into the dining and living rooms. Tony and Maria's furniture was traditional colonial and so spotlessly kept it showed that having the kids getting everything out of their systems in the rumpus room saved on wear and tear.

I also went to Nikky and Lina's house to help Theresa lug some things over. Again I saw the kitchen and main floor rooms, but it was much different from the others. Their only nod to marine life was a large aquarium. The youngest couple, Nikky and Lina's taste was modern and sleek and daring and bold, and being the most recently married with only baby Jason so far, everything was new.

Maybe one day Gregory and Doris, the middle George couple, would invite Gabe to their house and he could play with Phoebe and her older twin brothers. Then I'd have an excuse to see inside there, too. People's houses are so interesting. Without a word, they say so much about them.

It was a good vacation. Paula came over, and I went to the parsonage, on an empty stomach since Mrs. Bouchard went all out at the holidays. The glow came back into my cheeks, I put on pounds like the doctor ordered, I wore the sapphire dress two more times, and I went back to school feeling rested—only to find out mid-terms would be held.

CHAPTER 52

ALL MY RELAXATION FLEW out the window. Never mind the new year should have been a fresh start with new units in all the major subjects; instead, before moving on, we'd have exams on everything we'd studied so far.

"I wish mid-terms were held before the break at the end of the year," I whined to Mrs. Richardson.

Of course, my holiday vacation wouldn't have been quite as nice if I'd had to spend time studying, but now that I knew school policy was to keep that cloud hanging over your head, future holidays would include it.

"Some school districts do," was all she said.

I shrugged. I was only getting my gripe off my chest, but at least she took it seriously, even if she couldn't change anything.

"Don't exams count for a whole lot more?"

"They are weighted more than tests, but not unreasonably so, and your teachers will let you know what you'll be responsible for."

"They are. We're reviewing."

She reached to a shelf on her bookcase that contained a stack of booklets. "I recommend this study guide. It provides a variety of methods to help you prepare."

"Thanks. This looks good."

"It's what our student tutors use. Any time you need additional help in any subject area, they're available. Just ask your teachers."

"I remember you told me that at the beginning of the year. I'll ask if I need to." I almost did with math, but I caught on.

"Preparation is the key to success with exams, the same as it is with tests and quizzes."

"I'm just not sure I can prepare for everything." I needed some answers I couldn't study for.

"Oh?" She gave me her interested "How so?" look and waited.

"What would you do if you think one thing, but the teacher says another thing? Not like math, I mean subjects where the answers are more open-ended."

She smiled her gentle smile. "Since you ask what I'd do, no matter the nature of the question, I'd give the correct answer."

I let that sink in. I smiled back. "Okay."

I shared the ideas in the study guide after school, and we got right down to business. More than ever, it was practical for us to get as much work out of the way before heading home.

Theresa liked the extra hour she got on her own. It was a must for Margaret. She loved Kenny, but he was already a colicky crier, and that meant quiet for study and homework was hit or miss. Sometimes she stayed even later than the rest of us and went home with her father when he got done with work. Janice had a brother in second grade but she didn't have to babysit him, and she didn't mind forming fourth at all. She was doing more than studying; she was spreading her wings beyond Tina. Gabe was sticking to his nap time, so the hour worked out for me, too.

CHAPTER 53

FLASH CARDS WERE FINE for our study group, but I prepared for the open-ended questions at home. I knew they were coming in English and Social Studies, although I was less concerned about Mr. Shaw, since I hadn't butted heads with him.

After I had played my hand in English class, I'd also rocked the boat in my report about the book that took the Lord's name in vain. I know Mrs. Richardson said I'd learn things I didn't like, but that was just plain insulting to me as a Christian, and I said so. *According to the textbook, literature is open to interpretation. Some people may think blasphemy is entertaining, but I don't.* I used examples to point out that it didn't add any good value to the book, and I closed with an idea Julian wouldn't forget. *A lot of people say this book is a classic. I don't. As far as I'm concerned, a book that takes the Lord's name in vain many times could never be a classic to a Christian.*

I got an A-. I was spot on with everything he wanted in the report, it was spelled correctly, and he couldn't really tack on the minus because of my opinion, so I don't know why I got it. He didn't write any comment explaining. Unlike multiple choice and definitions, when it came to essays, exactly why you got a certain grade in English was anyone's guess. I planned to play it safe on the mid-term exam.

As much as I enjoyed the way Mr. Swenson taught geography, providing the answer to a certain question I expected on his exam was not as cut and dried for me as math, although it was presented as fact. English had just been the appetizer to the idea of evolution. Geography was the main course.

Mr. Swenson had kept us hands-on, even in the classroom. We got up and rotated stations to examine sedimentary, igneous, and metamorphic rocks. Just to prove that rocks were interesting, he unlocked a closet full of glass cases with samples where the minerals that made up the rocks had a physical property known as fluorescence; when he turned on a special light, the rocks lit up in different colors. But just like in *Inherit the Wind*, where a rock is ten million years old, Mr. Swenson said all the samples in class were, too. The earth had evolved over billions of years.

I didn't cotton to it. I'd already said straight out in English that evolution was only one way to explain how the earth got here, but when it came to Geography class, I had to think things all over again. Who was I to question it?

The best thing I got out of reading *Inherit the Wind* was that it's supposed to be about the freedom to think. I figured that included everything, even what you were taught. Sure, you had to learn from your teachers, but what if the teachers got some things wrong? Or not even wrong, but they just didn't have definite facts.

It seemed science was where that happened the most, which was surprising to find out, because I'd always thought science was pure facts. And I thought school was about learning facts. As it turns out, that's not always the case.

Science has areas where the answers can't be proven for sure, where only ideas about what might be true could try to answer questions. Maybe sometimes they did, maybe sometimes they didn't, but in the meantime, they weren't definite facts. Like Mr. Swenson said, scientists were always working to prove theories. It didn't make the theories wrong or bad, or right or good. Not that I didn't give the scientists the benefit of the doubt. Of course I did. Just like physical features, some ideas changed over time as people learned more. I couldn't figure everything out all by myself, but I still had to keep my thinking cap on.

And I didn't think the rocks were millions of years old, even if I couldn't prove it. But I had my reasons. One was a slab of rock mounted on the wall between the main circulation desk and the stairwell at Ward Memorial Library. In the middle of it was a dinosaur footprint. Talk about hands on. Everybody loved to place their palm in the fossil, right where some dinosaur had placed its foot millions of years ago. Or had it?

Ever since Theresa had mentioned The Dragon of Neston, and then Sue the Sturgeon surfaced, I'd thought a lot about dragons. Paula had said there were library books with drawings done by people who said they'd seen dragons or some such thing they thought of as a dragon. By now, I'd found several dragons in the Bible, like Dieter said I would, and I definitely trusted that source.

It was time to check out the others. I spent a Saturday afternoon at Ward Memorial Library. I must say, Miss Harrison was a big help. There wasn't much she didn't know. She showed me how to find information in books that weren't necessarily about dragons, which gave me a grip on the non-circulating reference section, and opened my eyes to special collections. It was all very interesting, and I'd only scratched the surface.

One thing I found out is that before somebody coined the word dinosaur, they were called dragons. After that, dragons turned into myths. There's just an eensy weensy problem.

People made carvings and sculptures and engravings and paintings of them, wrote and sang about them, and more, including something that especially interested me, made coats of arms with them. For centuries. All around the world. Including Île de L'eau in Neston.

All I'm saying is, a lot of people thought dragons were real for a very long time. And if they were dinosaurs, and I can't tell for sure if they were, people bumped into them a lot, which means they lived at the same time, not millions of years before people. That was quite the predicament, since some of them breathed fire.

Now, I know that's a whole other can of worms, but if rocks can fluoresce, and sting rays can shoot an electric volt, and fireflies can light up, then dragons could breathe fire. I just don't know how. Yet.

It seems the last of them was killed off not that long ago. In many of the pictures I saw, all the other animals looked just the same as they do today. The people looked the same, except they wore different clothes, and there were a lot of castles instead of federals. Everything looked regular, except for the dragons. And let's not forget the paper placemats at Chinese restaurants. You can just guess which one to circle out of the twelve animals of the zodiac because it—supposedly—doesn't fit.

They say great minds think alike. Well, when it comes to dragons, a lot of people who never knew each other or traveled to other places thought alike. Too often to be coincidence.

Much as I'd hoped Sue the Sturgeon was The Dragon of Neston, it was unlikely there were any dragons left in Île de L'eau. The lake wasn't big enough for some dragons to be hiding out without people knowing about them. But that didn't mean they'd never been there. It seems awfully unlikely that people made lake dragons up. Weren't all their drawings and stories examples of the same basic observation that Mr. Swenson taught us starting the first day of class?

But it's hard to buck the encyclopedia. It made all the stories about dragons untrue, just made up, and said myths were meant to teach us things, but they weren't real stories about things that really happened. That made the historical Dragon of Neston make-believe. I'm not exactly sure what we were supposed to learn from dragons if they hadn't been real. At any rate, you weren't supposed to take them literally.

Plenty of people said that about the Bible, too. Just as in English, once again I had to make a choice about whether I believed in the Bible or the other ideas that people said were how earth came into existence.

I knew it was important to learn everything I could, but it's possible to learn without swallowing everything hook, line, and sinker, and I wasn't about to throw Mr. Swenson out with the bath water just because I didn't believe it took the earth billions of years to come around.

CHAPTER 54

I MADE THE BEST of my situation. When I sat down to my first mid-term exam, I gave the correct answer. Both of them.

I not only followed Mrs. Richardson's advice, I stuck with God. I did it by adding a note to Mr. Swenson at the end of the exam. I hoped he would see that I was observing things from both viewpoints.

You taught us, from the textbook, that the earth evolved over billions of years. I don't believe this. The Bible says God created the heavens and the earth and all that is in them in six days, and I believe that. But I'm writing down what the book says because I wanted you to know I understand what scientists say about evolution. I read the material and took notes in class and studied for the exam. The class is very interesting and I'm learning a lot, but I think it takes as much faith to believe in the theory of evolution as in the Bible.

I didn't know how Mr. Swenson would take it, but I was on the lookout for attacks from that other Dragon of Neston.

As for English, I kept to my plan. I ticked off the black and white answers word perfect, and when it came to the gray question about poetry, which Julian had tossed things up with before the holidays, I included a creative example like Emily Dickinson that I thought showed I got it and liked it:

a small bite—
but then—
a big taste—

The Social Studies exam was the toughest of them all, and Mr. Shaw's choice of open-ended questions required us to take a position on civil disobedience or war or the electoral process and back it up. He wanted us to think about the issues, and I did.

Ever since I'd seen the protestors at the Fourth of July parade, the Vietnam war had stuck to the back of my mind like gum on the underside of a chair. It was unpleasant to discover and impossible to remove. The petrified residue was always left and you couldn't ignore it. You felt it every time you reached to pull the chair under your desk. It was like that every time I thought about the war, and with Dieter facing the draft, I thought about it more than ever.

Dieter had already turned eighteen, so he must have registered for the Selective Service. That didn't mean he'd be drafted, but Mr. Shaw said—and he said it was just his opinion, but an opinion informed by history—that once war was on the horizon, mandatory conscription followed. The sky might be the limit.

My answer to the open-ended question was as firm as it could be for the moment. Like science, new information might alter my view.

Loving your neighbor as yourself might mean going to war for them from time to time, but not in every instance. The reasons have to be clear-cut and the help has to be given by people who can afford to give it. If Neston was attacked tomorrow, it would be my responsibility to protect it, but I wouldn't expect anyone from places where there are riots to come do the fighting when they have their own problems that need more time to be taken care of. When it comes to Vietnam, it is more important for Americans to volunteer to help fix the problems we have all over the United States than for Uncle Sam to train them for war in southeast Asia.

I breathed better after the exams were over. We all did, but I wondered as much as everyone else what my grades would be. We kept waiting for them to dribble in, since exams take longer than tests to correct, but finally being handed your graded exam was almost as stressful as being handed the blank exam, especially because they're folded in half so nobody can see the grade but you.

We got Geography back first. I huddled around the folded pages like I was protecting my answers from a cheater trying to copy them. Under my comment about it taking as much faith to believe in evolution as the Bible, Mr. Swenson wrote, "I suppose it does."

What a relief!

That comment from Dieter helped me in many ways. Not only did it give me a new perspective, Mr. Swenson's response showed me it might for others as well. It was a good idea to keep in mind for the future. I wouldn't need to butt heads. It was the perfect middle ground between saying something nice or nothing at all. At least I understood that my note wasn't why I got an A-. I made stupid multiple choice mistakes about magma and lava.

Julian did not provide any feedback, but I got a regular A. I was glad I played it safe. You have to pick your battles, and when it came to an exam, which does count a lot more than class participation, he had the advantage.

Mr. Shaw stretched grading out over a week. I was as excited and afraid as when I was waiting to find out if I was accepted to attend high school a year early. When he did hand them out, our exams were folded lengthwise just like all the others, but not until just before the bell rang. Although it dragged out the suspense even longer, those of us who had studied together did not open ours during home room. We had agreed to wait, and as soon as we were released, we met up in the library as usual.

"I'll go first," said Janice.

She smiled immediately. "I got a B+," she said happily. "It must have been the study group. I never expected to do so well in Social Studies."

The only person who might have was Margaret. Social Studies were basically history, including current events, with other things mixed in, and Margaret had history in her blood, and sure enough, she got an A+. Theresa got an A. I hoped the study group helped me as much. I unfolded my exam.

"A+. You have a grasp of the material and you express your ideas well," wrote Mr. Shaw.

My grade was important, but not nearly as much as his comment.

CHAPTER 55

AN INSERT MADE THE Sunday *Neston News* thicker than usual. *The Summer Camp Issue*, read the insert's front page. I'd put camp out of my mind, but I skimmed the insert to see what I would not be missing.

After the Pine Tree Camp brochure had arrived in the mail and the topic came up at lunch, I said nice things about it. However, now I'd have to own up to not wanting to go there, since the topic was bound to come up again. The cover of the insert was done so kids would notice it and then pester their parents to go to camp. All of my friends would look to see if Pine Tree Camp was in the insert, and if it had a better ad than the other camps. It was, and it did, and sure enough, Sophie followed up with us.

"Remember to get your applications in before the fifteenth," she said. "The earlier, the better."

"I sent it already," said Theresa. "The dates are perfect, before my brothers take their vacations. Papa and Mama loved the look of the place. I'm finally going to camp!"

Atta girl.

"Then we'll be there together," said Margaret, smiling. "It's a go on my end. I'm sending the application this week. It will get there before the deadline."

Sophie looked sheepish. "I'm really sorry you won't be able to spend much time with Theresa and Margaret," she said to me. "I'm so used to thinking of you as the same age as us, it never crossed my mind."

"What do you mean?"

"Didn't you see the application form?"

"No, I only looked at the brochure."

"I hate to tell you this. The bunks are assigned by age, and many of the activities are, too. You'd be in the eleven-twelve group, not thirteen-fourteen."

"Are you sure?"

She grimaced and nodded. "I'm sorry."

"That's okay, it's not like it's your fault. I'll have lots of fun things to do here at home when you're gone," I said, which made it clear I wouldn't attend.

"I wish you could be with us, but it's only two weeks," said Margaret. "Except for our family vacation, I'll still have the rest of the summer to get together with you."

"And I'll be around most of July," said Theresa.

The door to camp was closed firmly, and I didn't mind one bit for this year, although our age gap got me to thinking. How soon would it be before I was left out of fun girl things they were ready for that I didn't care about yet? Margaret and Theresa already liked fashion magazines almost as much as my sisters did, and Paula was way ahead of the curve when it came to boys. I doubted she would want to bike Île de L'eau again this summer, but maybe we could get in some time on the water with Theresa. Margaret would be sure to like that. I'd have to come up with more activities all of us were interested in until I caught up with them—especially when they turned eighteen and I would only be sixteen.

The good thing was, the older we got, the less the gap would show. There wasn't a lot of difference between a thirty year-old and a thirty-two year-old. It made a difference now and might for a while, but it wasn't likely to divide us later.

Much as I didn't mind the loss of camp, what I did mind was what I'd never had, and it was something I wanted badly: a real summer vacation with my family.

Before I was born, they'd spent a whole five days in Boston; naturally, I've seen the photos. Since then, we took shorter trips to Montreal and Mom's nearby home town of Saint Anne de Bellevue any time of the year. Once, we took a day trip to Lake Winnipesaukee; I have no idea why we didn't just didn't go to the beach at Île de L'eau, since with all the driving, it was not very relaxing for Mom and Dad.

We would have taken a real vacation to Atlantic City last year during Easter break, but we had to cancel it because Gabe and I had colds. And even then, it was all about working around the needs of the Arms. The only thing we could have gotten out of it were strolls down Mom and Dad's memory lane—on a cold empty beach. Although I was eager to see the ocean, I doubted Atlantic City during the off season was much fun.

But Marcia and Donna didn't miss out on vacations. It all started when the Wendells, some real estate bigwigs in New York, came to the Arms. Frieda knew them from way back when, and she and Carl were good friends with them. The Wendells had been to the Arms enough times that not only had they seen Marcia working in the dining room, we Durands and the Meyers had dinner together with them in La Terrasse more than once. Marcia was already planning to go to the Fashion Institute, and Mrs. Wendell had some connection to it, so they invited her to visit them in Manhattan. You'd think they would have seen how snooty she was, but the Wendells were too, the way some rich people are, so it worked out on both sides. She'd spent more than one school break at their luxurious apartment.

It wasn't long before Donna caught on that our vacations would be few and far between, so she went with Kimmie's family, who were as happy to have her along as the Wendells were to host Marcia. Half the time, Donna and Kimmie and Betsy and Mrs. Hart saw the sights and went shopping while Dr. Hart attended meetings or toured hospitals. She had accompanied them to Baltimore, Cleveland, Chicago, and Washington, D.C.

It wasn't fair. By all rights, I should get my own vacation with Mom and Dad and Gabe. Marcia wouldn't care, and anyway, she made no secret of the fact that she planned to leave home at the beginning of summer. Donna might care, but I wouldn't mind if she came along.

Frieda said things usually came down to time or money. In our case, sickness had also interfered, but the reason we never found the time was people—more specifically, coverage. The Durands and Meyers had opened the Arms eighteen years ago. That was way too long not to have other people to hand the reins over to more often, and not just for four days. For a whole week or two.

I got to work brainstorming what fun things I wanted to do over the summer. For starters, I wrote *picnics* and *bicycling* and *vacation* to my prayer journal. For good measure I would send away for some brochures. I know, brochures make places look even more ideal than postcards do, so I'd just have to take them with a grain of salt, but they were still good for finding out about where to take vacations. Travel magazines at the library had ads where you could get a brochure if you sent a SASE, and even better, tear-out cards where all you had to do was check off all the places you wanted information about.

Some came off the top of my head. Dieter had sent a postcard from where he had spent Christmas on Long Island. It looked like a nice area. Of course, Atlantic City was still on the table. And why not Cape Cod? Theresa made it sound fantastic.

Mom and Dad would get my drift when they took the mail out the box, and then the seed would be planted in their minds. It wasn't any different than Sophie had done with Pine Tree Camp.

CHAPTER 56

NEVER MIND I DIDN'T let him carry my books or go to the cast and crew party with him, Denis persisted. A handmade card was on my desk on Valentine's Day, signed *From Your Admirer*.

"Thank you, Denis," I said.

He turned around and smiled. "Any time, Etienne."

The love bug had bitten him badly. Despite how clear I was about not being available, maybe he was hoping his efforts would cause me to consider him as someone I might want to marry. We spent enough time together for his consideration of me to grow. In addition to our classes and his occasional lunch table visit, Phase 3 of our personal civics group met twice more on Saturdays at Meeting Room 1A at Ward Memorial Library to finalize the project. We stayed on track and got our work done, but for Denis, it was the next best thing to a date with me.

It just came with the territory. Our pegs had gotten mixed up like Pick Up Sticks thrown in the air—and we didn't try to put the colors back together again. We were an odd group, which broke all the rules. We also happened to be paired girl-boy, which Paula would approve of. That took Patrick some getting used to, but as long as we were on task he was okay. Bucky, who had practice talking to women drivers while he washed their windshields, easily adjusted to talking to girls of any age. And you know Denis; he was an ice breaker in any situation. We girls were fine from the start; Paula said girls mature faster. Plus, it was all above board. We were under the noses of the librarians and in full view of everyone else.

For me, it was the closest I came to an extracurricular activity. I enjoyed it, but I stayed very focused on maintaining my grades, which, contrary to what some people thought, was not a breeze for me.

However, I was surprised to discover there was one thing I might not have to work so hard at. I was naturally good at gymnastics. With the greater possibilities for falling, it wasn't clear if I would be able to participate, so Dr. Lewis had to give me another full physical exam.

I got the green light, but he warned me to be extremely careful. I knew that drill. After one giant conkeroo, even one small conk was likely to be dangerous. I don't know how athletes in head butting sports managed; it must catch up with them at some point.

I had more than a knack for gymnastics. As it turned out, being a string bean was just the ticket for prancing across the mat with split and scissor leaps, hand standing on the beam, and swinging on the uneven parallel bars. And I wouldn't have said so myself, but Sophie said I looked great in a leotard. In fact, I looked regular, since it seemed the least developed girls excelled at gymnastics. You outgrow a lot of competitive sports, like swimming, even ballet. Miss Brennan got too old, and she wasn't very old at all. Gymnastics was like a boy's voice changing. You can only make the high notes for so long.

What's more, gymnastics is not really a team sport. Your performance is pretty much on your own. And other than Miss Williams and Miss Brennan guiding us through the moves and catching a few off balance landings, there was no contact with others.

It was different in another way, too. Just about anyone can swing a bat or bounce a ball, but the uneven bars drew a sharp line between the can doers and the can't doers. The only competition came down to a handful of us can doers. It was like cheerleading in that way. I don't mind saying it felt good to be at the top of the heap for a change.

But I had to be extra careful not to let my head come into contact with the mat during a somersault and to land on my feet after a handspring on the vault. And under no circumstances was I to have any less than double the usual number of spotters, and that included the teachers.

Like always, a group of girls sat on the bleachers to watch while we each took our turns on the uneven parallel bars. When it was mine, I clapped the excess chalk from my hands, took my position, and was halfway into a step to hop up onto the low bar when somebody screamed "Wait! Stop!"

I stumbled forward as if a stair step was missing, and Miss Williams and Miss Brennan threw their arms out to break my fall, but I landed intact, if a little heavily.

While I was catching my breath, Tina jumped down from the bleachers and came over to the uneven bars.

"This brake isn't set," she said. She pointed.

The bars were portable, and sure enough, one of the high bar wheels was not locked into place.

"Oh no!" I said.

In the stunned silence, it practically echoed off the gym walls. If I'd gotten on the high bar and it had swung out of parallel, the spotters might not have reached me in time—it was too frightening to think about. We were stock still for a good five seconds, mouths agape before Miss Brennan sprang into action and set the brake.

Miss Williams had her hand on her forehead. "Oh, Tina. You might have saved her life."

Tina looked away. "I only saw it," she said.

"You did more than that," said Miss Brennan. "You spoke up in time. Good job. Shall we check all the brakes?"

Tina took one side and she took the other, checking the brakes and shaking the verticals to test their stability.

I was shaking myself.

"Now we see the importance of equipment safety," said Miss Williams. "If any one of you sees a problem, follow Tina's example and report it at once."

Tina and Miss Brennan finished, and Tina went back to her seat.

I chalked my hands again. I took my position again. I took a couple more deep breaths. Before I mounted, while all eyes were on me, I minded my manners, and far from duty.

I looked straight at her and said loudly, "Thank you, Tina. Good eye."

CHAPTER 57

IN MY DAYDREAMS, I saw Patrick reading the letter our personal civics group had written to everybody who would be attending Town Meeting. In reality, none of us read anything.

All the reading had been done in advance. Our project had taken much more work than we had originally planned. Instead of writing the Chief of Police to ask for an officer to direct traffic at the intersection of Connecticut River Road and Neston Avenue, we wrote to the Town Clerk, the Town Treasurer, the Road Commissioner, the Overseer of Street Lights, and the School Board. The traffic problem was getting worse, and a police officer would not be a good, permanent solution—like the one we had.

The background information in the introduction of our letter was the same for everyone we sent it to, but in the body, we looked at the issue from their perspectives. Our closing salutation also was uniform: *Yours truly, the future of Neston*, followed by our individual signatures, all in our best penmanship.

To top it off, we wrote to the citizens of Neston. Our letter to the editor of the *Neston News* was printed the Sunday before Town Meeting Day. Perfect timing, plus the Sunday paper was always thick and had the most readers.

If anyone ever did see us working in the fish bowl room, they never said anything to us, but the letter to the editor revealed our personal civics project to the world. We expected kickback at school but it seemed no one we knew was bothering to read the editorial page. I didn't myself, usually, but I was getting in the habit of at least flipping every page of the paper to see if there was anything I ought to pay attention to.

All our work was summed up in the form of two ballot items in the *Town of Neston 1965 Annual Report.*

Dad and Frieda and I and Margaret and Mr. Fortin sat in a row in the middle of the room, each of us with our own copy. Whatever the outcome, my treasured copy would be kept in a steamer trunk in our attic. Across the aisle and a couple rows back, Theresa sat with Papa, all three of her brothers, and one of their wives. Far in the back were Denis and Patrick and Mr. Humphreys. I looked around and saw Bucky with his parents, Mr. and Mrs. Franklin, Mrs. Racine, Mr. Shaw, people from the Arms, and from every walk of life in Neston.

The Moderator pounded his gavel to open the meeting, and we followed along as he moved through the proceedings and officials stood to report on the Budget, Library, Historical Society, General Fund, everything including the Poor and Cemeteries. You'd be surprised how much discussion those topics got. Finally, he got to Roads.

"*'Shall the Town of Neston vote to appropriate $150 to purchase one-half an acre from Leonardo Napolitani, to be used as a parking lot upon the removal of the parking spaces on Connecticut River Road in front of the Sawmill Apartments, with said removed spaces converted to a lane for through traffic?'*"

"The floor is open for discussion," he added.

Someone stood. "A mite high for a half-acre, isn't it?"

"It's commercial land," said one of the listers, "and with limited parking on the street, residents of the Sawmill Apartments, as well General Store shoppers, have been parking on Mr. Napolitani's land as if it were public parking, although it is clearly marked for patrons of his businesses."

Frieda stood. "The handful of spaces on the road have been insufficient for Sawmill residents for years, but they are sufficient for another lane, and their loss will be more than made up for with a safe off-road parking lot," she said. "Mr.

Napolitani's land has been encroached upon for years, so he has already given away its use. The asking price is more than fair."

Leonardo Napolitani was none other than Leo of Leo's Pizza. He had an enormous parking lot to accommodate his customers, both the pizzeria and the roller rink he owned that was attached to the side of his restaurant. We all knew he was nice, but not that nice. Although his lot was more than big enough to sell off that corner, it would mean he couldn't use it in the future if he wanted to put in more businesses.

"'Bout time he got his due," somebody agreed.

A lot of murmuring and head nodding followed, but the room fell silent.

"Being as there is no further discussion, I present the resolution for vote. Those in favor vote aye."

"Aye."

The whole town spoke in unison.

"Those opposed vote nay."

"Nay," said a single voice. Everyone looked to see who it was. Mr. Jakes, JJ's father. I didn't see JJ himself.

I gripped Margaret's hand. She squeezed back. It was all we could do not to jump up and down.

"The ayes have it, and we shall move on to a related vote.

"'Shall the Town of Neston install a left turn traffic signal on the south side of the intersection of Connecticut River Road with Neston Avenue, with said traffic signal having its own lane?'"

"The floor is open for discussion."

A man in denim overalls stood. "I'm not against it, we got to move forward, but people will be asking for more signals. They'll be sprouting all over. Just think a that 'fore you vote."

"Should additional requests be made," said the Town Clerk, "each request will go through the rigorous review this one has undergone. No stone was left unturned in due diligence."

Mr. Shaw stood and looked over his glasses. "As we all know, 'necessity is the mother of invention,' and voting to approve a designated left turn lane and signal will provide a much-needed solution to long lines and waits, as well as improve safety for drivers and the many students who cross at Neston's busiest intersection. This request is thoroughly justified. Your vote of approval marks an historic moment in the progress of Neston."

Frieda stood again. "What's it going to cost? I don't see any figures in Appropriations."

"And how long's it going to take?" somebody piped up.

The Road Commissioner said, "Connecticut River Road is both a town road and a state road, and as such, the costs, which are minimal, will be paid for through the state's general fund for roads. The process is simple. Installation of the light requires nothing more than changing the signal out from the existing light. Creating the new lane is only a matter of repainting the lines, which should be done at the time the parking spaces are converted to a through lane. However, the Public Service Company does charge for service, and the line item in your report on page seventeen lists it as $33.92 per month, for an annual total of $407.04. That's Neston's cost."

"Well worth every penny," Frieda said.

Another man stood. "Until the interstate highway is completed, Connecticut River Road is the major eastern thoroughfare to the Canadian border. We need a safe corridor."

Mr. Jakes stood. "That's exactly why it I voted against the lane. It might be safer for drivers and pedestrians, but it'll bring through traffic that much closer to my front door, and no light is going to change that."

A woman stood. "I'd rather see the traffic moving. I live in the Sawmill Apartments, and there are more fumes from idling than driving by. The sidewalk is plenty wide, and we've got a strip of dirt going to waste. We'd be better off if there was a nice row of bushes planted along the yard, and it would be a lot prettier, too."

She got a lot of positive murmurs. Margaret and I nodded.

"As there is no further discussion, I present the resolution for vote."

With Mr. Jakes' single dissenting vote, the ayes had it again.

Mr. Fortin and Dad and Frieda looked so proud of us. Dad patted me on the back as Margaret and I hugged sideways.

"This might never have happened if it hadn't been for you," I said.

"I couldn't have done it alone," she said.

We turned around. Denis and Bucky both gave us thumbs up, and Theresa was smiling. Patrick turned red but he was grinning from ear to ear. His father also looked proud of him.

Converting the parking spaces into a through lane—which made the left turn lane possible—had been Patrick's simple but brilliant solution. The physical changes would be the result of nothing more than repainted lines.

It solved more problems than any of us initially realized. Leo would get his due—overdue, really. The public could park in the lot, the Sawmill Apartments would get its own section, and hopefully, nice buffer bushes would be planted. That would be just the job for Eugénie Cote's beautification committee.

But the solution also came with a different kind of cost.

According to Bucky, trucks clipped rear view mirrors of cars parked in front of the Sawmill Apartments pretty often. The Buckminsters would lose that steady stream of repairs after the cars moved to the parking lot. Wanting to see the traffic problem fixed showed he cared about a lot more than the Buckminster wallet.

Paper rustled and people chatted for a minute, but there was one more item on the agenda that kept us glued to our seats.

CHAPTER 58

SELECTMEN MEETINGS HAD NOT resulted in a clear-cut decision over whether the North Shore Marina could build an addition for a museum. Now it was up for vote.

The Moderator read the resolution, and deliberations dragged on. Some people thought Sue should go on display at the Neston Historical Society Museum.

Tony George, who was such a hothead when it came to protecting the honor of the females in his family, had cooled his engine, and he calmly took his turn and said that the Marina Museum would feature more than Sue the Sturgeon, and the Neston Historical Society Museum couldn't provide what was needed to display all of it.

Mrs. Racine backed him up emphatically. "Indeed we could not. The Historical Society it is not a marine museum, and we could not train the volunteers needed for one."

A man stood. "What's more, putting it in the heart of the Historic District would bring more traffic and create a problem like the one we just voted to eliminate."

On the surface, Theresa's choice of observing traffic at Lakeshore Drive for her Geography presentation appeared to be a copycat of what The Traffic Group did, but it stood on its own. It had served double duty in the letters we wrote by illustrating that its left turn lane and light worked well. Now it was doing triple duty for Tony, which I'm sure was her real reason for observing traffic.

Tony pointed out that Lakeshore Drive already had a left turn lane with flashing yellow lights. Just as the left turn light at the intersection of Connecticut River Road onto Neston Avenue would alleviate traffic backup, the Marina Museum location would divert traffic to a less congested part of Neston. There was plenty of parking in the Lakeshore Drive lot; it stretched from the North Shore Marina and Restaurant, along the road behind the tree line and beach, to the far side of Tedeschi's Bait & Tackle.

In fact, Tony said, it was already used as the school bus turnaround. There was enough parking for more school buses to bring kids to the exhibit. Students in every grade would be interested. Sue was just the main draw, but an important one that would bring scientists from all over.

I thought I heard echoes of Theresa in that, too.

But things were still touch and go. The final argument against the Marina Museum was that a new building would spoil the beach. This time Gregory George answered.

"It wouldn't be a new building, just an extension of the existing one. The footprint of the Marina Museum would be minimal, since we plan to reconfigure the space inside the Marina. The addition's exterior would be weathered to blend into the existing building, which is fully in line with the look of the lakeshore buildings."

A couple of teachers spoke of the benefit to the education system of Neston, and someone said marine life in Île de L'eau would interest just about everyone in the area. A Marina Museum on the water made sense.

The tide turned.

Sue the Sturgeon got her building permit.

The voters had made more history.

The Georges won in another way, and I didn't hold the business advantages they got against them in the least. Not only was the location a natural fit, Sue and the Marina Museum would help the North Shore Restaurant maintain its competitiveness against the Bowl & Grill. When it came to advertising, they got a two-for-one. The North Shore Restaurant, right next to the Marina Museum, could promote it, and vice-versa. One hand fed the other. I had no doubt Theresa would be studying marine biology before the museum opened, if she wasn't already.

Town Meeting was a real eye opener, civics in action in every way, shape, and form. Now I understood why selectmen meetings were so well attended. It seemed Neston would not be running out of issues any time soon.

CHAPTER 59

THIS TIME, I KNEW what had happened before I got to Social Studies. I often did now. Frieda and Carl were only too happy to help me keep up with current events, so I had a standing invitation to watch the evening news on their television.

The Sunday following Town Meeting, I'd been and gone to watch the news and was about to go bed when Frieda called and said, "There's something you need to see."

I tucked my pajama bottoms into my boots and threw on a coat, and Dad and I hightailed it over.

They had been watching a program about Nazi criminals on trial when the program had been interrupted to air the footage of hundreds of Negroes marching across a bridge in Selma, Alabama. The Negroes were met by state troopers in gas masks, who knocked the leaders down and tear-gassed the crowd while more troopers on horses pushed men, women, and children back across the bridge, striking them with clubs and tubing wrapped with barbed wire.

The Civil Rights Act had not done much to get the vote for Negroes. Another person had been killed in a different demonstration the month before, and violence against protestors was as bad as ever.

After President Johnson went on air and pleaded to Congress for civil rights for all Americans, Mr. Shaw warned us that the violence might remain for many years to come, "but, as Bob

Dylan so colloquially puts it, and I quote, 'the times, they are a-changin.'"

Bloody Sunday was just the first of a one-two punch, but by this point, I braced myself before the news came on. Anything could happen, and it could be more shocking than whatever happened before.

Somehow, I never quite braced myself enough, although the thousands of troops sent to South Vietnam was not a complete surprise, given how Mr. Shaw kept us following the situation in southeast Asia. From the beginning, when we studied the history and context of the war, we learned that the U.S. had been sending advisors over for more than a decade.

"However, these are the first combat troops to be deployed," Mr. Shaw informed us, "and mark my words, they will not be the last."

In fact, it was a one-two-three punch, and I never saw the third one coming at all. At our next meeting, Mrs. Richardson said, "Etienne, this will have to be our last session until the end of the school year."

I was surprised. "You said the meetings were mandatory."

"They were, but at this point, we must discontinue."

I was angry. "You could have let me know ahead of time!"

She looked at me more kindly than she ever had and said softly, "I didn't know myself until the last minute."

"All the same," I shot back, "you could have stuck up for me."

"If it was possible, I would have, but we have all seen that you've made the adjustment to high school very well."

I couldn't think of a time I'd ever disagreed with Mrs. Richardson, but my anger came back, and it showed. "That's only because we were meeting."

And she had never out and out disagreed with me, but she shook her head. "No, Etienne. Just as we always knew, you are a strong student, eager to learn and to adjust. You not only have adjusted to the normal stresses of entering seventh grade as well as any student can, you did so after skipping grades, and more importantly, far more importantly, you have overcome hurdles more challenging than anyone could have anticipated, emotionally and physically. You're very resilient, and I am confident you will continue to get on well."

I didn't care if I had to beg. "I just have to see you. Please, Mrs. Richardson?"

"This is a critical time for many students who are struggling academically, as well as socially, and school policy is to put them first, unless you have a specific reason to see me."

I had one straw left. "What about planning for college?"

"Next spring will be ample time for you to begin college admissions advising. Most wait until their freshman year at the very earliest."

Seeing as I had gotten only five Bs (all on quizzes) and one C (math, at the beginning of the school year), and I had friends, and I fit in, at least from her perspective, I saw her point, and where it left me. Since the school policy couldn't justify holding regularly scheduled appointments with me, I'd be out in the cold unless I went to the Guidance Offices for getting in trouble.

While I was pouting, she said, "We are in the thick of advising now."

"Well, but, isn't it always like this every year? I mean, we were supposed to meet until school lets out."

"May I tell you something?" she asked.

"Yes." A wary yes, but a yes.

"This year is unlike any other since I've been advising. Many boys who had not planned on attending college now have a strong desire to attend. Do you know why?"

I shrugged. "I don't know."

"Male citizens of the United States must register for the Selective Service when they turn eighteen."

"Yes, we learned about that in Social Studies."

"Good. Some young men volunteer for active-duty service after registering, but being drafted by the government has become a concern for others."

Just like Mr. Shaw said, mandatory conscription followed when war was on the horizon, and combat troops being sent made the "conflict" smell more than ever like war. "Because of Vietnam?"

She nodded. "Many of our students, and their parents, think that the draft will increase. In certain instances, it is possible to be exempted from service."

"What's that?"

"Exempt means not eligible, or excused, for specific reasons, such as health or for certain professions. Others, however, can defer entry—that is, they can put it off—while they are in college. They must still register for the Selective Service, but a deferment puts off the possibility of active duty until they graduate."

I got the picture. "So you're telling me the real reason is you've got a lot more college advising."

"Not only more in general, but a great many last-minute applications that students need help putting together for college entry this fall. For most schools, the deadline to apply has passed, but not all. Nonetheless, those students need to get ready for college in ways they had not academically planned for, and for many, it's an interruption of their plans to go to work. College was not their first choice, so it's not necessarily a second choice they want, but they prefer it to military service."

It sunk in now. "I guess they really do need you more."

"You're just as deserving of counseling as they are. It's a matter of priorities among differing needs. There is a short amount of time to meet their needs, and only so many counselors to go around."

"I understand, Mrs. Richardson." Once again, the problem came down to time and people, and not just counselors but civilians who didn't want to be soldiers.

"Thank you, Etienne. We will see each other once more though, to wrap up at the end of the school year, and of course, if any emergencies happen." She smiled. "Let's hope there aren't any more of those, but in that case, my door will always be open."

About the only thing that made me feel better from our meeting was that Dieter would be off the hook while he was in college. I couldn't really see him volunteering, although I'd have to ask. Like most things, you never know—and if the war was still on when he graduated from college, he could be drafted, maybe for a long time after that if the war dragged on.

CHAPTER 60

WE STARTED A NEW unit in Health class, and it looked like it might be a lot more interesting than what we'd covered so far. Mr. Gilbert had taken months to plod past personal hygiene, tobacco and alcohol, and first aid, which included a film reel showing how to make a tourniquet just in case you came across any compound fractures spurting ketchup blood. I had perked up when concussion treatment was covered. Although it was only about light concussions, everyone paid closer attention since Mr. Gilbert pointed out that sports concussions were not unusual. Once again, I was eyeballed as living proof of the almost-worst-case scenario.

I was excited to move on to human development, especially because I had a front row seat to observe Gabe going through the early stages, but let's just say that seating thirteen and fourteen year-old girls and boys next to each other during the puberty part of the unit tends to put a damper on their learning. They'd rather sneak peeks at the book at Ward Memorial Library, the one with the realistic anatomy drawings, the one I once found askew above the *Annals of Worcester* on the bottom shelf in the far corner of the Vermont Collections Room.

I understood. The book provided some important information not included in Health class. I took a peek myself before I returned the book to its proper shelf location, but it only confirmed what I already knew.

Eggs and sperm were also review. Mom had the birds and the bees talk with me before school started, and she told me that if I started to have a tummy ache but it wasn't really a tummy ache but tugged on my abdomen in way I never felt before, then an unfertilized egg had landed in my uterus, which would happen every month. I was prepared, although she didn't think it would happen to me very soon. I wasn't even a teenager yet, and like she said, we all developed at our own rate, and I was on the slow side.

If an egg got fertilized, however, then *voila*, a baby. When a woman's abdomen stuck out, it was obvious an egg had been fertilized. How it got fertilized was the most interesting part of the talk. The way Mom explained it, it sounded very nice.

But how a baby grew before it was born was news to me, so I sat up in class when we covered it. Howard, the boy dangling a worm at the beginning of *Inherit the Wind*, says we all start out as worms. Howard obviously had seen *Figure 51* in our Health textbook: cells developed into the worm stage, got gills in the fish stage, a tail in the amphibian stage, and then it reached the human stage. Mr. Gilbert said the way babies grew before they were born was the same as the way man had changed from lower forms of life over millions of years until it finally became a higher form of life: a human.

"My mother had seven children," Margaret piped up, "and she said there weren't any gills kicking in there. They all came out boys and girls."

"Growth changes at certain points according to the stages of development," Mr. Gilbert responded.

Margaret and I looked at each other. We weren't buying it.

As soon as I could snag Donna without Marcia being around, I asked her if I could look at her biology textbook. Sure enough, the same development illustration was in there.

"Do you believe in that?" I said.

"Not literally," she said.

"But it says so right there, in your book, and Mr. Gilbert says so, too. How come you don't believe them?"

"I'd tell you, but you don't want to know."

"Why not?"

"It's serious, dead serious."

I really wanted to know what made her buck the experts and stand on her own two feet, thinking for herself.

"Try me."

"Okay, but don't say I didn't warn you. You know Kimmie's father is a maternity doctor, right?"

"Yeah, he was Mom's doctor. His office is right next to Dr. Lewis's." They shared a waiting room, so it wasn't unusual to see a woman showing signs of a fertilized egg.

"When I went to Chicago with the Harts, Dr. Hart took us to a museum where dead babies are preserved in glass jars."

I was out of breath for a good three seconds. No wonder she'd never said.

"In glass jars?"

"They're in a liquid preservative."

"How'd they get them?"

"They were donated. A doctor—a woman named Helen Button asked for them from women whose babies died before they were born. It can happen at any time in the womb. The mothers give birth, but the babies are dead."

"Oh, that's sad." I thought of Gabe when he came home from the hospital and the pictures of Suzanne and Kenny, all so tiny but born alive.

"It's called a miscarriage. What the exhibit shows are the stages of development. In the early stage of growth the baby is called an embryo. The youngest one I saw was curled up, and it didn't look like a worm or a fish to me, although I can see how some people might think so. But fish don't grow from worms and babies don't grow from amphibians. That's just ridiculous."

A light bulb went off. "That's what the Bible says. Everything grows after its own kind."

"It's true, things just don't turn into something else. At any rate, after a few weeks, the embryo grows enough that it definitely looks like a baby. From that point on, while the baby is developing, it's called a fetus, until it's born, when it's called an infant. They were lined up in the containers, from the smallest sample of human embryo, through development of the fetus, all the way up to a child that died during childbirth."

I was stunned.

"So if you want to know why I don't believe what my biology book says, it's because I've seen proof."

"It sure explains a lot."

"That wasn't the only time."

"What wasn't?"

"That I saw proof of how babies grow. If you're really interested, I'll show you. You can see the proof for yourself."

"I'm really interested. How soon can I see it?"

"Right now."

She opened her top desk drawer and carefully removed a tissue paper wrapped issue of *Life* magazine from 1953. In it were two photographs of a six week-old human embryo.

"Wow."

She unwrapped an even older issue, and the photograph of a forty day-old fetus clearly looked human. It looked like a tiny baby that was praying. It was followed by a series of photos, from the youngest embryo ever photographed, only two cells, up to the skeleton of a baby near birth.

Admittedly, the youngest didn't look like a baby, but then a pumpkin doesn't look anything like its twin-leafed seedling. That didn't make it a butterfly. It takes time even to tell it's not a zucchini.

I was shocked. It wasn't only the proof, it was the idea that somebody else thought it was a good idea to follow a person's growth, only they somehow took the pictures inside the womb. I couldn't wait to tell Margaret.

"I decided to go into nursing because of these pictures," said Donna.

"How did you find them?"

"I came across the old magazine issues in the living room cabinet. I was just having fun looking at them."

"They're in the attic now."

"So that's where they went. I suppose I should put these with the others, but they're just as safe in my drawer as up there. I've looked at them a lot of times, and once I saw the museum exhibit, I felt certain about studying nursing."

She definitely had thought it through and knew what she believed.

"Where?"

"I won't decide until after I make campus visits with Mom and Dad, but I've narrowed it down to two schools in Massachusetts."

"Oh." I thought about that for a second but didn't give up on my reason for talking to her. "There's just one thing I don't get. How come the books all say something different."

"I can't help you there, Ette."

Donna became a living, breathing heroine to me that day.

I also learned more about her and her goals than everything before put together.

I remembered when she first got interested. She'd read a book about Florence Nightingale and thought nursing would be exciting. Then she read all the Cherry Ames and Vicki Barr novels about nurses.

Marcia fed her whim. She said that, after airline stewardesses, nurses were at the top of the professional fashion ladder. Anyone could see that nurses' all-white uniforms and stockings and shoes would look as sharp on Donna as her cheerleader's uniform. And according to Marcia, the cap was the next best thing a common working girl could get to a tiara.

But Donna became more serious the more she got involved with physical education. She learned a lot about muscles and all, and she had practiced bandage wrapping on me when she had the sports injuries unit in Health class, which was back before Mr. Gilbert taught it.

Since the school year started, another reason surfaced that meant she really and truly meant to go through with it: none of her girlfriends was planning to go into nursing.

Kimmie Hart didn't plan to go to college at all. She was a whiz at shorthand and typing and she wanted to be a secretary for a few years until she got married.

And if Peter Jarvis went to school in Massachusetts, it wouldn't be because of Donna; it would be because he couldn't get into his top picks to study sports broadcasting. Mom and Dad often asked about Peter, and Donna willingly kept us in the know. He'd already made campus visits with his parents, including Bloomington, Illinois, and Syracuse, New York, and he kept up his grades so he'd get into one of his schools of choice. It meant Donna knew all along she would break up with him in order to study nursing at her own top picks. I was surprised she went out with Peter at all. Football was famous for injuries. But maybe that was exactly why she did.

Nursing is an important profession. I understood better why my concussion had such an impact on her. It wasn't just what happened to me; she spent a lot of time talking to the practical nurses. Along with the magazines and the museum, I had no doubt she would follow her dream. I was impressed. Who knows where her career would take her?

It sure wouldn't be The Neston Arms. And with Marcia's foot halfway out the door to fashion school, that made my path clearer by the day.

CHAPTER 61

THE TRIBULATIONS OF PE returned with warm weather. What with the Bowl & Grill construction complete, we were back on for track and field, and the track activities proved highly competitive. With the main exceptions of Sophie, who was good at everything, and Tina, whose long legs gave her an advantage, sprints and hurdles brought out the worst in most of us.

Field was more of a mixed bag, so there were some opportunities to shine—or not. I had the shortest shot put, and for me the long jump was an oxymoron, like jumbo shrimp. I held similar distinctions in track. I couldn't have cared less, and for all the girls who did, they were spared the humiliations of coming in last and slowing down their entire relay team.

Competitiveness came out even more when we returned to softball. The girls wanted to keep the Sharks and Giants. This time around, Miss Williams held a lottery for captains, but only added the names of girls who said they wanted to be included—all five of us. I threw my hat in the ring, mostly because my friends pushed me to. Martha Zeno and I drew the winning lots. This time around, we chose our own team members, starting with a coin toss for first choice.

Naturally, Martha snapped up Sophie. If I'd won the toss, I had no plan to pick her first. I would have chosen Tina even if she was terrible at softball, which was far from the case, but I wanted to show her that the truce still held between us. Choosing her as my first pick showed I wasn't against her, that I wanted us to be on the same team, in more ways than one.

Like they say, it was a fragile truce, but we had made some forward progress: we came into closer proximity of each other's presence in the hallways and looked at each other when one of us spoke in class. On the softball field, I hollered out—and instead of giving me the cold shoulder, she took the encouragement. From time to time, she smiled. I doubt if she saw it as a form of loving her, but I did.

The girls warmed up to her like they never had. They saw that the parallel bar brake episode changed things between Tina and me. It didn't entirely make up for the foul but it helped a lot. Tina got a big break when Sophie walked with her between classes. She admired Tina's athletic abilities, and vice versa. It was a start.

Although they didn't walk to and from the school bus stop together, Janice sat with Tina at lunch once, and Mary didn't seem to mind. I guess it was safer to try to make amends in public. But when Janice returned to the table with Theresa and Margaret and me, her choice of friends was clear.

All of the changes were partial answers to prayer. Tina and I were a ways from a complete thaw, and she still had some work to do on her end to be fully accepted and make more friends, but it looked like she wouldn't be a complete loner throughout high school.

I was encouraged. My overall attitude improved as a result. Knowing someone hates you can really grind you down. What's more, by now I understood that doing my best and enjoying school were all that mattered. Like Dieter said, the rest is in God's hands.

Thanks to Mrs. Richardson's explanations of competition, I could take it in stride. If most everyone wanted to best me, so be it. I especially learned that in PE in the weeks after the concussion, when I couldn't have competed if I'd wanted to. It wasn't until gymnastics that I got a leg up. I didn't even care that it looked like I'd get a B in PE for the year. I held the unofficial tippy-top place for being a good sport.

I was just happy to be outdoors again, especially when we got introduced to tennis, and not only because I liked it a lot and was quick on the court. Tennis signaled the end of the school year. I'd survived so far, I knew how to prepare for final exams, I'd make it to the end.

The Avon School held its commencement a whole month earlier than Consolidated Union High School did. Frieda and Carl went. After they returned, they put Dieter's framed eight-by-ten senior photo on their mantle and talked about how close to the top of his class he was and how he got special honors for outstanding athlete and best senior thesis.

The news tided me over while I waited for him to return. Our hearts were set on him spending the summer here.

CHAPTER 62

SOMETHING DIDN'T FEEL RIGHT. Everything was the same as usual, but something felt different.

My penny loafers were firmly touching linoleum.

No more numbing pins and needles from my legs dangling. No more shifting and slouching. I could get reprimanded for swishing the floor! I'd savor it at lunch, where it wouldn't be noticed.

Maybe things up top would start to grow, too, and I'd move out of the training bra stage, but I had more concern about that than anticipation. If I grew fast and developed too much, I might lose my place in gymnastics next winter. I was only too happy to change into an undershirt at home. For another thing, after the year I'd just had, milking maturing held unexpected appeal.

Mrs. Richardson and I met for the last time. It was a great meeting and went way over since we had more territory to cover than usual. I had put a lot of thought into how seventh grade had gone.

God really used Mrs. Richardson to help me through it. I could say the same things to her as I did to Mom and Dad, but they never said, "How so?" It took some getting used to, but it made me think things through. In the end, her support was just as priceless as theirs was to me.

Over the course of the school year, I had come to appreciate Julian more than I ever dreamed possible. I thought he was unfair about *Inherit the Wind*, and I didn't like all his methods, but he showed me that teachers could be outside the norm in a lot of ways yet you could still learn plenty from them, and I did. At the patisserie, he was just another beatnik, but at school, he had his own peg. I admired that.

Much as I hated to admit it, calling us by our first names had its advantages. In school, the alphabet is your destiny. I'd sit between surnames beginning with C and E for my high school career. Not in all classes, and not if I got into some advanced placement classes, where the cream rose to the top regardless of the letter your last name starts with. But by and large, unless there was an influx of new students, I'd be behind Denis, in front of Margaret, and next to Patrick—and Tina—often. But with English, as with Geography and Art, we could change things up. And that alone could change destiny.

Not only could, but looked like it would.

All year, on account of the way Luc bumped Denis so he could take a seat near me, and Denis got back as soon as he could, I figured Luc was a rival to ask me out. I wouldn't have minded, not that I actually would have gone. I was still too young, even if he was classic marriage material. Luc was the dictionary definition of a regular boy. He was like math. You knew where you stood.

Except I didn't.

It wasn't me he was always making a beeline for. It so happened that even when she wasn't assigned by name, Margaret always sat near me. Not until the last week of school did I get that lesson through my thick skull.

He came to our lunch table and presented her with a package wrapped in a flour sack and tied with twine.

She smiled and untied the twine, not the least bit bashful. "What a nice old flour sack," she said, casting the twine into a neat ring on her hand. She slid the flour sack off.

"Oh, this is..." and for once she was at a loss for words.

"It's not antique, like I know you really wanted," said Luc, "but it'll hold a dozen spoons."

She ran her hands over the rack.

"Feel it," she said, and we took turns. It was sanded as smooth as silk, stained mahogany, and varnished.

Being an unusual visit to our table, lots of kids took notice. Denis, who apparently also thought Luc was his rival, grinned when he witnessed Luc give Margaret the gift. I had a feeling it wouldn't be Luc's last project for her.

I just hoped Denis didn't get any ideas. You had to like Denis, but he was too much of a ladies' man. Throughout the year, he had asked a handful of girls to carry their books and finally got a taker. Janice was flattered, but she didn't cotton to how friendly he was with Martha. He really was, too. Denis and Martha were neighbors in Hinton and rode the same bus, and Janice wasn't ready for that kind of competition, so it put the kibosh on book toting in a matter of weeks.

Back to the year in review, Mr. Swenson, a shoo-in for most popular teacher if there ever was one, showed me it was possible to like a teacher even if my beliefs led me to question some of what he taught.

By no means did I think I knew more than any of my teachers, but because of my faith there would be times I'd be on the offensive in my thoughts. There is a time to speak and a time to write and a time to be silent—and so, from time to time I may have to fold my cards even when I'm sure I hold the winning hand.

I took Math and Health more personally than they called for. The teachers were both so dry, but Mr. Reilly was more of a relief to me than he possibly could have imagined, while Mr. Gilbert had so much work to do to gussy up his Health class, I actually felt sorry for him. He might also need to be prepared for a lot more students bucking the textbook when it came to the evolutionary explanation of human development.

The April issue of *Life* magazine was on the "Drama of Life Before Birth." A color photograph of a fetus is on the cover, and the photographs inside document the stages of development. They're so beautiful, even better than the pictures Donna had shown me. She bought several copies of the magazine and gave me one, which was just as well, since that issue sold out in no time flat.

I was reminded of a line from Psalm 139: "For You formed my inmost being; You knit me together in my mother's womb. I praise You, for I am fearfully and wonderfully made." With these photographs, there's no question of how wonderfully we are knit together.

I was not quite the cooking star in Home Ec that people expected or that I hoped I would be, although I excelled at sanitation. It took so long for me to get the hang of the electric range, it's a wonder the school tax wasn't raised to pay for the food I burned. Mrs. Spaulding patiently reminded me to turn the heat down, and eventually, I produced a pie with a perfect flaky crust, which is nothing to sneeze at.

No amount of patience was going to make me into an artist, but Mrs. Casey encouraged me all along. I learned that the weird drawing of her showed real talent. The triangle is a musical instrument, so, along with the piano, the drawing combined art with musical instruments to express her unusual facial proportions and actually was a compliment.

Mrs. Spaulding and Mrs. Casey and Miss Williams and Miss Brennan were champion role models to me. It's one thing to support students who show some promise, but their undying patience and kindness and respect throughout my failures and sheer lack of talent or ability buoyed me up day in and day out.

I admired and appreciated them and Mr. Shaw above all. For as different as they were, Mr. Shaw and Mrs. Richardson held special places in my heart. He didn't pull any punches. Like they say, he was just the messenger, but he wanted to be. He wanted his students to think through their positions on the conflicts swirling around them. His challenging assignments and tough tests trained me to be a better student—and what he taught changed my world.

I'd learned more than I bargained for. I'd grown up fast. I hadn't meant to.

It was an unforeseen consideration that never crossed my mind when I made my pros and cons list of entering CUHS a year early. Everybody had such confidence in me that they never mentioned it as being a possibility, but I couldn't blame them for a sadistic classmate, voyeuristic pedophile, psychedelics, Bloody Sunday, or Vietnam. Puff the Magic Dragon was long gone from Honalee, but that would have happened in its own time anyway.

But the world was crawling with dragons, and Neston was no exception. Like Dieter said, The Dragon of Neston is the same great dragon found everywhere. I just didn't expect to find him at school.

I knew now that slaying The Dragon of Neston was not a once in a lifetime event. I'd be in the battlefield again and again, whenever hate and lies spew their flames. Until God finally slays the devil forever and ever, the fires of little dragons, and some not so little, will need to be extinguished.

Now that the shock was over, I had to navigate the long haul ahead knowing I didn't fit in with any of the major groups that had taken on personalities of their own. Some of them toted heavy luggage. Even if they were admired, the people in them had to live up to the group, and that was true of most groups. If you didn't stay stuck in what other people thought, there were consequences. If you did, then they decided who you could be.

I didn't want to fit in with the hippies, who decided smashing guitars was cool, or the greasers, who had a bigger turnout for cruising Neston Avenue than for Friday night football. I saw them less as cliques and more as what Mr. Shaw called sub-cultures, and the directions they were headed in scared me.

Other cliques still had luggage, but it didn't seem to weigh them down. By now, I realized that Donna was queen of the cheerleaders, and Marcia was queen of fashion design and construction. At least their cliques were based on ability.

There could have been a lot more kids in the brains clique if they'd seen that really applying yourself to academics was mostly what it took. Not many brainy kids were actually geniuses to start with. Debbie wasn't the only person to call me Einstein, but he was born that way; I was mostly a worker bee. And I'd personally met the genuine article: Patrick Humphreys. It's no wonder he figured out the best and easiest way to solve Neston's worst traffic problem.

Sometimes a clique was the cost of making a friend, and sometimes cliques closed more doors than they opened. For a lot of people, they never opened because they weren't based on common interests or abilities, but characteristics they couldn't control, like where they lived, or how their family made money and how much of it they had, or how they looked. Having the so-called "right" characteristics didn't necessarily guarantee membership, though.

All the same, I saw for myself that kids who lacked pegs altogether were pigeonholed as loners or unfriendly or stuck up. They never managed to fit in well anywhere—or others wouldn't let them in, which is a whole other story. I felt for them and hoped they were just strong individuals who would turn out to be leaders everybody looked up to; then they'd be the peg others wanted to hang on. I had wanted at least a couple of good pegs myself. I got them.

What I never expected was to become popular. Now, I fully expected the curiosity and interest to fade, and it had somewhat, but less than I thought it would. It beat being branded Eddie, but I knew from first-hand experience that center stage had its drawbacks, and that people could be fickle.

What I figured out is that the students wanted to peg certain people as popular. It seems to be as natural a part of their human development as becoming more competitive. Come next fall, if they still liked me, I'd work around the lines of expectation they drew.

And if I had to stay a free agent in the extracurricular department for another year, *c'est la vie.* Personal civics were an option, and until God showed me something else, Gabe would always be my extracurricular activity. He was years away from flying the nest. The main thing was, as long as I continued to rely on The Helper, I would stay on course.

I had some wholesome company. I looked one last time at our names on the Honor Roll. Then I released the year behind me to the past, where I left it, and put the year ahead of me in God's hands, where it belonged.

Summer beckoned.

I stepped outside. The sun was shining high in a clear blue sky, and I felt as fine as the day.

But a bank of clouds was crouching on the horizon.

NEXT IN THE SERIES

#3 in The Neston Novels Series:
The Oasis of Neston

Dieter Norden must overcome resistance to return to Neston for the summer of 1965, but when his delayed vacation starts, it includes unexpected company and a change of circumstance. Ette Durand has her own surprise, and she must face far more resistance to see it through. The startling consequences are among many changes weaving into the social fabric of Neston. While the rest of the Northeast is suffering through a severe drought, the lush landscape of Neston puts it on the map as "an emerald oasis in a sea of straw." But there's trouble in paradise, and it hits close to home. Together, Ette and Dieter make waves when they challenge tradition.

ABOUT THE AUTHOR

Tess Adone holds an M.A. in English. Her background includes teaching expository writing and assisting executives. Her first novel is *Respect and Respectability: Susan Price at Mansfield Park*, a standalone Jane Austen sequel. Currently, she is writing The Neston Novels Series, a continuous story told in sequence, beginning with *Neston*. The series is set in her home state of Vermont. Learn more at www.tessadone.com.

www.ingramcontent.com/pod-product-compliance
Lightning Source LLC
Chambersburg PA
CBHW050355260626
47156CB00003B/743